RODDY

MACLEOD'S LAW

a Scottish Thriller

woodlord

www.ebooks-uk.com
www.ebooks-america.com
www.woodlord.net
eBooks-UK Ltd., P.O. Box 36, Chesterfield S40 3YY, UK.
First published in paperback edition
by Woodlord Publishing 2011

A CIP catalogue record for this book
is available from the British Library

Designed and typeset by Kate Mason
for eBooks-UK/Woodlord Publishing
Chesterfield, Derbyshire, U.K.

Cover Image: Kate Mason
Cover design Copyright © Kate Mason 2011

978-1-906602-18-5

Dedications

To my father and mother:

Dear Father, no longer the need to tolerate that debilitating illness, suffered quietly with dignity, without complaint. Your spirit flies free like that of the Freeforester observing neither boundary nor restriction. You were the excellent rôle model of reliable provider despite your own abandonment in childhood. Look down and enjoy the successes you forged.

Dear Mother, I hope this novel helps to satisfy those writer ambitions you cherished. Your care and love were, and continue to be, spontaneous and generous.

To a close friend and one of the last traditional Freeforesters: for the adventures and the many fine memories you made possible. Like the eagle and the raven your spirit will guide the apprentice on mountain forays: for your friendship, and for inviting me into your world, my simple but sincere thanks. God bless.

Acknowledgements

To Shona Arthur who suggested numerous improvements to the original manuscript. Thank you for your reliable and unconditional friendship.

To my wife, Joan, thank you for your tolerance and support.

ONE

Life in remote Highland villages was often harsh. Despite a paucity of possessions, these were shared; likewise emotions. Tragedies were never unique to one person or family: the community grieved and supported those directly affected. Each person was valued for who she/he was. Unfortunately there would be one or two who showed disrespect; invariably they were incomers, victims of an anonymous town environment.

The laird, (often absentee), owned thousands of acres that could include part, if not all the village. How could one person with no ancestral links to the area and little interest in its people command 'respect' other than through fear? Often police and judges were rewarded for safeguarding the estate's salmon and venison. A 'fish' or haunch of meat enriched an otherwise meagre diet, but the prospect of being caught 'in possession' of such a windfall brought anxiety. Consequently there was only whispered appreciation in trusted company of the gift's source. Most locals questioned why a privileged few claimed outright ownership of resources provided by the Lord to benefit the needy.

The laird claims ownership of deer which cross onto his estate but revokes ownership of any that collide with cars. The contradictions continue: can the laird identify 'his' salmon as they follow the coastline before they enter the running (and hence ownerless) water of 'his' river? Few lairds show interest in conservation to guarantee healthy, renewable resources: instead they plunder and make no investment for the resource's future.

Some locals did more than question: a few dared to pursue what God had provided and risk the consequences;

their exploits were recounted in the privacy of the cottage as family members huddled around the peat fire. Few villagers had the ability to gain venison and carry it miles over rugged terrain; even fewer had the inclination to attempt such a venture. The stalwarts who dared, invariably shared their gain with others. Those few occupied a special place in villagers' affections. They were never identified by name but were christened 'Freeforesters'.

The Freeforester belongs to a bygone age when attitudes were different, and survival was raw and real. Improvements in living standards have removed the *need* for the hunter-gatherer, but their legend survives. Occasionally legend becomes reality.

This story relates the activities of a Freeforester who unwittingly stumbles across activities so sinister that they threaten a Highland community and its traditional family values.

Another wave pounds the black buttress of hard basalt. The volcanic intrusion had proved more durable to the onslaught of sea and storm than its sedimentary neighbours. The battle between sea and land had raged for millions of years; the physical forces beyond the comprehension of most humans.

The relentless pounding by the sea continued. Eventually it would win.

Like stranded flotsam, a forlorn figure stands in the shadow of the gigantic needle. Wind-borne spray flecks the reddened skin. Two hours earlier that complexion had been grey and wan, drained of vitality by darkness and alcohol.

Wind blows the damp, unkempt hair into curls that streak the broad, intelligent forehead. Stubble shadows the chin and cheeks. The dark eyes look up; searching, appraising to identify dangers and a possible line of ascent. Yesterday there had been little interest in anything. Now his eyes are vibrant.

Lips tauten; eyes narrow, cracking and crazing the white deposits of sea salt that encrust them; the irregular lines emphasise the depth of character etched so prematurely in the nineteen year old.

His sea kayak, recently abandoned, rises and falls on each huge swell. Its brittle, fibre-glass carcase crunches on sharp toothed rocks. Ragged holes are gouged; tears rip its splintered body. With its shell breached and with no buoyancy, the kayak lists badly. Its air bags had been removed and left in the battered van, itself abandoned two miles back where tarmacadam stopped: not even a track to soften the isolation; quite literally, the end of the road.

He'd looped a climbing rope around the van's front axle and lowered his sea kayak the sixty metres to the shingle beach. His lean, muscular figure had abseiled from the same belay. A frayed woollen sweater and ragged shorts hacked from kneeless jeans were functional but barely presentable; only the tight fitting climbing boots approached respectability.

He'd worn no buoyancy aid: the obligatory paddle plus a spray-deck over the kayak's cockpit to withstand the pounding waves were his only concessions to reach his destination.

The sixteen foot kayak had risen over creaming wave crests before plunging into deep troughs; swamped, somehow it had emerged, surviving that test many times. Stinging salt spray had blinded his vision of the next towering wave before it dumped onto and over his deck: his eyes had smarted, but his spirits had risen, fired by the challenge. The recklessness of daring youth had returned. Physical challenges were his raison d'être; this adventure the prelude to a cause and to a release.

Initially the abandoned van would be ignored; only two tapered flotation bags thrown onto its rear seat might attract interest from a casual passer-by. Later, the van would command attention, not only from the public but also the police, especially its forensic department.

The holed kayak sits lower in the sea, less responsive to the buffeting swell. Tendrils of seaweed snake back and forth in the lee of his rock island. The yellow colour fades as the kayak sinks from view; now a mere memory; its disappearance a reminder of his commitment.

The sea stack rises vertically: a pinnacle of defiance; a statement of independence. The figure understands. No rock is conquered. Rather, inner depths in the human psyche are explored ... revealed ... unless, of course, the challenge is beyond the mental and physical capabilities of the pretentious daredevil. Rock and climber share

6

secrets. Police and press guess.

Reverentially the figure fingers the rough rock. Sea birds nesting on ledges, others in flight, bear witness to the start of his perilous ascent.

The small day-sack appears ridiculously light: a backwards stretch to negotiate a slight overhang produces space between it and climber. Despite his choice of sheltered, leeward side, the swirling wind continues to glaze the rock with spray. Slimy algae coat the shaded underside of the overhang. His boots, smooth soled to maximise friction on dry rock, slide, unable to hold.

Both legs drop into space: a human pendulum is suspended on thin, muscular arms. His right foot swings up, scraping contact with the shelf but finds no purchase. Another pendulum action, and this time his right heel lips the shelf and holds: that all-important third contact against which both arms pull. He grimaces: forearm veins and sinews stand proud through taut skin. His head moves higher... now level ... and now above the shelf. Pressing down, his midriff is dragged onto the horizontal outcrop.

Safe, a well earned rest is taken despite the shelf digging into his lower ribs; the painful fulcrum is aggravated by the weight of legs dangling in space. The acute discomfort is tolerated; he needs time to recover, to reduce the lactic acid in forearm muscles.

The guillemot, now only twenty feet higher, no longer ignores the castaway. It's agitated; its ledge no longer safe. Falling forward it skims its 'assailant's' head, its tiny wings whirring frantically as it strives to clear the rocks to gain the sea.

A better swimmer than flier, the figure concludes. A smile creases his rugged features. Humour, lacking for so long, has returned, courtesy of that bizarre attempt at flight. He pulls his body onto the ledge and sits. The small black and brown bird with the white belly looks happier in the water: likewise the climber on the shelf despite his vulnerable station. Now is a time to reflect, to enjoy and to consolidate this return to a semblance of his former persona.

He recollects his first days in Tor'buie, a small fishing village on the north-west coast of Scotland. He'd been smitten by its beauty and its setting. He'd known nobody but been warmly welcomed. While his energies recharge, he recalls those first weeks.

He pictures the village hall where the wedding dance is in full swing. Although the famous uisge-beatha (whisky) is playing its part, the main source of the exuberance is the music as it fires the blood.

Two fiddlers, an accordionist, and a pianist are inspiring the dancers of an eightsome reel to ever accelerating spins. Laughter is spontaneous, and banter abounds.

George MacLeod is seated with friends at a table. His dark good looks and lean muscled physique make him an attractive dancing partner, but he is content to be a spectator. Indeed, as an incomer he is honoured to have been invited to the reception: his invitation, a token of acceptance in the community. A fine-set middle-aged man approaches. He is dressed in full Highland costume. His gait and unassuming manner command attention: a man of natural dignity, a true Highland gentleman, who, without vanity of any kind, has never had cause to doubt his worth.

"And how's Seoras tonight?" Stuart raised his voice to be heard. The ceilidh band's music compelled the guests to greater endeavours. George, addressing his Gaelic name, turned, honoured to be addressed by this intriguing character.

"Stuart, you were in my thoughts. It must be telepathy."

"Mary was just saying that she'd not seen you tonight. Did Maggie and Jessie release you from that wilderness they call a garden?"

George smiled.

"Oh, Maggie and Jessie are very good to me…"

"Och, I know. They're the salt of the earth. Mary and I couldn't ask for better neighbours. When Jessie's husband was alive he tended the garden well. They must have thought an angel was sent when you offered to tend their ground."

"Not exactly my offer, Stuart. Maggie and Jessie offered me a room and food in return for work. Remember I was stuck in that rusting caravan at a sky-high rent."

"Aye. Some incomers have no conscience when it comes to charging."

8

"Are incomers not to be trusted then?" George's smile and easy tone belied his wistful longing not to be considered an incomer.

"Och, Seoras. You know fine we didn't take long to recognise you to be one of us. For starters, you're a MacLeod. It was bad luck that your grand-dad had to go south to earn a crust. Now the blood has called you back home." Stuart smiled. "Now for a dram," and off he went, his kilted figure weaving easily through the crowd.

"Will you look at that son of mine!" he said, returning to hand over a double whisky. "He'll have that lassie off her feet if he birls her any faster."

George raised his glass to acknowledge Stuart and took a swig although his immediate thought was that it had been some time since he, himself, had had a lassie off her feet. Reprieved from the high decibel conversation, he cast his eye across the village hall.

In that sea of flushed and smiling faces that moved to the beat of the music, Sandy stood a head higher than most other dancers. The white shirt was unlacing across his broad, heaving chest. One hand held a glass of whisky aloft while his other embraced the lithe waist of his partner. Their dancing brought them nearer Stuart and George. The amber nectar defied the laws of physics as it remained in Sandy's tumbler.

"Slainte mhath, father, and you too, Seoras."

With raised glasses Stuart and Macleod returned the toast.

"Slainte, son."

"Slainte, Sandy, and strength to your arm, my friend."

The tumblers' contents disappeared in one well-practised swallow before Sandy and his partner merged into the swirl of the dancers. The music was intoxicating. The swinging kilts provided a continuous flow of colour. Occasionally a guest commandeered the microphone to sing or recount tales of the two uniting families: tales of moonless nights lying in deep heather beside river pools that held salmon; the despised ghillie passing, unsuspecting, within yards of the adrenalin seekers. More stories of greater daring refered

9

to hill sorties that ended with a stag over the shoulders at the end of a successful day. MacLeod felt the wary glances of some locals. He winced as he considered they might believe him duty-bound to report such transgressions. If only they knew how he longed to join their risky exploits. He had seen city life, drunk its success, breathed its atmosphere and rejected its superficiality. *Here* he felt content. He was carving out an identity. Soon he'd gain everyone's trust.

"Slainte mhor, Seoras." MacLeod, already feeling hazy, turned. There, for a second time, was the bride's cog, an ornately decorated small half-barrel with the names of bride and groom inscribed on a plaque. During his first drink he'd experienced unidentifiable tastes amongst the more familiar flavours of Guinness, rum, and, of course, 'uisge beatha', the Gaelic 'water of life'.

"Well, George, have you decided what's in the cog yet, or are you going to drink it dry?"

He grinned at Sandy's banter and handed back the cog, still unable to identify the fleetingly suggested flavours as they teased his palate.

"I'm damned if I can make it all out myself, man," said Sandy, his six foot three-inch frame towering over MacLeod. To the accompaniment of cheers Sandy proceeded to empty the cog. His dark, short-cropped hair and fresh complexion enhanced his boyish appearance, but his deep chest and powerful physique belied that impression.

Then Sandy looked regretfully at the stain on his shirt.

"I'll bet thon wis the stuff I couldna mak oot." His laughter was infectious. "Ach, it's aboot time I said somethin' afore I'm beyond it." Sandy strode purposefully towards the microphone. "Ladies and Gentlemen, for the bride and groom I offer a song that's rarely heard, except at the end of a long day on the hill and in the company of Freeforesters. For those who have no Gaelic I offer no apologies and attempt no translation. The song's magic is best appreciated through our true mother tongue. To Jamie and Mairi I dedicate the song on this, their wedding day."

With no accompaniment, Sandy sang from the heart. His eyes looked up, and he was spirited elsewhere, enjoying a freedom appreciated only by those who scorn boundaries and shackles.

Macleod's attempt to learn Gaelic had been slow, but, as he listened, he pictured the soaring eagle and the baying stag in a habitat of crags and crystal clear streams. The fresh smell of the chill morning air and the striking purple of heather-clad hills were vivid to his inner eye.

All were silent, enthralled by the gentle lilting voice akin to waves lapping a sandy shore, but also there lurked power and threat, like a dark crag piercing the enshrouding mist, its appearance ominous, a momentary intimation of peril before it disappears in the swirling, dank clouds; the mystery, intrigue and anxiety effects linger but become engulfed and confused in the audience minds.

Sandy finished. The silence remained unbroken as the haunting melody lingered. It was Sandy who broke the spell.

"Take the floor for an Orcadian Strip-the-Willow, and that's an order."

A loud cheer followed, and the action resumed its hectic pace. Sandy, apparently unaffected by the contents of the cog, danced and laughed while MacLeod became aware of legs that no longer responded to his brain's commands. He needed fresh air, but at the hall door Christine appeared. In his tipsy state she was the last person he wished to see.

"Are you bent on escaping then, just when I thought you might ask me for a dance?"

"Och, Christine, I'm afraid I'm in no fit state for dancing. I was just going out to clear my head. I'm really sorry."

He strived for the light tone to conceal his deep disappointment. Since delivering a package to her father's croft, he'd been smitten by the natural beauty who greeted him. Her delicate features were emphasised by fair, blemish-free skin. Long strands of shining, jet black hair had wafted in the gentle breeze, several straying over her high brow and finely chiselled cheeks. Sapphire blue eyes had pierced that scant dark veil, the contrast so striking and unusual it was compelling. He'd found himself staring, completely besotted. Her body, so slim and lithe, was perfectly proportioned and radiated health. Poised and elegant; she was, to MacLeod, perfection personified.

"Head so bad you don't want company? Or can I join you?"

"Of course."

Formal, stilted - he guessed that was how he sounded. A clown; he'd avoid alcohol next time.

The cool night air was refreshing, a clean sensation to the new setting.

"It's beautiful isn't it?" Her words were whispered. Christine had spent her life in Tor'buie, but familiarity had not dulled her appreciation of the picture before them.

From their vantage point, they enjoyed the clear moonlight shimmering along the expanse of Loch Breac, itself reflecting the shadows of the Cuillin Mountains to the south. A walk beyond the end of the building revealed the Ben Eolaire range to the north, while the hills to the east were dominated by Cnoc a'Caoirich, 'the hill of the hawk'. Romance and mystery were in the very names, but it was the view to the west that always caught MacLeod's breath. There, the rounded form of Meall an Laoidh dropped steeply to the sea, exactly where Loch Breac opened into the Minch, all illumined by the glowing orb that sailed serenely above them in the sky. Beyond were the Gannet Isles, cushions on the horizon to calm the harsh Atlantic weather.

The Gannet Isles: MacLeod had witnessed gale-driven Atlantic waves expend themselves in high flying streams of silvery spume against its grey buttressing rocks. Tor'buie, with its idyllic natural harbour, gave sanctuary from the ravages of storms and well deserved its name, 'Pearl on the Sea'.

"Yes, it's really beautiful."

The moment lingered as they enjoyed each other's company in those romantic surroundings.

"And is it these beautiful surroundings that drew you here?" Her west coast lilt was soft and musical. "Or ... am I sounding nosy, rather than interested?"

"No, right first time. When I drove up I took the tourist route from the north."

"Ah, so you drove past the peaks of Rainich and the Eolaire ridge and were smitten by the balcony view of Tor'buie?" MacLeod nodded. " *'So picturesque'* the tourists say....."

Was she teasing him?

"I guess I was hooked." He passed his arm around her, his hand against the small of her back, adding, "Beauty is bewitching."

Christine stood still, quietly resisting the pressure to move her closer.

MacLeod dropped his hand. "I'm sorry, I shouldn't have done that."

"No, you shouldn't." There was no reproof in her tone. "It must have been the whisky."

He moved back to sit on the old wooden bench, in need of some physical if not psychological comfort. After a brief delay, Christine joined him.

"George, I must ask. Are you married?"

"Mmmmarried?"

"Yes," and this time there was amusement in her voice as she mimicked his "Mmmarried" stammer.

"Why do you ask?"

"Didn't you know we all have the second sight in the West?" She tried to look serious but couldn't maintain it. The corners of her mouth quivered with merriment. "Do you remember the day Stuart and Mary asked if you'd take a, a..." Here she lowered her voice, "a venison roast to father and me?"

Well he remembered that day. Jessie had called him in for his mid-morning srupag (cup of tea). Their home baked pancakes and scones layered with butter and jam were always a treat. Making his way into the kitchen he'd met Stuart who was about to leave.

"George, it's a grand job you're making of the garden, not to mention the house. No wonder you're the talk of the village."

MacLeod glowed inwardly. He'd never known a father's approval, and Stuart approached that missing foundation

13

in his life.

"Cheers, Stuart."

"Now, to keep your fine physique in good trim, I've left something. Perhaps you'll find time to take a parcel to Christine and her father? We'll hope for a good day tomorrow." Then Stuart had gone.

Macleod's questioning look was answered by Maggie pointing. "It's there, under the cloth."

MacLeod raised the cover to reveal a large cut of crimson red, lean meat, its blood still oozing. He looked to the sisters for explanation and found two warm, but slightly conspiratorial smiles.

"It's venison. You *do* like venison?"

"I've never tasted venison. Is it different from other meat?"

"You'll find the answer in about; let's say three hours when we have our meal."

He watched Maggie place the meat in a large roasting tin before wiping oil over it and placing it in the Rayburn. For three hours the aroma from the slowly cooking joint became a torment of anticipation.

At long last MacLeod was seated at a table that supported a spread fit for a king. Small talk would ruin a good meal, and MacLeod said little as he attacked the thick slices of meat. Crispy fat melted in his mouth; the richness of the venison and gravy was complemented perfectly by the fluffy potatoes and vegetables, and all washed down with a bottle of his favourite wine. How had Maggie and Jessie wheedled that information from him? He recalled Maggie's innocent mentioning of Stuart's favourite tipple.

"And would you agree with Stuart's choice?" she had continued in an absent-minded, careless fashion, appearing to be more interested in filling the kettle than listening to his reply. Obviously, she had filed away the information he provided, and now he had the entire bottle to himself since the ladies never touched alcohol.

However, of all those memories his most vivid was the striking beauty who accepted his delivery and captured his heart.

He nodded again as Christine remained quiet, and added, "Well I remember that day."

Christine drew in her breath. "Returning to my question - the first thing I noticed, like many women in the village, was the mark left by your wedding ring, and so that helped the second sight. Then I heard the usual kind of speculation ..."

It was an inevitable part of village life, and one not appreciated by MacLeod.

"And what conclusions were drawn?"

"Och, don't sound so defensive, George. You showed no signs of grief so the men said you probably had something to run from, and the women said wasn't it terrible that you had probably walked out on your wife, but weren't you handsome, though?"

His lean features relaxed into something approaching a smile.

"And what do you think?"

"I don't think. But I'd like to know, if you'll tell me."

Another silence ensued.

"Okay, I did run away from my wife. She was something to run from, as far as I was concerned. I've no regrets, and ... of course, I am *devilish handsome*," affecting an English accent for the last words.

Christine burst out laughing. "You're joking about something which is not really funny. Are you going to tell me more, or is that it?"

"What do you want to know?"

She studied the toes peeping from her sling-back sandals.

"Well .....What was so terrible about your wife?"

"Nothing was really bad about Flossie. God, she even sounds like a pampered poodle."

"And is the Lord to blame?"

He was momentarily confused until he remembered the religious background shared by so many in the community.

"Sorry."

"We had reached the pampered poodle stage."

He hesitated and then continued in a slow, laboured way, as though regretting the telling, but he felt relief as he unburdened to someone who seemed genuinely interested.

"Well, for a long time I didn't want to go to work. I was a supervisor in a leisure centre that was used mainly by women in the mornings. They always seemed to be bitching about their husbands, and many expected me to listen. After work, I didn't want to go home. I felt trapped: claustrophobic. I tried to talk to Flossie about moving away from the city. She ...well, she just looked blank, didn't know what I was talking about, and said if she didn't hurry she would miss her bingo."

Distress showed in his face. He hesitated ... and then ploughed on. "I found myself thinking I was just the three Ps Flossie: 'Pectorals, Pelvis and well ......'."

"Well?"

"Well. 'Penis'. Sorry."

"I'm disappointed in you George."

"You think I should have stayed?"

"Oh no - it sounded like a slow attrition. I meant the comparison you made with those three Ps, especially the last. And your wife ...what will happen to her?"

"I left a note ... left her everything really, except the car. She works for the council and has a good wage."

"Children?"

"No, no children. Flossie didn't want her lifestyle disrupted."

"She'll manage, then?"

"She's a born survivor. She'll maximise the sympathy vote portraying herself as the wronged woman, then ensnare the right man. She's a good looker. She'll be fine."

The music in the hall had stopped. Through the open window they could hear the beautiful clear voice of a woman introducing a Gaelic poem she was set to deliver.

"Quick, George, we mustn't miss this. Oh no! You won't understand it, will you?"

"A few more months, Christine, and I'll have enough

Gaelic to catch the drift."

Mairead was about to start her recitation as they slipped
back into the hall. The poem was delivered in steady, beat-
perfect rhythm. Only the rising and falling modulations
of Mairead's voice and the occasional tremor of emotion
gave MacLeod clues to the fleeting expressions of awe, grief
and gladness unconsciously reflected in the faces of several
listeners. The language was central to gain admission to this
different world. MacLeod determined he'd become part of
it.

He did not see Christine home as he had hoped.
Someone else would. Sad to relate, after a few more drams,
MacLeod himself had to be helped home by Stuart. At the
cottage door, Stuart said cheerfully, "Ach, you'll be fine by
the morning. You'll see." Then added, "I'm thinking it will
be a nice overcast day tomorrow," before leaving MacLeod
to stumble upstairs to his bedroom.

What did Stuart mean? The last time he'd wanted an
overcast day concerned an outing to the hill. As he collapsed
into bed, MacLeod recalled that epic first day on the hill
with Stuart.

That day had been doubly memorable. Firstly, Maggie
and Jessie had sprung a surprise. They'd lingered over the
mid-morning srupag.

"You are such a blessing to us, George."

"No. I'm the one who's grateful for sharing your home
with me."

"Please listen. You see ... John, Jessie's man, now long
gone, and our dear brother, Murdo, taken in the first war,
we ..."

"You had a brother ... killed in the First World War?"

"They say he died ... in the trenches; probably from
exposure, possibly disease, or, more likely, a combination.
Murdo was very clever. Just eighteen years old, he was in
his prime and should have been enjoying life."

MacLeod struggled to find something to say but failed.

Words were meaningless and inadequate to address the grief then etched on the faces of these two gracious ladies.

"Here's his medal for rescuing a soldier, lying wounded, still under fire...." Jessie brought out the Mons Star, their material link with the brother who still stimulated vivid memories. Macleod touched it lightly with a forefinger as though he too could make a connection.

"We have something else of Murdo's. We want you to have it." Jessie proffered a polished wooden box.

MacLeod hesitated. Reverentially, he raised the lid and gasped.

Inside, a magnificent hunting knife; the steel of its finely honed blade gleamed quality as it dazzlingly reflected the light. MacLeod was stunned.

"It's .... perfect."

The words, 'It's too much. I can't accept', were contained as he looked at the kind, loving eyes. Words of rejection were not appropriate for this gift so precious to their hearts. His eyes had not known the healing power of tears since he was a child, and he strove to contain their gentle escape.

The silence was pregnant with meaning but, before it became too prolonged, Maggie, through a slight sniffle said, "We're pleased it's yours now, George. Murdo would approve. And it'll prove useful ... some day."

Jessie, with a choking "Please excu..." hurried from the room. A nod of understanding passed between George and Maggie, who then followed after Jessie. Before they reappeared there was time for MacLeod to compose himself.

They exchanged smiles, but little was said, the silence communicating their deepest thoughts and feelings.

Eventually Maggie changed tack. "Stuart will be pleased to know you enjoyed the venison."

MacLeod's eager enquiry followed. "Does Stuart go out stalking, then?"

There was a brief pause. "We never ask, and so remain ignorant, lest the police enquire." Maggie smiled sweetly: a lesson on reticence clinically delivered.

These charming ladies would never lie, nor would they

betray a friend. A deer from the hill, a salmon from the river; neither is regarded as a crime by the true Highlander, more a God-given right, intended for family and friends and those in need.

"But you're not the local constabulary, George," Maggie added, her eyes twinkling. "Stuart trusts you, and 'yes' is your answer."

MacLeod had returned to his task of repairing the drystane dyke around the garden before the second memorable occasion. Concentrating on his task he'd been unaware of Stuart's approach.

"Seoras."

Startled, MacLeod spun swiftly, left arm raised defensively over his head, his right fist balled with his arm cocked, ready to strike. The conditioned response from combat training embarrassed MacLeod. Taken by surprise Stuart had stepped back but was too much of a gentleman to question his friend.

"Ah, it's yourself, Stuart." MacLeod normalised contact and acted as if nothing unusual had passed. "Maggie and Jessie gave me something special. I'm a bit lost."

"The knife?"

"You knew?"

"Well, they asked me what I thought, and I said it couldn't go to a better man."

The older man's trust and affection, especially after such a short acquaintance, inspired humility and further eroded the barriers MacLeod used to keep people at a safe and detached distance.

"Thank you, Stuart."

Stuart smiled. "I was wondering if you'd like to go to the hill after lunch?" Reading Macleod's surprised but eager expression, he continued, "I've cleared it with Maggie and Jessie. Two o'clock?"

"Excellent. What do I need?"

"A warm top, waterproofs and a bite to eat: I'll see to the rest." He turned to go. "My back door at two."

MacLeod entered the house to be met by a knowing smile from Jessie. "We saw Stuart and yourself speaking.

Lunch is ready. Maggie has just nipped out to the shop for some sweets. Just why you'll need energy foods we can but guess." She assumed an amusing air of impish innocence.

A bemused MacLeod sat at the table. So Jessie and Maggie had colluded with Stuart to arrange the adventure he'd wished.

His mind elsewhere, MacLeod had picked up his knife and fork to tackle the plate of steaming food before his eye caught Jessie's. He'd almost forgotten.

"Sorry. I'm elsewhere."

"Will you say grace today, George?"

MacLeod felt uncomfortable. Hypocrisy was not part of his character.

"Well, maybe not yet," said Jessie brightly, "but the day will come." Then she bent her head. "Dear Lord, thank you for all your goodness to us. Thank you for the food on our table. And bless George and Stuart as they ...in all they plan to do today. Amen."

MacLeod rushed the lunch then threw waterproofs into a day bag before vaulting the dyke to rendezvous with Stuart.

Stuart, still relishing his pudding, enquired, "Let's see what you're taking, George...... Well now, I think we'll just swap these for your red cagoule and over-trousers, if you don't mind?" He rose and looked out olive green counterparts. "These are less conspicuous. Better not forget the sticks. Hopefully, we'll need them. Sandy will be here soon."

MacLeod fought to contain his questions. He told himself that participation would be the best education. A brisk westerly wind prevailed that day. MacLeod wondered where Stuart would go to take advantage of that wind direction.

"While we're waiting, see what you think of the rifle, George," passing across the .222 bolt-action Brno. "Treble two, the calibre favoured by the Eskimos. A bit on the light side for stags but adequate if you're able. Recommended calibre is .243 but it's noisy for us." Knowing nods and smiles were exchanged. MacLeod's education continued.

20

"And then the telescopic sight by 'Schmidt & Bender'; very good, but Zeiss is the best although a tad pricey for me. Sometime, though," he confided, "I'll have a new rifle, probably a .243 Sako Forester fitted with a Zeiss scope with a cross-hair reticle to pinpoint the target even in failing light."

MacLeod absorbed the information with an empathy fuelled by keen interest and deep affection for his mentor. The sound of a car slowing to a halt heralded Sandy's arrival, and then they were heading out of Tor'buie on the north road. The rifle had been carefully placed in the boot along with two long, stout hazel wands. The day sacks sat on their laps.

White emulsioned houses, their gable ends facing the prevailing westerly winds, slipped past as Sandy eased the car through the village. Beyond the bridge there were a few isolated houses. As the car lipped the north brae summit, Macleod cast an admiring glance back at the panoramic view below them.

'Tor'buie really is the jewel in the crown,' he thought.

"Aye, a fine sight, George." Sandy guessed MacLeod's thoughts. "After today you'll have more special memories. I feel it. One thing's for sure; you'll not get a better man to show you."

"Well, I'm flattered, son. I hope you're right about the day bringing success. We can only try."

Stuart's remarks were typically understated. MacLeod smiled and nodded. He was living the occasion, breathing its atmosphere, appreciating the setting. The heather had recently bloomed and covered the hillsides in its rich purple mantle. Clouds scudded past to disappear behind mountains. Hillsides loomed larger on either side, some breached by rocky outcrops. The rock climber in MacLeod stirred. He'd enjoyed some of the classic routes in Scotland. He recalled Ben Nevis's Tower Ridge, the longest rock climb in Britain. Bivvying overnight beside the C.I.C. hut in Coire Leis had allowed him an early start before other climbers arrived. Excellent scrambling interspersed the climbing sections, the most memorable being the Great Tower, followed by an exposed descent and step across Tower Gap where a look down Glover's chimney set the pulse racing. He felt the same tingling sensation as he anticipated the day ahead.

Stuart interrupted MacLeod's daydream. "You're about to experience the 'Sport of Kings' without it costing a king's ransom. Freeforestry pre-dates the law, and no one asked the locals about changes in favour of those who have wealth and no connections to the area. Anyway it matters little. Today the weather is perfect: a nice breeze and overcast. We don't want to be spotted by any beast, especially human."

MacLeod mused. A good day for a hard rock climb was a bad day for stalking. On the stalk, sunshine improved visibility but made concealment more difficult. On a crag, sunshine warmed hands as they explored the rock for a small finger hold that could raise a faltering spirit and revitalise aching arm muscles before their last reserves of strength failed.

"A penny for your thoughts, George?"

"Sorry, Sandy. I was reliving some routes I've climbed."

Father and son exchanged looks before Stuart added, "We were thinking there was more to you than being a townie. You understand the adrenalin rush. That's good. Today we hope it'll be just the stag that's at risk."

"So the landowners don't exactly encourage this type of foray?" MacLeod's banter translated to 'tell me more'.

"Aye, despite most of us being conservation minded, it's not all that long ago that the lairds evicted poachers, real or just suspected, plus their families."

"I thought lairds were clan chiefs who looked after their people?"

"There may have been something like that at one time, but once the clan chief started to send their sons to English Public schools, and money became the main consideration in every decision, all of that came to an end. Ach, we wouldn't want a return to the old kind of system, but we do resent being branded criminals for exercising a right that's always been practised."

The car was flying downhill and almost failed to negotiate

a sharp turn at the bottom due to Sandy's excessive speed.

"Sorry, lads."

Labouring uphill the old Austin coughed in protest. Without warning Sandy struck right, off the main road and onto a narrow dirt track. Ruts were either side of a vegetated ridge which threatened the Austin's floor, but, apart from slapping contacts with sedges and one ominous scraping sound, the car continued unaffected, apparently used to such treatment.

They gained height quickly as the road twisted in serpentine fashion up the steep hillside, often skirting precipitous drops. MacLeod, alive to the panoramic views, hoped they would not distract the driver. The Austin snaked around corners and hairpin bends so convoluted in places that they almost met.

Below, nestled snugly in the valley of the river Eiteach, lay several ruins. Small, scattered peat stacks bore evidence that the track was still in use. Otherwise the tranquillity remained undisturbed. Suddenly several golden plovers burst from the heather, the whirr of their wings just audible.

Sandy slowed the car over a blind rise to reveal a large turning circle. There the track ended. Bringing the car to a halt, Sandy left the engine idling.

"Right, Sandy, nine o'clock at the usual spot. Let's go, George." Stuart was out and had the boot up. "George, bring the sticks." Stuart dashed off to disappear down a slope. MacLeod, grabbing his own gear and the sticks, slammed the boot and followed at speed. Glancing back he saw the rear of the Austin, and then it had gone. Sandy would be home in half an hour. Behind a knoll Stuart waited MacLeod's arrival.

MacLeod's adrenalin-charged senses were in overdrive, keenly alert to his surroundings. In August the ling heather was at its best. The mountains were two-toned, the deep purple of the lower slopes fading to the grey of the summits. A skylark filled the clear air with its vibrant song as it continued its vertical flight. Nature had her oil painting interrupted by the movement of two hunters as they approached 'Cnoc a' Choilich', the 'hill of the grouse'.

Steadily they advanced through the heather. MacLeod was enjoying Stuart's tales of previous outings.

"There were more Freeforesters then. Now the number is three who practise true, traditional Freeforestery." Stuart regretted a way of life that was disappearing, but he enjoyed educating his apprentice about what to do and what to avoid. "The lie of the land is very broken with lots of ground not visible. Anytime we could disturb a beast," he warned in a low voice. Thereafter little was said.

Skirting a ridge they kept below the skyline to avoid being silhouetted against the sky. In that fashion they continued their ascent, gaining altitude and inceasing their range of view. Occasionally Stuart scanned the ground through his binoculars. A raven 'cronked' as it flew overhead: twisting in flight it eyed them carefully.

"A good omen, George," Stuart muttered softly. "The deer aren't far when you see the raven or the eagle. There are hinds grazing in the corrie beyond the lochan. Have a look."

It took MacLeod time to focus the binoculars and form a search image for the intended quarry. With Stuart's patient guidance he located the small herd of deer that were grazing in a hollow where the vegetation was green and lush. As he watched, hind after hind lay down until only two continued to graze nonchalantly.

"I should have brought my own binocs," MacLeod murmured as he returned Stuart's. "They're essential."

"Without them your first and last sight would be backsides in flight. Now I reckon there's a good chance of staggies close to those hinds, but we'll need to take care. A running deer will take the rest away. We'll follow this gully until we're almost opposite the lochan, and then we'll go left into the next gully. That way we'll stay hidden. That short, flat expanse," pointing straight ahead, "is the short cut, but there'll be no deer waiting if we take the direct route."

Stuart paused as he scanned the ground again, allowing his apprentice an opportunity to assess the approach route.

"See how they're positioned high up the corrie? From there they can see all the lower ground and, by keeping the wind over their backs, they scent anything from behind, out of their sight. You'll have to think like a deer, George, if you're ever to get a shot. Their senses are so astute that there's no room for error on our part."

Carefully they moved down the gully, pausing frequently to spy the immediate terrain. MacLeod, wary of being surprised by anyone else on the hill, glanced back. To his astonishment the head and shoulders of a stag appeared to his left. It was grazing, apparently unconcerned, and heading in a direction at right angles to their own line of advance and no more than three hundred metres distant.

"Stuart." MacLeod hissed, pointing in the stag's direction as instinctively he crouched lower. Immediately, Stuart shrank down, grimacing at being caught in such an exposed position. They watched as the stag continued to graze. It was moving very slowly, periodically stopping, its head raised to view the slopes. Soon its whole body was silhouetted on the ridge. What a magnificent animal. Effortlessly it held high its wide spreading antlers. Stuart's mouth silently whistled his admiration.

"He's a topper," he breathed.

Would it be wrong to shoot such a noble animal? MacLeod's thought was so fleeting that it scarcely registered. He was gripped in the hunter's primeval passion for the chase.

Another set of antlers confirmed the presence of a following stag as its raised head scanned the ground while it sniffed the air. Stuart and MacLeod had sunk belly down into the heather. The wind was in their faces carrying their scent away from the stags. The shadow of a cloud darkened the hillside. Rising cautiously, Stuart saw the heads of both stags down, grazing contentedly as they moved steadily into the wind. Beckoning MacLeod with an upward facing palm, Stuart led the stalk.

The hunters checked their progress to remain out of sight. Repeatedly they backtracked and made long detours to follow topography that gave them cover. With a more favourable lie of the land, and the wind still in their faces, they began to close on their prey, slowly edging closer to that position where the beasts were last sighted. At that point they crawled to move within range of stags they could not see. That they were close was certain, but how close?

MacLeod's heart beat double time, and, it seemed, double volume too. Perhaps its sound would alert the stags? He quickly dismissed that fancy and concentrated on Stuart's command, "Keep your ass down."

He'd rather have black, greasy peat smeared across his belly than risk scaring the stags and ruining any future chance of being Stuart's guest.

Stuart had whispered that there were probably only two beasts there: a stag and a younger beast or fag, as such an association was known in the stalking world. Still crawling, occasionally raising his head, Stuart's progress was very slow. MacLeod shivered as the cold oily wetness of the peat hag penetrated his clothing. Lying immobile, his adrenalin rush was being replaced by a feeling of acute discomfort.

Stuart was beckoning MacLeod while fixing his own gaze firmly ahead. Hugging the ground, MacLeod squirmed closer. His heart rate accelerated again, and his breathing became fast and shallow in anticipation of them being close enough for a shot. Stuart gestured MacLeod to raise his head. Slowly and tentatively he obeyed. No further than sixty metres, stood the fag with the big stag a further eighty metres. To MacLeod's surprise Stuart offered him the rifle; such was the generosity of the man. Declining the invitation with a shake of his head and a smile, MacLeod wriggled higher on the side of a knoll, avoiding its top where he'd be more easily seen. There, he assumed the role of spectator.

Carefully pushing the rifle barrel forward and clear of the peat, Stuart wormed into a good firing position. Nothing was rushed. MacLeod kept his eyes on the fag.

The report was followed immediately by a hollow 'plop' sound. The fag jumped and moved several metres before stopping to look around in a startled manner. It didn't appear to be injured. Looking quizzically at Stuart, MacLeod then realised where Stuart had aimed. Stuart continued to lie prone, the rifle still pointing uphill. The big stag had taken a couple of steps before turning its head to lick behind its shoulder. Then its legs crumpled. The gaze of the fag shifted towards the hunters. A sudden shift of MacLeod's position was enough to send it speedily racing over the rise and out of sight.

"Well done, Stuart!" Any doubts MacLeod had about stalking had been removed. That stag had no sense of pain. Stuart had remained ready, had a second shot been necessary. There had been no thought of trying to take a second beast before making sure of the first.

Macleod learned how to clean the stag. As the final preparations were under way to prepare the carcase for carrying, Stuart sent him to find a hole for concealing the gralloch and other discarded parts to escape the attention of crows: circling birds would alert the estate's stalker to the Freeforesters' activities.

The carcase was separated behind the shoulders to avoid the heavily boned area and also to discard meat spoiled by the shot. On each hind leg between shin and the tendon of the calf muscle, slits were made for slotting the stick. Seated, Stuart manoeuvred the carcase onto his back, his head in the triangle between the hind legs and the stick which he held across his chest. Satisfied with both the balance and the weight of the load, Stuart set the haunches aside and set about cleaning his arms and hands with water-laden sphagnum moss.

"Well, George, it's a good beast. You did well, although I think we had some luck. We've earned a feed."

Their early success meant there was ample time before the prearranged pickup.

While they ate and drank, Stuart recounted more tales. As he listened, MacLeod realised that he was learning as much about Stuart as he was about stalking. Their communication was through words but also beyond them.

"You saw me placing the liver and kidneys on that rock. Did you wonder why?"

It had crossed MacLeod's mind at the time. He had no

wish to seem foolish, but he offered his thought despite it seeming far-fetched.

"Perhaps it sounds fanciful, but I guessed you were thanking the raven."

Stuart shot him a quick, sharp look. "You thought that, did you?" His fine face softened with approval. "I'm thinking I was right when I told Sandy that we might have discovered another Freeforester in the true spirit of the name."

MacLeod felt his face redden.

"You're right about the eagle and the raven never being far from the deer. There's a chemistry of interactions, and we're part of it."

Nothing more was said. It was a time to reflect. The sweet biscuit signalled the end of the break.

"Now, George, there's ample time for another stalk. The hinds in the corrie remain undisturbed. I reckon a stag'll be sniffing close to them. The next shot's yours."

With meat guaranteed, MacLeod was ready to accept the invitation if it presented itself.

A large white rock served as a marker, and the carcase was covered with heather. They kept to gullies as they headed down from the summit, towards the corrie and the unsuspecting hinds. Near the floor of the valley the gullies petered out, and they were forced to make a detour about a mile downwind to avoid exposed ground. Slowly they ascended to gain a position immediately above the hinds.

Stuart had guessed well. "Two stags," he mouthed, raising two fingers.

"Looking after ten hinds," MacLeod grinned.

"Possibly more will be in the hollows behind these knolls. We have the advantage of the higher ground but we could be highlighted against the sky."

Thirty minutes of ultra cautious approach were followed by ten spent crawling. Antlers of resting stags were all they could see. A hind rose, looked around, then grazed camly.

Stuart slid the rifle over. MacLeod settled into a comfortable position. Twenty minutes passed as he waited for the stags to rise. His patience was sorely tested. Should he move closer? His silent question was conveyed by raised eyebrows while inclining his head. Stuart's smile and slow head shake reassured MacLeod that patience was all that was needed. MacLeod remembered the adage, 'the hunter has to be more patient than the hunted otherwise he goes hungry.' Turning to look at Stuart again, MacLeod saw him grimace and point downhill.

They'd forgotten about that hind. There she was, standing alert, ears raised, looking straight at them. Her sharp cough alerted the stags which stood up. Although startled they did not know the nature of the danger or its location, and so they stood still, nervously scanning the ground.

Gently, MacLeod raised the butt of the Brno rifle. It fitted comfortably onto his shoulder. Sliding the safety catch to the firing position, he sighted the nearest stag, but it had been spooked by sharper coughs of alarm from that nuisance hind. Moving in short uncertain dashes, it slowed to a stop a further thirty metres uphill as it checked to seek out the threat.

The cross hairs of the telescopic sight zeroed to a point slightly behind the shoulder. MacLeod talked himself through the mechanics: 'exhale a little, hold the remaining breath and squeeze *gently*, avoid jerking...' The trigger squeeze continued, his grip remaining firm and comfortable. The bang was followed by the solid thump as the bullet found its mark. The stag lurched forward, and, to MacLeod's disbelieving eyes, ran downhill. The other deer were off.

Stuart moved with amazing speed.

"Quick, George. Follow it," he called as he took up the chase. Stumbling to his feet, MacLeod was not as nimble as the older man. He felt deflated by failure. How could he have made such a mess? Downhill, then up and over the top of a knoll he followed, and there, barely ten metres away, was Stuart bending over the dead stag, his pleasure expressed by an enormous grin.

"A heart shot, Seoras." Stuart addressed George by his Gaelic name, a sign he was particularly pleased. "Heart shots always run a short distance. You've got to keep track or you'll lose them when they drop in the heather." The dead stag, its tongue sticking out in its last act of defiance, blended with the heather and peat hag into which it had fallen. Had Stuart not pursued, there would have followed a long and possibly fruitless search: another lesson for MacLeod.

MacLeod squatted next to the stag. He felt a spiritual connection.

"Aye, George, you can pray your thanks before sleeping tonight, but right now we have work again." Time was passing. It would not do to have Sandy waiting, possibly attracting attention.

Stuart had cut the jugular. Dipping his forefinger into the escaping blood, he marked MacLeod's forehead, the customary baptism for a first kill that bonded hunter and quarry.

With the stag prepared, MacLeod shouldered the haunches, the day's exhilaration easing the heavy burden, even during the uphill stages as they retraced their steps. He was glad when they reached the white rock and the earlier cache.

"You deserve a rest, George."

They sank into the heather, and took time to relax and refresh themselves with the last of their supplies, all the time admiring the beauty of their surroundings. The welcoming 'cronk, cronk' of the raven thanked them for the tasty morsels and endorsed their symbiotic relationship.

Two men rested; talk was unnecessary.

The minutes passed too quickly. Haunches were hoisted onto shoulders, the hunters grinned, and the homeward journey resumed.

Within a mile of the pick-up point they rested again until the light faded sufficiently to make it safe to move nearer. A large rock sheltered them from the prevailing westerly and from prying eyes. From the vantage of their hidden station they could observe two twists in the track as it snaked downhill, giving them ample warning of an approaching car.

Ten minutes later, Sandy arrived. The carcasses and gear were loaded into the boot, and they were off. Stuart described their day. Sandy was visibly delighted at MacLeod's success.

"We'll have a good dram tonight, George, once we've dealt with the venison."

Sandy backed the car up the garden drive to the shed door where the contents of the boot were unloaded. Using a rope and pulley the carcasses were hung from the roof beams. Skinning followed. Bloodied meat was cleaned with a damp cloth, and then the carcasses were sawn down the spines, the freely hanging halves left to dry and tenderise. The welcoming hot shower helped to soothe away sores. Later they met to savour a good dram and to recall the day's events.

The whisky tops of two bottles once removed were thrown aside. "We'll not need those again!" The night was young.

TWO

Those had been good times; the best. What had happened since? He shakes his head; time to push on, time to forget.

Resigned to whatever fate the cards deal, he continues his assault: a dark shadow, he moves unobserved on a darker wall; a spider without its silken thread. His rope had been deliberately abandoned with the kayak. Here is a purist confronted by his ideal of free climbing, of working with the rock, ignoring personal safety. Nature's edifice would not be desecrated or scarred. He respects these ancient monuments.

Pleasant, dry rock offers excellent holds and allows rapid progress for thirty feet. The climber pauses to admire the pact between artist and evolutionary design: the olive-green egg with brown scribing sits on a narrow shelf, itself devoid of nest material. There, the hand of God (more plausibly, natural selection) has forged the perfect pear shape to safely retain the object despite its precarious perch. If only the climber enjoyed such reassurance.

Above, looms the start of a narrow fissure that bisects the pillar for twenty feet. He identifies a broad overhang, on his left and just above the crack, as his next rest station.

The sensation of extreme exposure hits home: thin, very thin holds; the possibility of peeling is very real. Without warning the rock has become smooth, its insecurity aggravated by dampness and slime, the treacherous consequences of rain and greasy secretions from the vegetated crack.

His heart pounds and thumps against the breast bone; his mouth and throat dry and feel like sand paper. He thrusts his right hand above his head and into the gap. A crude grope reveals the slightest of grips. Cold beads of sweat pepper his brow; a chill shiver runs down his spine. Forcing his hand inside the cleft he forms a fist: the hand belay permits a needed rest.

With his weight balanced against one fist, the rock cuts into *flesh; blood trickles down his forearm. The pain is worth the security the engineered hold provides. He shakes out his left arm to increase its blood flow and remove cramp. In such fraught circumstances he questions his sanity, but this venture was conceived during a time he endured a long, dark tunnel that is despair and depression.*

Now that he's found himself, he faces an unexpected dilemma. Sensations he'd long believed dead have been resurrected. Now he fears death before he's ready. Ready? How ready had he been? When, or rather, if this mission is accomplished, will be the time to decide. In the worst case scenario the personal message in his day-sack will explain.

Also, he'd posted a letter to Paddy, a school friend, now a successful journalist. He hopes that Paddy remains the same independent spirit who pursues truth regardless of barriers or threats. The letter contains evidence of murder and drug peddling; it names a senior judge and an Assistant Chief of Police. Paddy's reputation would be enhanced if any editor dared to publish the corroboration that Paddy's expected investigation would reveal.

The throbbing pain in his right hand compels him to move. The beauty of the pink thrift flowers scarcely register. His left hand moves higher, looking to repeat a fist belay, but the cleft has narrowed and permits only finger entry. Feet slip, mercifully not simultaneously. Adrenalin surges and sets alarm bells ringing at siren decibels. Fear and failing strength stimulate an attempt at a lay-back; feet and knees push against rock, countered by the curled fingertips pulling inside the fissure. Bulging forearms threaten to burst the skin. How long can he endure?

Head abreast of the overhang, he struggles to rise another foot before his left arm lunges over the shelf, his right fingertips maintaining their tenuous grip. His right boot moves higher, its toe nicking the crack and gaining enough friction to encourage him to throw his right arm over the shelf; at the same time his torso twists through ninety degrees. With both arms pressing down, his right toe skims rock before plunging into space. Gravity enters the equation with a vengeance.

Years of guano deposits litter the shelf; its stench is but a faint impression as he feels himself slipping; slowly, but very definitely slipping. Feet flail seeking some invisible purchase, but their jerking action only accelerates, in spasmodic fashion, his 'contact' with space.

Desperation forces him to pull back his left hand to allow fingers to grip the shelf's edge. Able to twist his body he moves his right foot onto rock and feels for a toehold. His stomach churns. His right foot makes reassuring contact before slipping into the vacuum of space. He dips lower; a sinking feeling that courts feelings of the inevitable.

Sustained contact? Please, God for a solid base. Calf muscles gently increase their tentative push: his body regains lost height. 'Maintain that foot angle; retain that contact,' he commands.

Using the high jumper's Straddle technique he advances. His right hand explores the shelf. A blind, greasy bump is scraped of guano to reveal a solid grip. Confidence rises: left foot moves onto right to maximise that precious, albeit precarious, toe hold. Ignoring the greasy, stinking waste that coats the platform, a grateful climber lies prostrate on that bed of bird faeces, his left cheek enjoying its cool dampness.

Unwilling; too exhausted to move ... just enjoying the physical support that his body no longer needs to provide, his thoughts drift. Bird cries are close but fading; sleep answers his exhaustion. Distant memories flood back.

He recalls how much he'd enjoyed his introduction to the hill and his disappointment at not having managed to take up Stuart's second invitation to go out. If only he'd gone, things might have been different.

That first day on the hill had produced a feeling of contentment, of inner satisfaction, almost bliss. But the insistent voice calling him to surface was anything but bliss. He tried to weave it into his dreams, but its increasing volume and anxiety "George, George, are you awake?" began to penetrate. A gentle knocking which had accompanied the voice became a loud 'rat-tat-tat', followed by an even louder banging to torment his thumping head.

MacLeod groaned and pulled a protective pillow over his ears. Confused and disorientated, he lay trying to gather his senses, but the pain cleaving his skull made this difficult. Gradually he grasped where he was, and that the torturing voice was really the worried tones of Jessie. He had no recollection of how he had arrived in bed or what had reduced him to such a pitiful state. Through a haze, events began to be recalled.

He vowed never to drink with certain locals who appeared to have cut their first teeth on a whisky bottle. MacLeod lacked stamina and needed to avoid future excess consumption of 'The Famous Grouse', but he found it difficult to ignore a challenge.

Jessie's voice had become fearful. Against her natural inclination, she dared to push open the bedroom door.

"George, are you ill?"

A coarse croak grated from MacLeod's throat. The rasping and incomprehensible noises galvanised Jessie into action. She threw the door wide open.

"What's the matter?"

MacLeod's pale, drawn face looked back at her.

"Well," she went on, relieved to find MacLeod was not dieing, "I've seen healthier corpses."

That such genuine concern could change to scorn when 'illness' was 'self-inflicted' was a point not lost on MacLeod, even through his mental fog.

"Whether you deserve it or not, I've brought you a srupag, *and* it's the *third* trip I've made to see if you're in the land of the living." Off stormed Jessie, leaving MacLeod wondering if he were indeed 'in the land of the living'.

The mug seemed within reach, and after a few failed attempts he captured it. The tea did wonders for his throat but nothing for his pain-battered temples. Death seemed imminent, and would not have been unwelcome, but that avenue of escape remained closed. Half an hour later and MacLeod has manoeuvered his legs to dangle over the bed, toes scraping the carpet, gingerly testing the floor which seemed stable, but objects around the room blur in and out of focus. *How much* had he drunk last night?

Five more minutes and objects became discernible and static: next goal the vertical position, but not too quickly. Cautious steps are taken; each jarring move registering on the Richter scale. MacLeod slides his feet to avoid the tremors. He intends to greet the sisters in a normal 'everything fine' manner hoping to salvage some respect. Progress goes well until the bedroom door where a controlled collapse ensues.

The stairs invoke further purgatory, aggravated by self-doubts over his inability to recollect his behaviour the previous evening. Had he upset Maggie and Jessie, he wondered? Tentatively he pushed open the kitchen door, to be greeted by the lingering smells of bacon and egg. The effect was instantaneous, but he managed to reach the downstairs toilet before parting with what little remained of the previous evening's poison. Retching, breaking sweat and drawing breath all contributed to a much improved MacLeod. Submerging his face in a sink full of cold water concluded the remedy. Wet fingers preened his locks. He convinced himself he was presentable. Mustering an apologetic half-smile, he re-entered the kitchen.

"Are you planning to stay this time, or will there be something more interesting elsewhere?" Jessie's tone was tart. She certainly knew how to put the boot in, for such a sweet old lady. Anyone foolish enough to succumb to the demon drink got no sympathy.

Maggie, more solicitous, "I don't suppose you'll want breakfast, George?"

"Thanks, Maggie, but I'll miss breakfast today, if you don't mind."

"No problem, dear. Just let me know when you'd like something."

('Dear Maggie.')

At that moment Stuart appeared and smiled knowingly.

"Seoras, you're looking a bitty pale about the gills!"

MacLeod groaned in self-reproach. "I'll never touch another drop."

"Go canny now, George. Not so hasty. Perhaps it wasn't the whisky? Maybe you mixed your drinks? .... and that's bad. Just remember, we don't want you giving offence by refusing hospitality when it's offered. Best stick to *one* good whisky *all* night, and you'll *never* suffer a hangover, no matter *how much* you drink."

Such advice from the wiser campaigner moderated MacLeod's hostility to the amber nectar. At the same time his self-esteem received a boost when he was assured that he had not made an exhibition of himself and had conducted himself very correctly. Perhaps he would be able to look Christine in the eye again, he thought, and his spirits soared.

"Will you manage the hill after lunch, George? It's shaping up to be a good day: a nice wind and not too bright."

'Damn!' Inwardly MacLeod cursed. He felt acute disappointment.

"Well, Stuart..." but he struggled to find the correct words ... and their correct order. Stuart saved him the trouble.

"There'll be other days."

"I'm sorry, really sorry, but I'd just be a handicap. Maybe I could call this evening?"

"Grand. You'll be fine by then."

George followed Stuart to the door, and watched him depart. A cold shiver cut down his spine, but he considered the eerie sensation to be yet more protest from his poisoned system.

By early evening he was 'more like himself' and celebrated by demolishing a chicken drumstick and savoury snacks. With the light fading, he realised Sandy would be on his way to pick up his father and so he headed upstairs to watch.

His bedroom window commanded a good view of Stuart's back-garden as he watched for Sandy's car. His thoughts involved Christine before a check of his watch showed forty minutes had passed in his role as observer. They should have returned. Perhaps Stuart had taken a late beast which would explain the delay, but Stuart had always stressed the importance of being at the pick-up spot at the agreed time.

MacLeod maintained his vigil for another half-hour, becoming increasingly anxious as time passed. With no sign of Sandy and Stuart he sought explanations: mist disorientated all who became enveloped in its shroud, and that could explain Stuart's non-appearance, but his unease returned as he remembered the mountaintops had remained clear all day. Perhaps the old Austin had finally packed in? MacLeod went downstairs to ask the sisters if he could borrow their car. They required no explanation. They, too, had become anxious.

"Are you sure you'll be alright on your own?"

"I'll be fine. Don't worry."

"Then take the keys. And may the Lord go with you."

He had just persuaded their yellow Volkswagen to splutter into life when he saw Sandy reversing the Austin into his parents' driveway.

He cut the engine and was about to leave the car when he saw Sandy *alone*. Fleetingly Sandy entered and then left the house with waterproofs slung over one arm, a rifle and torch in his hands. He looked agitated as he hurried back to the old Austin.

"Sandy, where's Stuart?"

"No time to explain. Dad's missing."

"Hang on, Sandy. I'll come."

"I'd appreciate that, and Mum will be relieved to know I'm not alone."

It took MacLeod no more than five minutes to collect his gear and tell Jessie and Maggie of Sandy's news. The sisters would sit with Mary until the men returned: in fishing communities the women provided comfort and support during times of uncertainty. All too often it was a vigil that ended in tragic news with the loss of a husband, a brother, a son. Again that cold, unnerving shiver ran down MacLeod's spine as he watched Maggie and Jessie prepare to go next door. Yet the night was not cold.

"Mum's really upset. I've tried to reassure her, but I'm concerned myself."

"Twisted ankle?" The words sounded hollow, but MacLeod needed to respond with some plausible explanation. Sandy sped the car through the village.

"No. A sprained ankle wouldn't keep him from the rendezvous. A broken leg's different. If that's the case, you'll

38

go and fetch help. I'll stay with the old man."

Anticipating scenarios and considering appropriate responses relieved some of their concerns.

"We'll use the torches and hope that Dad'll see the lights. And I've brought the .22 so he'll hear the shots in case he's lying out of sight in a gully."

Despite the emotional trauma, Sandy had analysed the situation calmly and had remained practical. The car turned at speed onto the twisting peat road. Perilous plunges skirted the track one side or the other. Sandy braked hard at the first corner. MacLeod's sharp intake of breath alerted Sandy to the possibility that adrenalin was pushing the accelerator, and the remainder of the peat track was taken at a more sensible speed. MacLeod relaxed, as the threat of a drop into black space waned.

On reaching the lochs, they decided to skirt around and up Cnoc a'Choilich using the torch once they were half way up. Stuart might see its light and fire a shot to draw their attention. If they'd no success by the time they reached the high saddle they'd continue to the flat summit and so cover as much of the ground as possible.

The darkness was intensified by pregnant clouds. The two conversed but sporadically, each immersed in his thoughts. Occasionally, moonlight pierced the dense cloud curtain and illuminated the terrain with its glow. Ghostly reflections of grey cumulus clouds glided across lochs. All around, dark peat hags emphasised the colour 'black' with its associations. Again a cold shiver unsettled MacLeod.

For long periods the moon and stars disappeared making progress ponderous and heightening the risk of an accident befalling either man. In the inky darkness many a slide was taken into holes that looked no different from the rest of the uniform blackness that surrounded them.

Eventually they reached the plateau. Apart from the roaring stags bellowing challenges to each other, all was quiet. The small arms' fire from Sandy's .22 had attracted no response. Little was said, their anxiety increasing as the area that offered the greatest chance of finding Stuart petered out.

The return trek was one dreary, despondent trudge. They resolved to resume at first light. Then they'd cover the far side of the hill and include the corrie on the adjacent mountain. Stuart would not have progressed further since the sound of a shot would carry to the stalker's cottage.

The returning car brought Mary running from her house, but the faces of the searchers told her what she dreaded. Her head sank and her shoulders shook as she headed indoors. Never had MacLeod felt so inadequate. Nothing could be said which would not have sounded trite. Sandy tried to comfort his mother with positive talk about renewing the search in the morning. Maggie and Jessie would stay all night with Mary to comfort and support her in this crisis.

MacLeod retired to bed. It was three am. Another three hours and there'd be sufficient light to return to the hill. Although tired, sleep proved impossible. He lay awake, his mind racing, question following question. With only suppositions for answers, he found poor solace. The unthinkable needed consideration. If the morning search proved fruitless, they'd need to inform the police who'd organise a formal search with its advantage of numbers and the possibility of search dogs, even a helicopter.

Dawn found them on the mountain, both feeling they'd abandoned Stuart. They tackled the search with fresh determination. Despite Sandy's frequent use of the rifle and much shouting, their efforts yielded nothing. The hill, the heather, the entire environment remained uncannily quiet. As the day wore on the light deteriorated, and the spattering of rain turned into a steady downpour.

Dejection exacerbated by fatigue told in their faces. As they entered the police station their bedraggled appearance prompted the duty sergeant to respond sympathetically.

"You look bushed, boys. Take a seat. Billy," turning to the duty constable, "two mugs of hot, sweet tea and make it snappy."

Sandy described events as briefly as he could without revealing the reason his father had gone to the hill. Stuart would be found and, hoped Sandy, hear the approach of a search team. Forewarned, he'd be able to hide the incriminating rifle before being discovered.

"You've only decided to come to us now?" queried the sergeant. "I'd have thought…"

"We didn't want to trouble you," said Sandy. "We never dreamt we wouldn't find my father …" His voice stuttered and broke. MacLeod completed the necessary details.

"Best go home and get some rest. I'll contact the mountain rescue and log a report. I'll be in touch to let you know what's happening as soon as I'm told."

A bath and hot food were welcome. Word of Stuart's disappearance had spread. Numerous phone calls to Sandy and Mary raised their flagging spirits; many wanted to be part of any search and rescue operation. Sandy thanked them and requested they register with the police.

Police marshals organised volunteers into three groups, each directed by a member of the rescue services. Sweep searches would be conducted with lines of individuals at ten metre spacings on open heather, that gap reduced to five metres over undulating ground; impressive organisation in such a short time. Sandy's and MacLeod's hopes were raised.

The army of rescuers set off in police transit vans with a land rover in the vanguard. The rain became torrential; splashes that hit solid ground rebounded to ankle height. Near the mountain a rising wind threw sheets of rain that thrashed the sides of the shuddering vans. All the time the wind whined its disapproval of the rescuers' intent.

Sandy's and MacLeod's concerned expressions spoke more than words. How would Stuart withstand such conditions; to what extent would such hellish weather limit the search; might Stuart have crawled into shelter and then lost consciousness? Stuart was well known and liked by all in the village. Each volunteer harboured personal concerns.

Strain and fatigue were telling on Sandy. When all three transit vans stopped, he yelled, "Come on. What's the problem?" Regret followed immediately; "I'm sorry, but we're running out of time…."

The 'walkie talkies' picked up Sandy's outburst. One

of the leaders from the advance land rover battled back to board the transit carrying Sandy and MacLeod.

"I'm sorry for the delay, Sandy. I'm Angus, the main co-ordinator. I've been trying to contact the helicopter from Lossie. I'll want you and your friend to join me in the 'Sea King' once it arrives. The conditions are causing grave concern."

"I just lost the place. Sorry."

"We understand, Sandy. Think you'll both manage the chopper trip for a couple of hours? I'm worried you might not have the stamina given what you've both been through, especially you, Sandy."

But Sandy's gaze was focussed on the floor of the van; away in his own world, his spirit seeking his father.

"We'll manage, don't worry." MacLeod's 'reassurance' only raised Angus' concerns.

A bellow from the land rover confirmed contact with the aircrew, and Angus, forgetting his immediate reservations, left. The procession continued its winding ascent.

The weather deteriorated further. The wind became a howling gale, driving the rain with such force that it sounded like buckshot peppering the van. Side and rear windows were misted with condensation. Through the windscreen slanting lines of rain angled past. The driver struggled to keep his van on the track as a particularly vicious gust hit the transit broadside. Perhaps it was just as well the passengers could not see the perpendicular drops first one side and then the other.

After what seemed an eternity the transits reached the hill lochs and the end of the track. The men huddled in the shelter of the vehicles as they awaited instructions. Angus bellowed to make himself heard, informing all that contact had been established with the chopper pilot.

"He should be with us in ten minutes, lads, so let's run through the routine. It's too wild to be heard out in the open, and there'll be no chance when the chopper's overhead, so listen in."

Sandy became totally alert and focussed once more as he and MacLeod eagerly absorbed the information and instructions peculiar to their special role.

"Crouch down when the 'Sea King' is settling, and stay that way until I give you the signal to move. The machine won't land but will hover just above the ground. That will mean a jump up and a clamber in. On board, move to the opposite side, sit down, strap on the seat belt and stick on the ear mufflers."

Angus paused to read their faces. They nodded their comprehension, allowing Angus to continue.

"Sandy will be given a set of headphones to communicate with the crew of the 'Sea King' and myself. George, I'm afraid that you'll just have to leave the talking to us, but we'll need your eyes to scan the ground. Okay? "

MacLeod nodded again. It was only correct that Sandy be the main contact. He was glad of Sandy's firm grip on his arm: a grip that communicated their unspoken, but implicitly understood feelings.

"Okay, there's the chopper, three o'clock. I don't think he sees us yet." The two-way radio crackled again.

"Glenlivet-Angus here. We're at the south end of the loch where the track ends. Do you locate us? Over."

More static, and then, "I have you. Will complete a circuit before descent, just in case. Over."

"We'll be ready. Over and out."

Like some predatory dragonfly, the helicopter approached, its bulbous bulk increasing. Then it headed off in the direction of the mountain. Sandy looked at Angus in anguished disappointment.

"No problem - he's just checking for down-draughts and other hazards before his final descent," Angus reassured him. "There could be lots of trouble with these bloody gales, but don't worry. They know their job. That's how they survive."

Eventually radio contact was re-established with a crackled "Coming in."

Again the huge, yellow bubble of the Sea King drew closer, the staccato beat of its whirring rotors making verbal communication impossible. Angus gestured a reminder of agreed procedures. The metallic clamour suggested the machine was about to shake itself apart.

Prostrate and leaning out of the main hatch two crew members talked to the pilot to guide him still lower. By the time the chopper was within ten feet of the ground, one of the crew was dangling halfway out to survey the situation, all the time informing the pilot via the radio link in his helmet.

The pilot inched lower until the machine hovered just clear of the ground. A beckoning wave from the crew signalled the crouching figures to jump aboard, ably helped by a well timed tug from the helicopter winch man. Sandy was fitted with the headphones. Even with the ear mufflers on, MacLeod found the rattling vibrations deafening and wondered about meaningful communication.

Leaving the three separate groups to scour the ground, the helicopter headed towards the mountain. MacLeod could only watch and second guess the conversation as Sandy's lips moved. The Sea King dropped lower, almost brushing the heather. Slowly, it skirted the mountain, rising occasionally to get an overview before it returned to its low search pattern. The bogs and hags were given priority by the pilot as Sandy directed him over the most likely areas. All eyes strained to pierce the gloom for any signs of Stuart. Radio contact was maintained, albeit intermitently, with the ground search teams.

Time passed, and with it, a rewardless exhaustion of the most promising areas. The pilot started to sweep less favoured ground. Sometimes an outline, vaguely visible through the sheets of rain, raised hopes; only to have those hopes dashed soon afterwards when closer inspection revealed a deer or a mound of bare peat.

The search on the ground had proved no more fruitful. Hope and despair alternated, with despair more frequent and more intense as the slow moving line of searchers covered more ground. By dusk the walkers had reached the summit of the Cnoc. Although the rain had almost stopped, they continued to be strafed by the high wind. Five hours of unproductive searching in those conditions had taken their toll. After consulting Angus the ground leader ordered a retreat.

Not long afterwards the helicopter returned to the transits. Once Angus, Sandy and MacLeod had hit the ground, the machine whirred back towards Lossiemouth. Angus informed Sandy of his decision to withdraw the ground team.

"Five fresh men have arrived at the police station to offer their services. Three are mountain rescue workers and two are dog handlers with their four-legged friends. The handlers will cover ground not yet searched to avoid the dogs confusing searchers' scents with that of Stuart." Sandy looked despondent. Angus responded, "The dogs have an acute sense of smell, Sandy."

"I'll go with them," Sandy said. "I can show them where..."

Angus, reading Sandy's ashen face and deeply shadowed eyes, interrupted. "Sandy, *you* are going home for a rest. I will call you *immediately* we have news. You'll join us again *tomorrow*. That's a promise."

Reluctantly, Sandy realised that his present state might render him more of a handicap than an asset. The palms of his hands covered his cheeks. His fingers stroked eyes that were blood-shot, tired and felt gritty.

"Okay." Turning to MacLeod, Sandy pleaded. "He's out there somewhere, George, but where?"

"*We shall find him*, Sandy. Keep faith."

During the journey home little was said. Thoughts and prayers occupied their minds. Deep in his own thoughts, MacLeod's reasoning faltered. He understood that every hour strained the survival time for an injured man in such hypothermic conditions. Feelings of guilt and betrayal troubled him. If only he had accompanied Stuart, there would have been help immediately to hand. Would Mary and Sandy think him guilty too? Those thoughts weighed heavily.

When the transit dropped them, Maggie and Jessie appeared at Mary's door.

"It's good you're back. Come in."

They found Mary sitting, her gaze unblinking as she

stared into the glow of the coal fire. Finally she looked up, registered that her son was present and, wordlessly, went to Sandy. He held her close. Minutes passed, but time stood still.

"We have some chicken broth." Maggie's voice was low, practical and comforting. "You must eat before you go to bed."

Alone in his own room MacLeod prayed, the first time since those innocent years of early childhood. Comforted by a warm bed, exhaustion overcame him.

He awoke to the sound of a shot, followed by a groan, and found himself sitting bolt upright, sweating profusely: a nightmare but what did it mean? He had no wish to speculate. How long had he slept? What news? The vicious truth hit hard. There could be no news, or he would have been wakened.

Turning his eyes to the window, he realised that the rain had become drizzle. A feeling of nausea welled up from his stomach. It was the worst possible weather. The hill would be shrouded in mist, visibility down to just a few metres.

After dressing, he crept downstairs, glad to find that Maggie and Jessie were still asleep. Taking a scrap of paper he left a note on the kitchen table.

'6.30 am. Went for a walk. George'.

He found himself seated on a sandbank, gazing out to sea. He had little recollection of his journey. He watched the waves roll in, over and over again: gently, soothingly, they washed over the stones. The sound of tumbling shingle was muffled beneath the froth that creamed before each breaking wave. The tide had turned and the waves were in retreat. The further they withdrew, the further MacLeod withdrew from reality. A numbness that defied concern about how or why he was there, or for how long, crept over him.

At first the gentle pressure on his shoulder didn't register.

"George ..... George."

Who was this figure intruding on his peace? He had no wish, no wish at all, to be disturbed. Slowly reality began to re-establish itself as a loved voice said again, "George".

His vacant expression changed slowly as he regained the moment.

"Chr ... Christine?"

"You're okay, George." She sat down beside him, concern furrowing her lovely brow as she searched his face. "George ..... my love." Her voice was breaking. Her arms encircled and drew him to her. Her closeness, warmth and love broke his protective barriers. Emotion surged through him once more, like a dam bursting. His body shook uncontrollably. As his head sank into Christine's lap he began sobbing.

"Stuart ... we couldn't find him." He broke down weeping unashamedly for a friend but also for himself.

Christine's fingers stroked his hair as gently and steadily as the waves of the sea had lapped the shore. The sobs subsided to be replaced by heaving sighs.

"George, dear George, you and Sandy did all anyone could expect. It's terrible facing the loss of someone you love. You feel guilty, but it's not justified. Believe me, I know."

"How could you?"

Christine looked out to sea. She needed to distance herself before she started to explain. "Almost two years ago ... but as clear in my mind as if it happened yesterday, we were on the beach, watching a lad in a small boat. He was called Robbie. He was rowing to the shore. For no apparent reason he leaned over the side. A wave, much bigger than the others, turned the boat over. He was no more than twenty metres from us. We watched helplessly as he clawed at the boat, struggling so hard to get a hold on its curved base. His efforts grew more desperate. He coughed and choked as he inhaled water. Those noises still haunt me. All we could do was watch as Robbie drowned."

Silence. Christine turned her back, looking upwards for something, anything to relieve the anguish of reliving that tragedy. "There was *nothing* we could do. None of us could swim. So you see," she swallowed, her eyes welling with tears. "You see. I *do* know."

The comfort of his arm around her shoulders signalled

she'd said enough.

"What trials … and none our making? I'm sorry you saw me like that, Christine, and yet, I'm glad you found me. I just …"

"You just needed to cry, George, to lessen the anguish and rid the guilt that's been gnawing inside you. No need to apologise. I'm just relieved I'm here. Come home with me. A bowl of father's brose will work wonders. I need to let Jessie and Maggie know you're safe."

Without question or hesitation he followed to her car. She drove past the bay at Ardroan and then turned to negotiate the rutted track that led to the croft.

Preparing to meet Christine's father, MacLeod attempted a veneer of composure, but images of recent events invaded his mind.

"Do you mind if we sit a while before we go in?"

Christine nodded to the bench in front of the cottage. It offered a peaceful view over croft land that gently fell away towards the sea.

For several minutes they sat in silence, side by side, their body contact providing comfort and strength. Christine stole an occasional glance at his face. She needed reassurance he was recovering. At last he turned to look at her.

"George, please tell me what you're going through."

By nature, MacLeod was not a communicative man, especially when it came to expressing his feelings, but Christine's eyes brimming with concern encouraged disclosure.

He recounted the horrible nightmare of how his sleep had been violently interrupted by the rifle shot that sounded so loudly, and how he'd felt the desperate grasp of a reaching arm, as though a drowning man was straining for a lifeline that was an inch too far. Those feelings were so close and strong that he smelt fear and sensed an evil presence. Then he'd found himself awake, shouting, shaking and sodden with sweat.

Christine's eyes widened. "Oh, George," was all she said but with a wealth of compassion and understanding of his inner turmoil. Her hands gripped his arm transfering strength and reassurance.

"Christine?" A wavering voice emanated from the cottage.

"Coming Father," she called, lightly touching MacLeod's arm. "Father will be worried, not knowing what has happened." But MacLeod needed more time.

The cottage and its outhouse stood nestled against a crag. Its location, small windows and storm doors were designed to withstand the prevailing westerly wind. From the shingle drive a rich green meadow sloped down to the road; beyond that the shoreline and the distant Gannet Isles rising from the grey Atlantic. MacLeod's eyes moved from that tranquillity and security to engage the spectre of the hills. Ominously, mist shrouded their summits, the final knell to any hope that had sustained him through the trials of the last two days.

"Stuart, I'm sorry, so sorry," he whispered, unaware of Christine's light-footed approach. She touched his arm before holding him close for a moment.

"Come and meet father."

MacLeod drew several deep breaths and followed, ducking below the door lintel to enter a short hall with a cloak stand on one side and the faded photo of a well-presented lady and gentleman opposite. Following the voices, he entered a dimly lit room: its walls and ceiling were clad with traditional pine panelling that had mellowed with time to a rich, deep hue. The flickering flames from the peat fire illumined tapestries and photos that punctuated the otherwise bare walls.

By the hearthside Christine was seated on a small stool next to her father's chair. The grey haired old man looked up. MacLeod's advance stopped, transfixed by those piercing blue eyes. The high intelligent forehead housed an alert brain. The grief-ravaged lines in MacLeod's face did not escape detection, and the old man's expression softened immediately.

"Come in, friend," beckoning with frail hands. "You've been through the mill. Christine's told me. Stuart was a true gentleman."

'Was', past-tense: the way Macleod was starting to think.

They shook hands, and MacLeod sat next to Christine, facing her father.

"You'll be sick with worry.": statement rather than question. "Christine, the kettle is on the boil." Addressing MacLeod once more, "Greta, Christine's friend, phoned this morning to say she saw you looking out to sea, and that you seemed unaware of her, even when she spoke. Naturally, she was worried and contacted Christine knowing how much she cares for you."

"She spoke to me? ... I can't recall. Please say I'm sorry."

With nothing to add, he felt vulnerable again. The sight of Christine pouring boiling water into a bowl was a welcome diversion: a stir of its contents and then he was presented with a white paste. His cautious inspection did not go unheeded.

"Brose - some folk add whisky, but we can offer you better." Mr MacKenzie's eyes twinkled. Was he having fun at MacLeod's alcohol abuse? "Our cow's contribution."

He poured a generous helping of rich cream over the brose. His hands shook slightly: their grey skin, mottled with brown flecks, was stretched thinly across prominent blue veins and swollen rheumatic joints.

"No need for a grace. Enjoy." Her father's mischievous smile occupied Christine's own features. MacLeod's face grinned, the humour not lost on him even if he was the butt of their amusement. The bowl's contents proved tasty and were soon dispatched, but no food was taken without tea. Accepting the cup from Christine, MacLeod sipped the strong, sweet liquid and gazed pensively into the fire. He decided that further talk on what was uppermost in his mind was useless. Instead he asked about the croft.

Suddenly, he realised that Jessie and Maggie wouldn't know where he was. "I must tell..."

"I've already phoned, but they'll be glad to hear you." Mr MacKenzie anticipated well.

Jessie answered. Yes, they knew he was at Hector

Mackenzie's. No, there was no news from the rescue party, but Jessie would phone as soon as they heard anything. Sandy had fallen asleep in front of the fire; drained both physically and mentally. MacLeod replaced the phone and looked at two anxious faces. He shook his head. They sat, quietly mesmerised by the flickering firelight. Surreptitiously MacLeod studied his host.

Hector Mackenzie had a large frame, but he was thin, almost gaunt. He suffered from a wasting illness, but his eyes were as bright and alert as a falcon's, and his face was fresh. His general appearance belied the serious nature of his condition. Multiple Sclerosis is the curse of the Highlander. Hector would have lived an energetic life before it struck. Now he was fated to endure the cruel torture of an astute mind imprisoned in an inactive body. Yet, there remained vibrancy about the man, an inner strength derived from his faith in God. Thank goodness, thought a sceptical MacLeod, that religion could serve good purpose.

Lunch was a wholesome plate of broth, accompanied by thick slices of buttered wholemeal bread. Beef had been cooked in the broth and was then served up with swede in the emptied soup plates. A large pot of boiled Kerr's Pink potatoes, some with their skins peeling to reveal fluffy white centres, sat in the centre of the table, inviting people to help themselves. MacLeod had been unaware of his need of food, but soon he'd replenished those energies lost on the hill. Repair to his inner self was also underway.

"Thank you, Christine, for a lovely meal and for everything."

Her colour deepened, and she smiled. "You're easily pleased, Seoras MacLeod" as she began to clear away the dishes. MacLeod followed her into the tiny kitchen, intending to help, until Christine whispered, "Father doesn't often get the chance to talk to other men, George. I know he's enjoying your company."

So MacLeod returned to listen to stories of croft life in bygone days. Hector was a good raconteur, but an underlying anxiety about his own place surfaced. There were outstanding repairs that Christine couldn't tackle, although she did her very best.

Suddenly, the phone shrilled. Hector nodded, and MacLeod picked it up hastily and with some trepidation.

"Sandy, here, George … just to tell you that …well, there's still no news of Dad."

"But the dogs … surely?"

Sandy continued in a low, strained voice. "The rescue party's back. The dogs followed a scent that took them over Beinn Donald, but then lost it, probably washed out by the rain. I've never known Dad go so far as Beinn Donald. I can't understand. The mist made a helicopter search impossible. … George, I can't tell you how much your support has meant …"

"Sandy, it was little enough in the circumstances. If there's anything, anything at all…you know you just have to say."

"I know that and I'm grateful, my friend."

Christine, Hector and MacLeod all shared the same fear, but Hector put matters into perspective reminding MacLeod that Stuart had enjoyed life and would have wanted his friends to recall happier times. Hector's repeated use of the past tense reinforced MacLeod's sense of foreboding.

"You're not leaving already?" challenged Hector. "The ladies know you are here and can easily get in touch. We'll be disappointed if you don't stay for supper."

Macleod remained in that precious haven, relaxing as his recuperation continued. Keen to show his appreciation, MacLeod offered, "Would you like your peats moved from the byre to the lean-to? They'd be handier there."

"That would be a great help. Sometimes the baskets Christine fills are barely adequate if she's away longer than she expects. It'll be a pleasure to have the peats so near, especially when it's raining."

Christine smiled. Hector needed constant heat, and the transfer of the fuel to a more convenient shelter would considerably lessen her daily work. The task was started. Hector's appreciative smile boosted MacLeod's self-esteem.

Supper followed: chicken and potatoes then Christine's crowdie cheese and pancakes, and then they returned to the fireside seats. Conversation flowed, encouraged by a couple of malt whiskies. Hector's eyelids grew heavy and finally succumbed to the combined effects of whisky and warmth.

Christine moved quietly. "Come." She took MacLeod's hand and led him outside.

Darkness was falling. Standing, hands held, they watched the blood-red glow from the sinking sun warm the sky above the Gannet Isles. Slowly the fireball disappeared into the purpling sea.

"Isn't it beautiful?" Christine was still whispering. "Oh, it made me so happy to see Dad content and relaxed." Impulsively, she gave MacLeod a hug; its warmth reached deep.

Much later Macleod returned to the village to find Jessie waiting up. Assured that MacLeod was well and in no need of food, Jessie bade MacLeod goodnight.

MacLeod slept well, but, on wakening, he felt guilty that he was capable of uninterrupted rest when anxiety kept others awake. Perhaps, in this case, the whisky had helped. Certainly he felt physically restored, and his time at the croft had improved his mental health. Yet, still there lingered that feeling of guilt at his failure to accompany Stuart to the hill on that fateful day. A quick breakfast was taken before he made for Stuart's and Mary's. Through the window, he saw Mary still gazing fixedly at the flickering flames. He hesitated but decided it was better to visit and break the trance.

The door was unlocked. Quietly he entered and sat in the chair opposite. She looked uncomprehendingly in his direction. Several long minutes passed.

"Oh, George," she trembled. MacLeod took her hands and gently raised her from the chair. Leaning against him she let her tears flow. Her frame shook with every sob. "I'm so terrified he's dead. What other explanation is there?"

What could he say, when his own thoughts mirrored Mary's? Body contact offered comforting support that words could never express. Finally composed, Mary moved to the table while MacLeod put on the kettle. A cup clasped in both hands, Mary looked at the photos that faced her: a beach snap with infant Sandy proudly holding a shore crab; a hill scene with Stuart cutting peat; Sandy on the back of a cow, and Mary raising her hands in protest at having her photo taken.

MacLeod encouraged her to talk about the photos and her fond memories of the past.

"Can you stay awhile, George? Sandy's out again with the search party, and I'd like you to be here when he returns."

And so MacLeod stayed, grateful to feel needed in some small way. The long day passed with Mary comforted by his quiet but solid, male presence so much that she even managed to sleep for an hour, although her sleep was troubled.

In the early evening Sandy returned. His concern weighed heavily on him although he tried to hide it for his mother's sake. He embraced her warmly and spoke encouragingly about his plan for the next day but he lacked conviction. Mary knew. How often had she anticipated the possibility of Stuart not returning? The hill held dangers. A number of walkers, and even stalkers, had failed to return for the ultimate reason. Indeed a small number had failed to be found at all.

"You've done all that anyone could possibly do, son. We have to consider the unthinkable but we'll continue to pray."

MacLeod felt like an intruder at that moment. Excusing himself, he made for the door. Sandy followed, grasping MacLeod's shoulders to turn him. Their faces were inches apart, their gazes direct and unblinking.

"Dad was very fond of you. Will you join me tomorrow?"

The burden of guilt rolled from MacLeod. Sandy had used the past tense. MacLeod guessed the invitation would be to share a private farewell.

The next day the winds were light. The rising sun gently warmed them as they stood surveying moor and mountain.

"If you don't mind I'll walk on a wee bit, George?" With that gentle dismissal, Sandy, rucksack on his back and rifle case on his shoulder, strode off. MacLeod followed at a respectful distance. Both needed time and space to deal with their thoughts and emotions. On the summit of the Cnoc they stood together, their spirits stirred by the strengthening wind.

"Dad would have wanted you here, George." A bottle of the 'Famous Grouse' and two glasses appeared from Sandy's rucksack, and then he uncovered the rifle; a .243 Sako Forester fitted with a Zeiss scope.

"Fill the glasses, George." Sandy placed three rounds in the magazine, pulled the bolt and slid the first bullet into the chamber.

"Dad had only ten days until his fiftieth birthday. This rifle was to be his present; what he'd wanted for years, but was too frugal to spend such a sum on himself." Pensively, Sandy caressed the walnut stock. "And now, dear Father, a final farewell..." Sandy raised the rifle to his shoulder; his lips muttered some private message before he fired three rounds skywards. "Your freedom, Dad." Glasses were raised and contents drained. The rifle returned to its cover, Sandy looked into the distance, further than eyes might see, before turning, a tear glistening. With a nod he indicated the conclusion to his personal moment.

MacLeod stooped to pick up the empty shell casings.

"If it's okay, Sandy, I'd like to keep one?"

"Of course."

Long periods of silence accompanied their descent. Stories concerning Stuart provided some welcome comfort on their homeward journey. Before they parted, a look that expressed shared sorrow and mutual understanding was exchanged.

"He graced our lives, Sandy. I'll cherish the memories." They hugged and then turned.

It was the end of an era. With a hollow, sickening 'thud' a special chapter in life had closed.

THREE

'Kwa .... Kwa,' its crescendo increases, single complaints merge into hysteria ... 'Kwakwakwa': cacophonous din. Shrieks and rants break his slumber.

Right foot pushes ... space. Automatically his left hand seizes ... air ... panic.

'Freeze,' he commands. 'Gather your senses, avoid blind reaction. The dangers are imagined. You're fine.'

The source of the raucous abuse that tripped his panic button? - herring gulls, a.k.a. avian yobs. The figure explores his surroundings cautiously; his movements grow stronger, more confident. The gulls' flight signifies their abandonment of an inert body that had promised many meals.

Sea thrift's pink flowers provide relief from the immediate squalor of the thick, slimy faeces, itself liberally peppered by equally disgusting pellets: regurgitations that failed to graduate into stinking guano; many had disintegrated to reveal bone, feather and fur as evidence of predatory and scavenging activities.

His raised head identifies the summit, a mere forty feet away; another platform for more disgruntled 'shit-hawks' squawking their obscenities. Below, and more disconcerting, a void is interrupted by white froth; the foam of swirling water smashing against dark, unseen rocks. Intermittent calm streaks dissect the troubled sea to identify inert water trapped in deep chasms.

A gliding seabird provides a welcome interruption to the awesome spectacle: soaring on an up-draught, its tail, a rudder, dips deftly to one side, producing drag and effortless direction control; such freedom the envy of dreamers imprisoned on terra firma.

Time for action: a series of strenuous moves with thin holds on vertical rock and then the incentive of an easy scramble to the summit. No greeting fanfare; only bare rock with white 'welcome' splashes from evicted avians. A few blades of coarse grass are *whipped by the strong breeze. What price this barren piece of real estate measuring no more than five metres by four?*

Across the short sea divide, the cliff-tops sprout heather and grasses that stoically survive the hostile influence of the Atlantic Ocean. On top of the stack the stooping figure removes the contents of his day-sack; a bottle of Glenmorangie and a crystal glass, each well padded by bubble wrap. The protective cover, once removed, is replaced inside the sack. A fine dram deserves a special container to complement its quality; just like fine bone china enhances the taste of tea. With the day-sack as a cushion, the supine figure eyes the amber nectar against a lightening sky; visual appreciation enhances the anticipated taste.

'For such special memories ....'

Deferentially the warming liquid is sipped: no longer the rushed gulp to obliterate bad memories, to satisfy an addiction.

Two large drams are enjoyed before the upturned glass is placed on top of the bottle, itself positioned in a hollow. His eyes close; memories return.

Shock and depression had followed the failure to find Stuart. It had taken a long time before life approached normality. Then everything was thrown in turmoil.

Asleep; his eyelids flutter; hands ball tightly, his knuckles white. Sleep is troubled.

MacLeod felt no urge to return to the hill. He had assumed the role of adopted son to Jessie and Maggie. As the number of tasks at the sisters' place diminished, he spent more time at the croft carrying out repairs and enjoying Hector's company.

Some weekends MacLeod would borrow Christine's car to rendezvous with John in Glen Nevis where the Polldubh Crags provided the challenge. There they would set up camp and let the weather and personal whims decide if climbing or kayaking took place. The Rivers Spean, Awe and Lochy developed their skill levels to tackle grade three rapids competently. Anticipation of these activity weekends with their thrills and spills kept MacLeod upbeat.

"I'd love to tackle snow and ice again, John. What about it?"

"You need to meet Dougie. He's done lots of winter climbing."

"You think he'd join us?"

"I'll get in touch and give you a bell."

MacLeod greeted the arrival of freezing temperatures with zest. Friends who led a more pedestrian life thought him crazy. Christine was none too happy either once she learned his intentions.

One Saturday MacLeod received word from John. Fort William was on for the following weekend, and Dougie would be there. That weekend exceeded MacLeod's expectations. Snow and ice skills were sharpened and improved on the relative safety of Ben Nevis' lower crags in Coire Leis. Suspended on ice walls gave MacLeod his adrenalin burst.

Exhilarated and exhausted the trio called it a day. With the light slowly fading to a shade of grey, they descended to the distillery car park. Ahead lay the unattractive prospect of a cold, uncomfortable night. They talked incessantly like excited children. Their drug was snow and ice.

After a freezing cold and distinctly unpleasant night in the cars, they rose early. A few jumps on the spot restored some circulation while Dougie made a quick brew. A greasy breakfast cooked on the paraffin stove set them up nicely for the day ahead. Stiff shoulders loosened and sore thighs disappeared on the walk into Coire Leis.

Dougie selected a moderate grade ice climb called 'Tower Scoop' which involved two pitches. Ghost-like, Dougie advanced up the ice-covered rock. However spectres don't use such language. Dougie had problems turning an ice screw into the frozen wall of snow.

"Jist ae lack o' practice, lads. Bit rusty, otherwise nae probs!"

Dougie disappeared from view, the moving rope indicating his progress. Soon John and then MacLeod enjoyed the freedom of suspension in crisp clean air. Dougie had hewn a narrow ledge at the Scoop and all three crowded that perch, secured on separate belays. A menacing ice wall towered above. Dougie's axe and hammer sliced into the wall. Each boot with fitted crampon repeated the move, the front spikes penetrating the hard ice. Dougie moved quickly and soon disappeared. Ten minutes of snow and ice showers followed as Dougie fashioned a solid belay. MacLeod got the call and was relieved to move numbed legs.

"Move min," Dougie glowered as MacLeod's head appeared above the edge. "I'm gittin' frost-bite in my arse."

With the crux pitch over they unroped and solo climbed to the summit edge. There, crafted by eddying spindrift was a massive curling cornice. A round window of piercing light showed the way to the summit. MacLeod bellied through the tunnel cut by previous climbers to be welcomed by sunshine and a clear blue sky.

A flask of hot, sweet tea to wash down chocolate bars and then they moved to number four gully to glissade down to the corrie. Wearing waterproof gear and using their ice axes to steer, all three tobogganed on their backsides: an exciting end to a perfect day.

Dougie pointed out classic routes such as 'Zero Gully' and 'Point Five'. In that amphitheatre they were mere mortals surrounded by raw nature. That weekend opened MacLeod's mind to his potential, and his confidence grew.

At the cars they enjoyed a strong brew and arranged a date and location for their next venture before parting.

Driving home, MacLeod realised how little he knew about Dougie. Not that that mattered. He'd learned that Dougie was a car mechanic who'd purchased a garage, and then his wife had run off with the car salesman. Dougie had been forced to sell the business to finance the divorce settlement. At least Dougie had managed to keep his house. Dougie's gruffness hid a caring side to a man who kept people distant to avoid further hurt, but special bonds are forged amongst individuals who rely on each other in dangerous situations. MacLeod had been allowed to bridge that barrier, and then he was reminded of Stuart.

Life on the croft resumed in a steady predictable manner. MacLeod's renovation of the barn progressed slowly but steadily. It had been Hector's suggestion to convert the barn as an alternative home for MacLeod who was spending more time at the croft than in the village. Hector worried that the sisters might feel valued purely as a bed and breakfast resource. Similar concerns had troubled MacLeod until he raised the subject with Maggie and Jessie. They assured him that he was welcome for as long as he wanted. Indeed there had been a twinkle in their eyes when they'd stated their expectation that MacLeod would depart one day. However Hector sensed uncertainty in MacLeod.

"You have reservations?"

"I'm flattered to be asked, and it makes sense to live here with all the jobs to be done. It's Christine … I'm not sure how she feels."

"Perhaps you should ask?"

MacLeod found Christine in the adjacent room.

"I heard," she said as MacLeod hesitated. Christine moved closer. "And my answer is 'yes'."

Their friendship had grown with neither wishing to damage the special relationship. Christine's encouragement was what MacLeod sought.

He took her hands in his. Facing him, she rocked gently on her heels, her cobalt blue eyes holding his gaze. That smile, the upturned corners of her mouth twitching ever so slightly, seemed to tease. Her rocking increased, bringing her hips into direct contact with his: a fleeting contact but enough for her to feel his longing. Her smile faded, replaced by a smouldering look. Slowly her head moved nearer, tilted slightly, her mouth angled towards his.

The warmth of her breath, her faint jasmine scent, the fullness of her breasts against him, increased his desire. Her eyes were questioning; knowing what she wanted but unsure of the consequences. Moist pink lips, so close to his, were parted invitingly. Gently his mouth made contact, his probing tongue heightening their states of arousal. He forgot where they were. Gently his left hand caressed her right breast while his right arm held her securely.

Suddenly she broke away, grabbed his hand and led him outside to the byre. Straw was their mattress; their passion all consuming. Their initial consummation was one of wild abandonment as they satisfied their deep need of each other. Afterwards they'd lain, caressing, exchanging secrets and wishes for the future before making love again.

Whispers, quiet laughter, lovers alone in their private world, completely oblivious to all else; their dream became just that as they fell asleep, secure in each other's arms.

A cat, searching for mice amongst the hay, startled them from their slumbers.

"Gosh, it's nearly eleven. We've been here for three hours. Dad will be wondering."

She stood up, the perfect proportions of her naked body silhouetted by the pale moonlight that entered the narrow window; the glow of light showed firm breasts and erect nipples. MacLeod continued to spectate. Christine finished dressing and stooped for a momentary kiss before making for the house. After several minutes MacLeod followed having checked that no tell-tale straw clung to him.

If Hector was worried, it didn't show. Hector had been raised in a religious household and was a practising Christian who accepted people at face value without trying to change them. Setting a good example (which others might choose) was his modus operandi. After a cup of tea MacLeod bade farewell. Christine escorted him to the door. Outside they embraced, Christine purring in his ear and laughing softly before pushing him away.

"Just make sure you get that barn ready and soon. Now go," the mock command more invitation than scold. His heart was snared. He had little recollection of the drive back.

Completion of the masonry work was followed by internal joinery and plasterboarding. Finishing to Christine's standards took considerably longer. Finally, an advert was placed in the local paper for basic, affordable furniture. Being springtime, guest house owners were renewing items prior to the bed and breakfast season. It didn't take long to obtain the necessary items, and then MacLeod moved in.

Their plans were well advanced. They'd decided that after a month MacLeod would approach Hector to explain Christine's and his intentions to cohabit with marriage their intent as soon as they could manage. MacLeod was confident that Hector would not object; neither would he openly welcome their decision which ran contrary to his beliefs.

In the meantime Christine needed income and a career to satisfy ambitions she'd abandoned when her father required constant care. With MacLeod using the croft as his base, Christine enroled on a hospitality course at Inverness College. The course was split between college and work. With a wide variety of catering jobs available in Tor'buie from early summer to late September, Christine would be able to stay at home whilst completing the practical placements. Their plans were shaping up nicely.

Spring merged into summer. With Christine spending weekdays in Inverness, MacLeod became restless, and his thoughts returned to the hill. The mouth-watering prospect of thick venison steaks sealed his decision, and he decided to go out the next day, a Thursday, despite the risk of encountering workers on a weekday. Also he wanted to be with Christine when she returned on the Friday evening without her being aware of his intended stalk on the very ground where Stuart had disappeared.

Despite many searches Stuart had not been found. The passage of time had lessened the anguish but deepened the mystery and inspired several explanations, some bordering on the supernatural.

MacLeod would set off at six am and hope for a morning kill and an early return. If his day lengthened, Thursday afternoon was when the nurse visited Hector so everything would be fine. Content with his arrangements, MacLeod spent the remainder of the evening with Hector and explained his intentions. Once Hector was safely in bed, MacLeod retired to his bothy and made preparations. The byre renovation included a secure cabinet that contained MacLeod's prized possession, his Sako .223 rifle, personally recommended by Stuart as the best for Freeforestry.

MacLeod caressed the walnut stock: its chunky beaver tail design afforded a firm, comfortable grip. The only scope worthy of that quality piece was the Zeiss 4 x 20 with centre reticle and cross hairs: its ability to catch and intensify sparse light had proved a prize asset on a number of occasions when he'd taken a beast late in the day. With its barrel cleaned of oil, MacLeod replaced the rifle in its case. The ammunition was Sako's own make: each round fifty grains in weight and soft nosed to expand in a controlled manner on entry, thereby maximising shock to increase its killing power. A quick honing of the lock knife on the oilstone concluded MacLeod's preparations. A good breakfast the following morning and he'd be gone.

He fell asleep, a smile on his face as his thoughts turned to Christine's return on Friday. Everything seemed rosy.

FOUR

Six am found MacLeod looking out the window. The sun was rising, and the sea was flat calm like the proverbial duck pond: ideal for sunbathing but not stalking. In such conditions he'd be easily seen, and any sane deer would be on the highest summit where air movement would reduce the numbers of nuisance flies. He could only hope that a breeze would pick up later. Against his better judgment MacLeod decided to go. His binoculars were the final item to be placed in his day sack for immediate availability.

There were no other cars on the road. Only sheep enjoying the warm bitumen witnessed his passage. The turn-off approached and still no other vehicles. MacLeod steered the van onto the peat road where the hairpin turns commanded his attention. One sharp bend overlooked a sheer drop and held slippery shingle to increase its threat.

Ice-cold needles pricked MacLeod's back, moved up his neck and down his arms. He shivered. Such was the eeriness of the sensation that he considered turning back.

'Steady,' he scolded. He'd been in the shade of the hill, but there had been no obvious temperature drop to explain that unnerving feeling. The more he analysed, the greater the failure of logic to explain.

One last bend and the lochs were reached. MacLeod cut the engine; the immediacy of the situation focused his attention. After all, he was not invited by the laird. Pulling the rucksack onto his back and, with rifle over his shoulder, he scurried out of sight.

Around the hillock he paused to catch his breath and enjoy the early sun's rays on his face. The skylark climbing higher into the blue sky sang a clear melody. The air was clean, and MacLeod breathed deeply. Tarns, their edges laced with wafer-thin ice, reflected the sun's acutely angled rays. The effect was spectacular. The mountainside shimmered: a dazzling cascade of diamonds danced to the rising sun as golden rays graced frozen dew drops; the slumbering jewels glittered brilliantly on contact with those solar wands.

Surrounded by treasures that no amount of wealth could purchase, MacLeod was the privileged spectator of the richness that danced and sparkled before his eyes. It was a breathtaking display. For several minutes he remained mesmerised, knowing his wealth was but transient, hoping that his memory would capture that picture for frequent recall.

Spell broken, he moved from artist to predator. The eerie sensation remained with him, and, as he ascended the Cnoc, he kept checking behind lest any person followed. Avoiding the skyline he reached the plateau, a vantage point to scan the lower ground. Apart from a sheep there was no other life visible. The increasing warmth had driven everything either to the highest ground or to the coolest peat hag.

The Cnoc itself resembled a hunchback: rounded near the summit with the ground falling sharply so most of its lower slopes were not visible. MacLeod moved over its plateau and down the other side stopping frequently to search, but his vigilance went unrewarded with no deer to be seen. Perhaps a wasted journey, but the hunter is always hopeful: MacLeod searched the clear sky for the eagle or raven, but nothing interrupted that blue expanse.

Now in the valley floor he moved upstream towards a lochan, a slight breeze wafting onto his face. Through the binoculars he spied a couple of hinds some two miles away; they were moving slowly towards Beinn Cailean. At that distance there was no need for stealth, and he moved rapidly over the undulating terrain. He'd no interest in the hinds but nursed the hope that a stag might be near them.

He'd identified a crag to mark the position of his last sighting of the hinds. As he neared it he stopped and removed the rifle from its case and placed five rounds in the magazine. Sliding the bolt inserted a bullet in the chamber, and then the safety catch was engaged. Progress became ultra cautious with MacLeod rising from a crouched position to inspect the ground frequently. He sensed he was very close. The binoculars were swung over his back to avoid any accidental rifle contact that would startle the quarry. Crawling, breathing shallowly, his heart thumped loudly; how near? With the heather so dry it would crack underfoot, he kept to rock and grass as he edged upwind into the faintest of breezes.

On the skyline he bellied his way to a rock that offered a commanding view, but only a bare plateau stretched before him. He was in unknown terrain and chose to enjoy a sandwich and a cup of tea as he observed and familiarised himself with its main features. The sun was high, and he stripped to the waist to enjoy its comforting warmth.

Nothing stirred until a peregrine falcon appeared. It turned deftly in the slight breeze to alight on a rock barely fifty metres away. Through the binocs MacLeod admired its powerful compact body; those yellow eyes so bright and alert. It faced MacLeod. Its drooping black moustache reminded MacLeod of a bandit. He identified strongly with that magnificent raptor; both were equally loathed by the laird.

As the peregrine stared back, MacLeod lowered the binocs to expose his true identity in respect for that monarch of the air. For a short time they gazed at one another before the peregrine gave one short, sharp screech before launching itself. Like a stone it plunged down the gorge before banking at an acute angle around the crest and out of sight.

MacLeod interpreted the encounter as a promising sign and penetrated deeper into the unknown ground. Systematically he quartered the area using the glasses, and there it was; a lone stag grazing nonchalantly. At last the spirits were smiling, but it would be a difficult stalk across open ground.

The slope descended to a valley with a steep rise on the other side. Gain of that convex slope would position him below the beast and out of its sight: a real shooting opportunity. MacLeod's problem was how to escape detection until he gained the valley.

Progress was painstakingly slow. MacLeod hardly checked his footing as he concentrated on the stag. He was prepared to freeze the moment the grazing beast raised its head. More than once he almost fell as his leading foot trod space where solid ground was anticipated. He changed style, reclining his weight onto the uphill rear foot to counteract imbalance. Despite constant vigilance he was almost detected. The stag looked up and stared in his direction. In a crouched position MacLeod remained immobile for minutes; endurance that emphasised his determination.

Eventually, the stag decided that the unusual shape posed no threat and continued grazing. Another minute and the white tush of the stag's backside mooned welcomingly. A few delicate steps relieved partly seized muscles, and MacLeod's descent of the slope accelerated. Another two pauses were necessary as the stag moved its head to either side to sample lush grass and young heather, and then it passed out of view.

MacLeod straightened and relaxed before moving quickly into and over the valley and then up the convex slope towards its brow. There he jettisoned gear that would be awkward in the final approach. Carrying only the rifle and his knife he moved cautiously forward. So close were hunter and hunted that each step was tested before he placed his weight.

Over the brow and MacLeod lay face down and squirmed forwards pressing deep into the heather: there, no further than thirty paces, the back and shoulders of the unsuspecting stag. MacLeod was too close. The rising ground would force him to stand to make a heart or lung shot, but the stag would be alerted and be well away before then. With the beast's position pinpointed he retreated to make for higher ground and the offer of a clear, unhurried shot. Reversing over the brow he adopted a half bent stance always keeping the light wind on his left cheek to carry his scent away from the stag. He continued until he estimated he was about eighty metres from his quarry.

Above and on his right, a small knoll promised cover for his final approach. He bellied forwards over a slight bog feeling its cold wetness spread through his clothes, and then the knoll was gained. Barely sixty metres away the stag continued to graze calmly.

Gently MacLeod nursed himself into as comfortable and steady a shooting position as the uneven ground allowed. Excitement had given way to a calm finality as he eased off the safety catch. The cross hairs zeroed behind mid-shoulder. The firm, gentle squeeze of the trigger, and the report was followed by a hollow thud. The stag jumped, took five paces and collapsed.

MacLeod walked to his prize, rifle poised in case another shot was needed. Touching the stag's eye with the rifle's nozzle produced no response. It was time to collect his gear before returning to gralloch the beast.

A couple of hundred feet below the kill his peripheral vision registered movement on the ridge. He shrank into the heather. A head bobbed into and out of view, followed by more heads. MacLeod's heart pounded. Fear dictated flight, as fast and as far as possible, but he resisted the panic response with its guarantee of detection, pursuit and possible capture.

The group could not know his position; he'd slipped below the skyline and out of their sight. He waited.

Four heads ... three ... two. 'Now, MacLeod, go.'

Recklessly he careers down the slope; panic catalysing speed, despite the risk of a fall in such broken terrain. He slithers over the edge of the slope, takes several deep breaths, and dares to check. Peeping above the lip he fears seeing a hostile face or someone in hot pursuit, but only hillside and clear blue sky are visible. Lying back he exhales some of the tension, but fear returns as he imagines the group encircling him. Again he risks a look. On the skyline are two figures: then another two appear pointing and sweeping their arms; but not in MacLeod's direction.

He sits tight anticipating a short futile search: after all, they had *his* stag which would be adequate compensation for not catching the poacher. As their search activity appears

69

to lose momentum, MacLeod reasons it would soon be safe to move. Never again would he stray from tried and tested ground. The penalty for ignoring that eerie warning was being exacted.

Cloud cover had increased to accelerate the failing light. A hint of dampness carried in the light wind. There had been no activity for twenty minutes. He appraises the twenty metre stretch of open terrain that leads to a sharp descent and the promise of cover and safe passage along the valley.

A final inspection confirms the time is ripe. He'd sprinted eighteen metres when a loud metallic 'clang' rang out and echoed; at the same instant a powerful thump smacked his back and somersaulted him downhill. Nausea clouds his senses as he slips into and out of consciousness. The repetitive 'boom' of a heavy gun torments his throbbing head. Darkness brings welcome relief from the pain and confusion.

The cool drizzle revives; awareness dawns. The bastards had shot him. Apart from intense pain and a warm, damp feeling in his back, he seemed to be in reasonable shape. Still undetected he could only have been unconscious for a brief time, but any delay increased his vulnerability. His assailants must be closing on him.

He rises and then collapses but can not indulge time to recover. Sliding down the slope on his backside his dizziness passes; he adopts the position of a sprinting crab to skirt the hillside and put distance between himself and pursuers.

A gurgling sound catches his attention. A gap in the heather reveals a subterranean brook. The hole appears too small, but the overhanging heather conceals its true dimensions: it'll be a neat fit but, in his beleaguered state, it offers potential refuge.

On his belly he reverses, the space is shallower than expected. His toes point back as he extends his legs in the direction of the flowing stream. Rocks scrape his shins. Trouser legs ride up chafing the recent cuts and grazes. MacLeod pushes until his rucksack jams in the tunnel. Barely concealed he cranes his neck but can see only grey clouds through the heather framed window.

"Come on, I reckon he's ower here."

Stomach muscles contract, toes dig in and knees bend to draw his body deeper under cover. Despite the stabbing pain between his shoulder blades he manoeuvers the rifle off his back: now the chance to fire, but moving the rifle has gained precious space, and he squirms further back. His rucksack drags against the tunnel roof pulling at his jacket, sweater and shirt to bare his midriff. Sharp rocks score his belly. The cold water numbs and exhausts. It's a struggle to keep chest and chin clear of the rising water.

Rising? His body is plugging the channel: voices again but louder; closer.

He daren't move: a bullet through his skull a distinct possibility. The ice-cold water engulfs his midriff. His elbows have no feeling, but they continue to support. His chin is now touching the rising pool.

The voices appear to be fading. MacLeod moves slightly. A dislodged rock cracks off another. Heart pounding, he holds his breath.

"I reckon you're away too far ower, Jim." The shout is near, so near.

"Ya reckon?" Jim's voice sounds directly above. "Thon other poaching shit went much further than you thought. Bloody good job that I didna listen to you then, or the Judge would have had oor balls for marbles. I'm gonna hae a shiftie ower here and then I'll work back. Dinna reckon he was as far as this but better check."

Was that confirmation of Stuart's murder?

The marshy ground trembles. MacLeod's chest is compressed; all his breath forced out. He almost screams at the searing pain. Jim's weight had collapsed the tunnel roof, forcing MacLeod's face down. Water trickles over and past his mouth. Taut neck muscles shriek, but can not withstand the pressure, and his nostrils submerge. Drowning brings panic, but he fights the urge to heave upwards and protects the secrecy of his sanctuary.

Jim feels the ground sink and steps to the side. MacLeod's ordeal had lasted barely thirty seconds but had

71

seemed endless. The impelling need to cough is choked to a faint rasping sound, but was it heard? He imagines a raised rifle, Jim gazing at the bolt hole: MacLeod screws his eyes closed.

A minute passes. Very slowly MacLeod raises his head to see Jim looking in the opposite direction. In the poor light his features are difficult to make out until he turns; then MacLeod emblazons them in his mind.

MacLeod's heart is pounding so hard it must attract attention. He shivers at the prospect of the damp culvert becoming his grave; its running water would remove scent and any scant chance of discovery even by trained dogs. He visualises Stuart's decomposing body. His eyes narrow. These bastards will pay.

Jim moves away, the vibrations through the boggy ground weakening. Five ... ten, probably twenty minutes pass. MacLeod is unable to tolerate his claustrophobic confines any longer.

He struggles forward on unfeeling limbs until his head is directly under the hole. His entire frame is shaking; cold or fear? With great caution he raises his head. His eyes, just above ground level, conduct a three hundred and sixty degree sweep. The mist has thickened. Only shadowy outlines of unrecognisible bumps appear through the grey swirl. He listens intently but hears nothing; the confirmation he seeks.

Up and out; silently he curses disobedient legs, needed then to assist unresponsive arms. Very slowly he extricates himself from that holding dungeon; finally free but unable to move further. Massaging legs helps to restore some circulation. Despite the reassuring rifle with its full magazine he feels very vulnerable. Rucksack removed, he feels his back: sore but no blood. So what caused the warm damp feeling? Mystified, he rummages in the bag. The flask is no longer cylindrical. Snatching it clear explains all as the steel body reveals a crater shaped dent. Thrusting deeper he finds the culprit: a splayed lump of lead, probably the nose of a .243 bullet. Perhaps God existed after all.

As muscles warm and blood flows his pain increases.

Waiting for his limbs to recover, he consolidates his image of Jim: a skinny runt with sharp features emphasised by that thin hooked nose; the image of an ill-kempt rat is reinforced by straggling greasy hair. Jim's guttural tongue and clipped dialect were repeated until MacLeod had them firmly memorised. MacLeod's account of characters and events would not survive cross-examination in a court of law, but MacLeod had already determined his personal and satisfying version of justice.

His physical discomfort persisted, but he attempted several shaky moves on legs that resembled lumps of lead; mechanically they thumped the ground, jarring his body at each step. It was a hundred metres before full coordination returned, and legs behaved as nature had intended.

Five minutes later a heavy drizzle started; the mist that disorientated walkers but would act to MacLeod's advantage. The condensation behind his watch face made it difficult to read, but he believed the time to be about six p.m; and still a long way from his van.

The mist, so recently blessed was soon cursed as MacLeod became hopelessly lost. He had as much chance of walking into his enemies as he had of finding his van. Logic told him to locate the stream, ford it and then ascend what should be Beinn Cailean. He set off. The stream was found and crossed, but the ground did not rise as expected. He was about to retrace his steps when he encountered rising ground, but much further than anticipated.

Visibility of one metre prevented any appreciation of his surroundings. Confused, his confidence was dented: about to backtrack he reasoned that the light wind had been a westerly. If he kept what slight wind existed on his left cheek, then he should be heading in the correct direction.

Lumbering on, he reached ground that dropped steadily: off the plateau so soon? If his understanding was correct, he should find a lochan or adjacent marsh. Twenty minutes passed without a lochan or marsh despite the ground being flat. Bemused and bewildered he sat down. The clever person would wait until the pea soup cleared, even if that meant spending a night on the hill and walking out at dawn,

73

but MacLeod could not enjoy the luxury of that option. He knew that Hector would contact the police if he failed to return, especially after Stuart's disappearance.

Damn that mist. It played such cruel tricks. He regretted not taking a map and compass. He pushed on and found 'another' stream. At least its water was welcome, and he drank freely. A momentary lifting of the mist revealed an unknown lochan. He retraced his steps but was unable to find the stream he'd so recently crossed. He fought the urge to dash blindly to find something recognisable reasoning that the mist distorts, and so nothing would have looked familiar. He rested again. Tiredness and despair made his eyes heavy.

A noise startled him: darkness. He must have fallen asleep with no idea of how much time had passed. Up and onwards: five minutes later the unmistakable gurgle of a stream drew him. He stepped into a void. Sliding down greasy banking he landed feet first with a reassuring splash. A breath of air on his *right* cheek signalled the return of the slight breeze. To be on the correct route, he should have been facing one hundred and eighty degrees in the *opposite* direction. Assuming the wind had not changed direction, that reasoning made sense.

He followed the watercourse back to its source. Twenty minutes found him on marshy ground. Picking up a fist sized stone he launched it. The satisfying 'plop' as it split the surface of the loch brought a smile of relief. Convinced he knew where he was he bore right and found rising ground that led to the flat summit of the Cnoc.

In the inky darkness, black peat hags were indistinguishable from space. Several times he failed to contact the expected solid ground. One bad fall found his right leg embedded to the thigh with cold, oily water oozing from the raw peat, his left leg twisted beneath him. His depleted energy reserves were further drained as he struggled to drag his weary body clear. Gasping, he lay on his back. Twinkling lights winked back; *stars*. In the long struggle to escape the sucking sludge, he'd been unaware the mist had cleared.

Comforting thoughts of a warm bath and a large dram inspired renewed efforts. Light from moon and stars was mirrored from the surface water and showed features on a moor that was otherwise unpredictable. He suffered no more spills, and a spring returned to his step.

Flat expanses of light signalled the lochs: near them his van. His tiredness was almost gone as he rounded the bay and neared the van's parking site. The van's outline was savoured for several minutes, and then that inexplicable shiver unnerved him. He sensed he was not alone, and that any company would not be the welcoming type. He retreated thirty metres and observed.

It was tempting to cast precaution to the wind, jump into the beckoning van and ignore potential threats just to get home, but his hunters had too much to lose to allow him that luxury.

'Shit'. If they'd found the van its registration would identify ownership. MacLeod's mind raced. One lead would bring others until they'd trace him back to the croft and Christine and Hector. There would be danger for those he loved, *if* he returned.

He hoped they'd believe him dead, undiscovered in the heather, but, with the absence of his body, they'd prepare for any possibility. MacLeod decided the peat road *had* to be guarded.

Cautiously he circled the minivan in a wide sweeping arc, stopping frequently to listen for a sound that might betray another's presence. The proximity of some sheep caused him to move further away in case they ran and alerted others: that detour proved a blessing.

Below, some thirty metres on his left, MacLeod saw the pinpoint glow as it brightened then faded. Again the glow as another drag was taken on the weed.

From hunter to hunted, now back to hunter, the pendulum vacillated. Emotionally detached, MacLeod felt no fear. The ultimate quarry is the armed human. MacLeod anticipated another attempt on his life was imminent. 'A dead killer is a safe one' he reasoned.

Crouching, he threaded his way towards the red glow.

His leading foot tested for hazards before he committed his full weight. Inching nearer, it took him fifteen minutes to reach a large rock ten metres from the two smokers. They appeared unconcerned, oblivious to the possibility that MacLeod might arrive, suggesting they considered him to be dead.

A dark outline stood up. It grew in size. MacLeod realised it was heading towards him. He sank down and held his breath: the tinkling sound of urine on the other side of the rock; a couple of minutes later the figure had returned to its seat. MacLeod breathed easily once more as he listened to the fuzzy charcoal shapes discussing their day.

"Well, Jim, do you really think we'll see our poacher friend tonight, or do you think your shot finished him?"

"Nae doot thon yin's deid, an if thon mist hidnae cum doon, then we'd huv goat 'im, an that's fur sure. I dinnae miss sitters like thon, or ma name's no Jim McGuinness."

"Mmmm, so what happened with the other poacher, Jim?"

"Listen, smart arse, dinna thee be tryin tae mak oot that I wis tae blame for that cock up. Thon shit o' a factor reckoned that I couldna shoot oot his richt leg, an' him rinnin fur cover. How wis I tae ken that he'd drap jist when I shot? Jesus Christ, the sicht o' him squirmin in the grass, an' thon moanin', fair seekened me, I can tell ye."

Had a shotgun been to hand MacLeod would have used its spreading pellets to avenge Stuart. In the dark his single rifle shot had little chance of success even at such close proximity.

"Bit whit really scunnered me wis the way the Judge taunted thon poor bugger as he wis sufferin'. Imagin' sayin that he'd ken whit it wis like tae get a taste o' leed, as he poked 'im wi' the rifle, an' laughin' a' the time."

"Yeah, I felt the same. I've always been frightened of the Judge, and I don't mind admitting that he's got me shit scared. We're all in this together. You've got to hand it to him. He controls us while remaining above the law himself. Yup, Jim, he knows we've all had it if word gets out. Fear of disclosure keeps us together. Even if somebody says you

76

killed those two poachers, there's a world of difference between an allegation and proof. The Judge carries some clout, even if he is an evil bastard. It's as much in his interest to look after us, as we need to look after him."

"So ye reckon we'll be okay, Bob ... if we a' keep thegither?"

"Not a shadow of a doubt. Who's stupid enough to tie the noose around their own necks? No, we're all in it, right up to our eyes. The Judge made sure of that."

Jim shifted his position and fidgeted as if uncomfortable.

"Bob?"

"What's wrong?"

"Where did you aim?"

"When the Judge took us a hundred metres away and told us to take a shot each so that nobody would know who'd actually killed the wretch?" Jim grunted confirmation. "I mean ... does it really matter? We all hit him, except the Judge, of course. He decided that his shot wasn't needed, especially after that bastard, Colin ....how many shots did he fire? He's a psychopath; enjoys killing. Where did the Judge find him?"

MacLeod almost vomited. He'd heard Bob's description of a death that must have been agonising. A bullet would be too quick and merciful for any of that lot, especially the Judge.

"Yeah, the jidge played it real safe. Even made Billy take another shot 'cos he reckoned that he missed on purpose. But, yir richt aboot thon bastard Colin bein' twisted. I saw 'im squeezin wan o' the plaything's tits, an' hur screamin' while he's smilin' awa'. A queer bugger and wan that I dinnae want tae git near. Reckon he's the jidge's last line o' defence. Micht even huv goat 'im oot the clink. Whit dae ye think?"

"It'd crossed my mind. But hey, what about Helga ...ever wondered how she gets so many bimbos for the parties?"

However Bob's interest in 'tottie' wasn't drawing any response from Jim who continued.

"Never thocht firther. Cannae get it oot ma mind. I

mean ....."

"Agreed. It was all so cold-blooded, calculating and smart. Now, we're all in his power."

"Naw, ye stupid shit. I wis meanin' how near thon guy wis tae the first yin we buried. There wis nae mair than a hauf mile a'tween them. Disnae that seem weird tae ye?"

"Coincidence, Jim; just coincidence: yes it's uncanny, but, we're the only five who know what happened so keep calm. We're in this together. Yes, and we'll be training together, possibly you and me sharing the same length of rope in a fortnight's time. You might be in need of a helping hand, so keep the rag. We're companions, like it or not."

"And so micht you need ma help, as weel, matey! Anyway whit's the idea o' takin' us ower tae thon Loch Aoil place tae hae us bugger aboot oan rocks 'n watter? A reckun the jidge's aboot tae flip."

"No, he knows what he's doing. He's instilling character and discipline. He wants to see just how well we handle pressure. Maybe he wants to find out who the weak links are when the chips are down ... eh, Jim? Remember he's got Colin who's done lots of this outdoor crap before. Reckons he might make us a bit more like Colin; dependable, reliable, good old, bloody Colin. And remember, there's the Judge's toy boy."

"Ya mean thon fair haired, bum boy? Well I reckon thon's bendin' ower fur Colin as weel."

"How come?" Bob appeared to relish the reference to sexual perversions.

MacLeod had gained some good character insight of the Judge's henchmen. Four of them, plus the Judge, had been directly involved in the callous execution of Stuart. After the Judge, Colin seemed the most dangerous adversary. The 'bum boy' remained an unknown quantity.

More followed, MacLeod learning that the Judge would be checking the van registration with the police: bending rules, including the Data Protection Act, is normal to the privileged and corrupt, but such influence suggested 'Judge' referred to profession rather than nickname.

Christine and her father would be involved once the

van was traced. MacLeod's vengeance would be insatiable if either was harmed, but, as he considered matters, he reasoned that Christine and her father would be safe, as long as the Judge believed that MacLeod had not contacted them. If the Judge believed MacLeod dead then MacLeod's damning knowledge had died with him, and so there'd be no reason to harm MacLeod's friends: that logic provided comfort. Evil though he was, the Judge was not stupid, but how could a 'dead' MacLeod exact justice?

The exchanges between Bob and Jim interrupted his chain of thought.

"So ye reckon that bum boy Luke kens a bit aboot canoein' an' climbin'? Masel, I widna be in frint o' thon on a rope or ony ither place. An anither thing, I ken thae fags he taks stink like burnin' syrup. He's nae athlete thon yin, unless he's high oan drugs."

"Ok, Jim, maybe the Judge has other reasons to send us to the outdoor centre. Perhaps he's looking after his business. Unusual forms of transport may suit the collection and distribution of the merchandise."

"Whit dae ye mean?"

Tor'buie had the usual problem associated with any port. The previous year an undercover investigation, 'Operation Glasnost', had netted a million pound haul of cocaine as it was transported by road out of Tor'buie. The cocaine arrived on the Klondykers, the fish-processing factory ships of communist countries. Each year those rusting hulks anchored in Loch Breac taking mackerel and herring from the British trawlers. It was rumoured that much of the fish off-loaded onto the Klondykers was 'black landing', the over-quota harvest by the trawlers with the skippers unloading their legal quota at Peterhead. Illegal transactions were common, and so it was no great surprise that Tor'buie had been contaminated. While the drugs were intended for the lucrative markets in the south, every contact stained and tainted the attitudes of all those involved. Despite its strong community spirit, Tor'buie was being damaged by a few making a quick pound.

After 'Operation Glasnost' there had been more

questions than reliable answers at the end of the day. Token arrests had been made, but the organisers remained free. A suggestion, (and one that had gained common acceptance), was of a police contact warning those behind the shipments to destroy evidence before the police swooped.

Bob's remarks made MacLeod wonder if the Judge masterminded the Tor'buie drug operation. The pair's talk turned to parties where drugs and sex were in abundance. Bob appeared to enjoy a spectator role while Jim liked privacy for his 'shag'. Lewd descriptions of party frolics followed. MacLeod decided he'd gleaned all the information that was useful and made to move but stopped as the conversation turned to the outdoor training.

"Well I ain't happy wi' the summer week, but as fur thon fortnicht in winter, canoein' an' snaw holin' wi' climbin' 'n a'! Weel he can fuckin' forget it."

MacLeod continued to eavesdrop, intrigued to learn about the outdoor training. He gleaned that January was the preferred month, although no dates were mentioned. MacLeod would check it out. While Jim and Bob showed little relish for the outdoor activities, they'd indicated that Colin and Luke had expertise. Also Bob had suggested that the Judge could use outdoor skills for drugs transport, but, such suggestion, while interesting, was speculative.

MacLeod appreciated how easily kayaks could collect small packages from the Klondykers under the cover of darkness. Kayaks were versatile and could be launched from any shoreline with little chance of detection. Waterproofed and attached to a submerged buoy, the drugs could be jettisoned if a police craft approached, and there existed a good chance of the packages being salvaged later. With no incriminating evidence, the kayakists' activities would continue, and the operation blossom.

The single road south from Tor'buie posed the greatest risk for the traffikers. There, MacLeod conjectured, was the value of the mountain training. A fit person with good navigation skills could easily carry twenty kilos over wild terrain to make connections elsewhere with no risk of arrest. There were many routes through the mountains, the easiest having been identified by drovers who steered cattle to east coast markets.

To MacLeod it all seemed so very feasible. Drug delivery was virtually guaranteed and with no danger of being apprehended.

With Jim and Bob posted to guard the peat road, MacLeod considered it most likely that a watch had been placed on Hector's croft, but MacLeod's immediate concern was how to escape in the van. Starting the engine would give warning. If he got past the sentries, MacLeod reasoned that the Judge would have a contingency plan, possibly a vehicle blocking the track further down.

With nothing more to be gained from his eavesdropping MacLeod moved off downhill to check. Five minutes later he came across a land rover parked in a passing place. Ten minutes' observation convinced him that it was unguarded. He advanced purposefully. A plan had formed: if successful it should remove Hector and Christine from the Judge's suspicions and attention.

Slipping off rifle and rucksack, MacLeod rummaged in the bag for the small hacksaw he used to butcher deer. Sliding beneath the land rover his fingers sought its brake pipes but found them accessible only near the rear wheels and in a very awkward position for his intentions. Wrapping his balaclava around one brake pipe he started to saw. The cloth muffled the sound of metal rasping on metal. Ten minutes and a few skinned knuckles later, his nostrils were greeted with the pungent smell of brake fluid. The action was repeated to partly sever the second brake pipe. MacLeod prayed that his hastily contrived plan would succeed.

He moved half a mile down the track searching for any obstruction before returning to his van, hopeful that the peat road was clear along its entire length. His immediate problem was how to get past the sentries?

His van was parked on a downward incline with an uphill slope to follow. He intended to let the van roll and hope to gain enough momentum to carry the rising gradient. Not turning the engine would reduce noise and delay alerting the sentries and so their ability to respond, but he still anticipated fireworks.

MacLeod checked the van: tyres okay, bonnet not forced; no sign of sabotage. Was his hastily contrived plan flawed? 'Yes,' he considers, 'because I'm depending on them doing what *I* want.' Other imponderables troubled him. 'Would the van gain enough momentum to free wheel up and over the rise? In the darkness would he see enough of the track without using the lights? How long before they'd realise MacLeod's impending approach and what would they do?' The risks were great, but he had no other option.

He removes the rifle from its cover; still a full magazine plus a round in the barrel. He thumbs the safety catch to 'fire' and places it on the passenger seat; immediately available. The ignition key is turned, the light glowing 'red' for 'ready' (*or red for danger*)?

A final check: any omissions? His heart flutters - the choke. The old van was temperamental; she needed choke to encourage her to start. Yet again he checks preliminaries. Sweat dampens his brow. His mind races; every muscle is tensed. He pushes the van out the lay-by. Very slowly, it moves down the gentle slope to face the next rise: clear that and it'll be downhill all the way to the gate. Shit, he'd forgotten about the gate: it had always been left open: too late now.

Running alongside, pushing, left hand on the steering wheel, door wide open, he reaches the top speed his tired legs can muster, but is it enough? Jumping in: breathless, gently clicking the door closed. Now it's momentum versus gravity. He is a helpless spectator. He listens to the rumble of rubber tyres over the rough track.

The van starts up the next rise. Its speed drops dramatically, and still a third of the rise to go. He winces at the continued slowing of tyre on track and wills the van on. His throat tightens. Breath held, he's fully focussed on the brow of the rise. The van crawls, almost to a stop, unsure – forwards, backwards? MacLeod jumps out and pushes; 'forwards' resumes. Jumping in, he knocks the steering wheel. The offside front wheel leaves the track and spins in air as it sweeps the bordering ditch. Automatically MacLeod corrects, and four wheels contact solid ground.

Window down he listens for any warning, but the van's free-wheeling is deafening. Grit crunches, wheels plop into and out of potholes. MacLeod grimaces, but still no sign the sentries know of his approach as he closes on their station. He depresses the clutch and engages third gear, the car gaining speed as the gradient steepens. His eyes are wide, both hands are firmly on the steering wheel, left foot pushing down but ready to release the clutch while his right foot hovers to slam the accelerator at the correct moment. Suddenly there are shouts; blurred movements on the track ahead and an orange flash.

MacLeod responds, flicking on the lights in full beam. His left foot releases the clutch as his right foot slams the accelerator. The van skids viciously and moves sideways, almost careering off the track.

Jim drops his rifle, hands shielding his eyes from the blinding headlights. Momentarily he stands rooted to the spot but, at the last second, throws himself to one side to deprive MacLeod of his first meaningful contact.

Bob, slower to reach the track than Jim, has his night vision unimpaired and heads for the land rover. MacLeod realises he'll not gain as much time as he'd hoped and roars past. In his mirror he sees Jim raise the rifle. MacLeod douses his lights and also drops a gear for the rapidly approaching bend.

The sound of the shot distracts MacLeod. He skids, overcorrects, and the front of the van slews off the track and mounts a pile of earth. The front offside wheel spins wildly in unresisting air, the nearside barely retaining contact with the ground. With the front of the van suspended, MacLeod panics and presses the accelerator; the front wheels spin faster and the engine whines its complaints before calm and sense return. He releases the accelerator, engages first gear and opens the driver's door to lean out. The van tilts, the near wheel contacts solid ground and, with controlled acceleration, the van inches slowly off the mound.

The land rover rounds the corner, the glare from its headlights dazzling MacLeod. Jim is as surprised as MacLeod to find their vehicles so close and slams his brakes. With the van's front wheels biting hard track, MacLeod switches on the lights and accelerates rapidly to put distance between him and land rover. He fights to hold the front wheels astride the grassy ridge that bisects the track.

Down the steep and snake-like track at breakneck speed, MacLeod hammers on: it's reckless and suicidal, the track twisting perilously close to rocky outcrops and sheer gullies on either side. Unwilling to ease up on the accelerator in case the gate's closed MacLeod can only pray it hasn't been touched.

The land rover is closing. MacLeod hears a couple of shots, but no sound of a strike on his van. Suddenly there's an almighty jolt as the land rover rams the van to thrust it forwards, the van tail slewing, MacLeod fighting for control. Using his rear mirror MacLeod anticipates further shunts and strikes the accelerator prior to each attempt.

Ahead a straight thirty metre stretch drops steeply. It ends in a hairpin bend that courts a deep gorge.

MacLeod accelerates rapidly to leave the land rover trailing. The hairpin is close. MacLeod brakes late and hard. The van's rear wheels spin throwing stones over the edge, down into the inky depths. MacLeod smells the acrid stench of burning rubber as smoke swirls around a van that's sliding sideways more than forwards. Is he about to be rammed or will the van's lateral momentum take him into the abyss?

Like some blazing eyed monster the land rover's lights loom large in his side mirror. MacLeod drops the van into second gear and snaps the accelerator to the floor. The sudden lurch whips his neck back; the van thrusts forwards around the corner and out of the land rover's path.

A brief look in the mirror shows the land rover, its speed unchecked, going sideways. MacLeod brakes and witnesses the unfolding drama in his side mirrors. Bob's arms cover his face. Jim, eyes wide, a look of sheer terror, sits, his straight arms locked to the steering wheel by white knuckled fists; a body rigid with fear. Dark space beckons: impending catastrophe.

MacLeod registers no emotion but hopes that, once

they realise their fate, those last seconds extend to minutes, just as they'd prolonged Stuart's suffering. It was surreal to witness the speeding vehicle, its progress unchecked, slide over the vertical drop.

MacLeod dowsed his lights, rolled down the window, and listened. The only noise that drifted through the night was a faint purring from the depths of the gorge.

Taking the torch from the glove compartment and the rifle from the passenger seat, MacLeod walks cautiously back. The flattened grass bears witness where tyres left the track. Flimsy railings have disappeared. Deep scars in bared earth are testimony to where the land rover has gouged and ripped out heather in its last desperate attempts to stop before it plunged.

The faint purring is slower, the sound of flowing water greater. The smell of oil and petrol hang in the air. MacLeod begins his descent into that dark fissure; devoid of emotion but remaining alert.

Progress is made dangerous by the greasy rock. Twice he slips; almost falling when he mistakes a wet, dark smear for a non-existent shelf. Immune to fear, detached, blinkered and completely focussed, he resembles the predator in its final approach to dangerous prey.

The land rover is upside down, angled slightly downstream, its sub-frame exposed. The purring sound comes from a wheel revolving in the night air. Water spills through the broken windscreen and swirls inside. The torchlight shows Jim suspended upside down, defying gravity. His head flops sideways. His eyes bulge with fear. In contrast to his loose, broken neck, Jim's body is pulled forwards as if some giant magnet holds it to the dashboard. Bright red frothy blood oozing between clenched teeth provides the clue; torchlight reveals a snapped steering wheel entering Jim's jacket: a red stain has spread almost to his shirt collar.

The petrol fumes make MacLeod light headed. He stands upright and gulps fresh air. Shining the torch on the stream reveals a lengthening rainbow that dances over the dark water. The leaking fuel continues to trickle through the damaged filler cap.

A low groan has MacLeod splashing his way to the other side. Bob is only concussed and is regaining consciousness. His forehead deeply gashed, the blood flows freely, but there appears to be no other damage.

'Typical,' thinks MacLeod, 'the Devil looks after his own'. MacLeod's skin crawls with revulsion as he considers the grossly overweight, self-indulged specimen but quickly checks himself. He can not allow emotion to cloud his purpose.

Bob's appearance suggests a harmless lump of little consequence. His morphology of immature male is enhanced by his baby face and rolls of puppy fat: prejudice blinds reality; Bob is bad news.

Splashing water over Bob's face revives him faster. His small, hard, dark eyes focus slowly and then are consumed by fear. MacLeod's penetrating glare never wavers.

MacLeod needs answers, and quickly. Bob's right hand moves to finger his throbbing forehead but is stopped, held fast by MacLeod's crushing grasp. Slowly Bob's head turns to look once more into MacLeod's unflinching stare. The menacing silence and threatening physical presence reduce Bob to a whimpering wreck that begs for mercy.

MacLeod looks at the miserable form of life that has played its part in the death of his fine friend and the subsequent destruction of a lovely family. His left hand grabs Bob below the chin and twists his face backwards and sideways forcing those beady eyes to meet his own.

"Now, who's the Judge, and where do I find him?" The hissed question aggravates Bob's terror. His fearful eyes seek sanctuary from MacLeod's glare, but that grip is firm and unyielding and pulls Bob's face nearer. Bob's sweat trickles onto his wrist, and MacLeod smells fear and experiences some satisfaction. MacLeod yanks him closer until their noses contact. The stench, as Bob's bowels void, is scarcely a distraction.

"I don't know. Honest, I don't know," blurts a shaking mass.

"I don't think," says MacLeod in slow measured

tones, "you fully understand. I'm tired. The police'll be surprised if anybody survives this: two corpses will raise no questions."

MacLeod shines the torch inside the land rover settling its beam on one item. Panic-stricken, Bob's head twists free and turns, his eyes identifying MacLeod's interest; a petrol-can. Instantly he turns back, his eyes managing to hold MacLeod's as the urgency of survival overcomes his immediate fear. Mutual understanding exists. MacLeod nods to confirm Bob's suspicions. Bob's desire for life reaches fever pitch.

"*No. Please*.......I *beg* you, *please* don't kill me." The wretched plea brings no response. "The Judge commands all of us. I really don't know much. *None* of us does. That's the truth. It's how he works. I'll tell you *anything* you want to know. *Please* let me live."

"I'm all ears."

Bob describes the Judge's team, allowing MacLeod to appreciate the dangers each might present. Undoubtedly, Colin, being strong, and, Bob believed, ex-military, was the most dangerous adversary. Colin enjoyed taking risks and dominating weaker individuals. Bob was frightened of Colin, although it was another, called Billy, who was the main target for Colin's abuse. Bob, astute and cunning, was very perceptive about people's strengths and flaws. He understood MacLeod's determination to gather information at any cost, using any means necessary. Bob gave his fullest cooperation.

Bob's knowledge of Luke was limited. Luke spent most of his time with the Judge, nurturing the belief of a homosexual relationship. "At parties they watch others having sex. They never join in; never take any of the bimbos to rooms; just sit together, often touching and stroking. Jim reckons ...." Looking at Jim, shuddering and then continuing, "...reckoned that they have the odd little ear nibble but Jim was fond of the drink and didn't see well. Not that he's ever going to see again," returning his gaze to the frame pinned to the steering wheel; Jim's head oblivious to the water that lapped its straggling strands of greasy hair.

"… and?"

Bob, imploringly. "You'll let me go, won't you?"

"Tell me about the parties."

"Saturday nights: there's the wealthy in-crowd, plus young fillies that Helga picks up. She promises a good night; drugs, booze, and generous tips to reflect the pleasures they provide. Helga always finds two or three."

"What 'in-crowd'?"

"Guests from London, friends of the Judge, but we don't know who they are. Sometimes, they snort 'Charlie', forget themselves and mention the legal profession and the stock market. Twice I heard the police mentioned and what would the press give for a picture of this guy as he snorted. The guy just laughed and said he'd plenty of shit on his superiors; enough to make murder appear angelic. I guess we get them from all walks, including the law. Colin reminds us that we heard nothing. Once, one of the girls was left naked on the floor, only to be found dead in the river the next morning. The police were called, of course, but the matter never reached the media. The Judge saw to that. A pregnant pause followed, Bob apparently elsewhere with his thoughts.

"You were fond of her?"

"She was … she was …" His voice petered out.

"How did the Judge keep the lid on the death?"

The mention of 'death' returned Bob to the present. His mood changed and he became increasingly unbalanced, almost hysterical.

"You bastard: you're not going to let me go, are you?" Wild, hollow laughter gave way to uncontrollable sobbing.

Bob's usefulness had ended. MacLeod's right fist shot through the open window to connect squarely with Bob's chin. The hysteria ended as abruptly as it had begun.

As he rummaged through Jim's and Bob's pockets looking for a diary or notebook, MacLeod found nothing apart from cigarettes, matches, and, in Bob's jacket, a wallet containing money in notes and coin. The notes might be useful and would not be missed, but he decided against emptying the wallet in case that raised suspicions.

Unable to open the doors, MacLeod leaned through the window, past the slumped figure of Bob, to reach the kerosene can. Liberally sprinkling its contents behind the front seats, MacLeod strikes a match, flicking it dismissively past Bob. A slight explosion of igniting fumes is followed by flames licking greedily at the vehicle's upholstery.

MacLeod retreats. Clambering up the gorge, he makes speedier progress as the spreading flames illuminate the rocky chasm. Suddenly he feels vulnerable. Any passing driver will see the burst of light funnelling up from the depths of the gorge; a spout of fire piercing the night's darkness; Danté's inferno. It will only be a matter of time before the police are contacted.

As MacLeod exits the gorge no car lights are visible on the main road. Starting the van he moves slowly downhill without lights. In the next passing place a feverish eight point turn is executed to face the van uphill. Phase two of his plan begins, although its implications weigh heavily on his mind. By then the flames are licking high, and the area above the gorge is aglow as if a tunnel to hell has opened: the spectacle will soon attract attention.

An almighty explosion follows his negotiation of the hairpin. Burning projectiles blown skywards are returning to earth, many still alight. A firework display peppers the hillside and bathes MacLeod's uphill passage in a swathe of light. MacLeod guns the accelerator, hoping that no cars will pass along the main road for the next few minutes.

In the rear mirror he sees several heather fires. Gaining the top of the track he stops to view the fiery glow emanating from the gorge. In the few minutes it had taken to reach his vantage point the inferno's intensity has increased: now it penetrates high, diffusing into the night sky to lighten its darkness like an aurora borealis. Around the gorge a sideshow of several expanding heath fires blaze.

Noticing car lights fast approaching, MacLeod drives over the rise to his original parking spot where he reverses, carefully placing the van in the identical position to its previous slot. Locking it, he heads west towards the large reservoir, at the far end of which is an old drove road which he intends to follow to Ardroan, then only a mile from Hector's croft.

The twinkling stars welcome him as they glitter brightly through breaks in the cloud. MacLeod marches on, buoyed by the turn of events. Lady Luck has not abandoned him, but he can not rely on her intervention again. Evil and danger jeopardise the safety of those he loves. The brightness of the moon penetrates the light cloud cover, and it isn't long before the thinning cloud has cleared. The full moon and its army of sparkling sentinels shimmer grey light onto the mica-filled stones that glisten along the footpath. MacLeod draws deep, reviving breaths of the crisp, night air. Invigorated, he makes speedy progress.

There was a spring in his step as he arrived at the reservoir's boulder shore. He flitted from one rock to another. In that sprightly fashion he moved around the body of water. The moon's reflection spread a silver sheen that masked a threat in the loch's dark depths. MacLeod shivered at the secrets those black waters might hide.

"Stuart, are you there?" MacLeod stopped, listening, searching. He heard the distant bellow of a stag as it warned potential suitors to respect the harem so painstakingly herded. An unknown bird flapped away into darkness and oblivion. An uneasy MacLeod continued his journey.

Resigned to the need that he must leave Tor'buie for the foreseeable future, MacLeod imagined life as a carefree drover to dispel thoughts of his enforced exile, and how long it might last.

His thoughts returned to the scene of carnage. Police and fire fighters would organise a search following the discovery of his van so near the incident. Their inability to find his body, coupled with the unexplained accident, would make the Judge deeply suspicious. MacLeod worried that an inspection of the land rover might reveal sabotaged brake pipes but hoped that the intense heat would have melted and welded metal, making foul play less detectable.

MacLeod willed the police to classify the crash an accident and remove any implication of his involvement.

Then the Judge might believe MacLeod was dead, pickling in a remote peat bog. To make his death more credible, MacLeod intended to disappear. Heartbreak and deceit, normally unthinkable, would be justified to safeguard those he loved while offering him a chance to bring the Judge and his thugs to justice.

The implication of the plan weighed heavily, and MacLeod trudged the last three miles, eventually reaching Ardroan, a crag that once served as a meeting place for drovers. There he left the track to strike northwest towards Hector's croft.

Ten minutes found him overlooking the shieling, a derelict cottage that had been home to a shepherd and his family long ago. MacLeod wondered how families eked a living from the poor land. The attractions of town life were understandable. Lured by the promise of similar comforts, MacLeod made for the croft.

Resigned to his fate as a fugitive, MacLeod considered how best to secure Christine's acceptance despite the bitter anguish his plan would cause. Concern was replaced by hatred and fury at the scum that had forced that situation. He'd make them pay.

Over another rise and below, the ghostly glow of whitewashed walls of Hector's cottage, a welcome sight for this weary traveller. His visit would be brief: just long enough to collect food and other items from his bunkhouse without disturbing Hector. Then he'd abandon that haven regarded as home with all its comforts, security and, above all, its promises for the future.

MacLeod rested behind a rock while he reflected on his plan. He had to be certain it had no flaws before its next phase started.

A yellow flash, followed by the telltale red glow; he had company. Circumstances dictated. He slunk to the other side of the rock and monitored the sentry's activities until he was confident there was no immediate danger of being discovered. His day sack served as a pillow, and, despite his circumstances, he managed to sleep.

Bleating of sheep and the high piping notes of a meadow

pippit interrupted his slumber. Slowly his senses returned as he languished in that pleasant state between sleep and wakefulness. Even his dire circumstances were not allowed to deny him a rare moment of bliss.

A stretch removed some soreness, and then MacLeod sought to locate the sentry. Quartering the ground with binoculars confirmed the previous position to be vacated. Sniffing the air for cigarette smoke and detecting none, MacLeod decided that the vigil was over.

The cough was so close it came as an immense shock. Startled, MacLeod shrank behind his rock. Barely fifty metres away a figure glanced between wristwatch and horizon.

Several minutes were needed before MacLeod regained sufficient composure to risk inspecting the enemy. The stranger appeared to be in his early thirties, of average height and medium build; the type who would pass unnoticed except for that flaming beacon of red hair. He kept checking his watch, suggesting a lapsed meeting time. Another ten minutes passed and his relief arrived. There was a brief exchange during which 'Red Hair's' face was visible; craggy, wind-burned features suggested a man of the hill, possibly a stalker. MacLeod had been very fortunate to have gone unnoticed.

'Red Hair's' relief sought immediate shelter with no attempt to observe the cottage. His face was pale and pallid: its wan complexion suggesting familiarity with indoors and nightlife rather than with the bracing effects of weather vagaries. The conscript's slumped shoulders and limp physique made MacLeod wonder how such a specimen could be an asset and branded him 'Pimp,' but he was relieved that 'Pimp' had replaced 'Red Hair'.

It wasn't long before 'Pimp' was extracting a half bottle from the folds of his overcoat. Breakfast was spiritual, in a manner of speaking. MacLeod was delighted to discover a weak link in the Judge's armour and hoped not to have to wait for dusk to make his escape, but he'd already decided not to collect personal gear from the croft in case 'Pimp' had a pang of conscience and glanced downhill at the wrong moment. Instead MacLeod would head for the road south of Tor'buie and thumb a lift only from lorry drivers to avoid being recognised.

In Inverness he'd contact Christine but worried in case she'd news of his disappearance and had already returned home.

About a mile from 'Pimp', MacLeod hid his rifle below a distinctive crag that he'd remember: the ammunition was concealed below a lichen encrusted rock ten metres due south. With his load lightened, he strode in the direction of the road.

Through the condensation on the watch face he believed the time to be about eight am. It took him two hours to reach the road about a mile south of Tor'buie. A slight incline provided a vantage point to view traffic and allowed him ample opportunity to dodge out of sight of cars but enough time to reach the road to hail an approaching lorry.

His good luck prevailed. The first lorry he thumbed slowed to stop on the crest of the hill. MacLeod threw his bag into the cab, thanking the driver as he boarded. The driver was cheerful and loquacious, but MacLeod was not listening and offered only an occasional 'aye' to maintain the monologue until the outskirts of Inverness.

The driver must have been glad to see the back of MacLeod when he dropped him at the Longman roundabout. No doubt he'd think twice before picking up the next hitchhiker until his thirst for company made him forget the dour, taciturn Scot from the northwest.

Ten minutes took MacLeod to Inverness College. Seated on a bench he pretended to read a discarded magazine while keeping a watchful eye for Christine. It was 12:30 pm, and he knew that Christine would soon be taking her customary walk prior to lunch. He hoped she'd be alone.

Loud shouts from a motley bunch of youths signalled the lunch break. Christine appeared chatting animatedly to another female. Her relaxed manner showed she'd no news of MacLeod's disappearance.

Christine and her friend headed into Inverness,

MacLeod, trailing eighty metres back, checked that nobody was following her. If he was seen making contact the Judge would know that MacLeod had spoken of the attempt on his own life and the likelihood of Stuart's murder, and Christine's fate would be sealed. Several hundred metres further and Christine and her companion parted company. MacLeod, confident of no third party interest, made his approach. Gripping her by the arm he ordered her to behave normally as he steered her into the multi-storey car park.

Her startled expression at his unkempt appearance and strange behaviour was understandable, but she played along. The obscurity of the carpark gained, MacLeod relaxed his grip. Christine contained her urgent need for an explanation for his antics and unkempt appearance when she looked into eyes that were troubled and fragile. She shielded his body in her warm, protective embrace, once more his strength.

"It's all right, Seoras. Everything's fine."

He lingered, enjoying the comfort of her body, but time was short.

"We've got to talk, somewhere more private. Here might be okay if we move higher; fewer cars, less people."

"What's happened? You look terrible!" Christine needed answers now that MacLeod seemed better composed.

He outlined events. Christine's expression was quizzical. She checked his eyes. Was this a prank? Had the man she loved lost his senses? 'No' to all questions, she decided as his story unfolded.

When he described having been shot, she could not help but question again his sanity. She looked for a half smile, anything that might contradict his words, but her disbelieving stare received only a questioning look in return. She started to raise his jacket and shirt but stopped when he gasped with pain.

"Forgive me, George. You *are* hurt. You need a doctor."

It took persuasive talk, together with a brief inspection of his back, to allay Christine's anxieties and convince her that he was not going to drop dead. The sight of the disfigured thermos flask made them shudder. Lady Luck had been magnanimous.

Christine tightened her grip on his arm as he continued his saga.

Twice Christine required support when it appeared she might faint: the first time concerned Stuart's fate; then she reeled when MacLeod described events leading up to the blazing land rover while omitting that he'd torched it. She'd enough to digest without complications.

Several minutes allowed Christine to regain composure.

"Come," her inviting hand reached out. "I know a quiet place we can eat. The students will have left."

They walked to a corner café and ordered fish and chips. MacLeod was ravenous and after finishing his own meal he helped devour Christine's, following it with two jam-filled doughnuts washed down with a mug of hot, sweet coffee. Christine watched in amazement as he demolished the calories, understanding better the physical demands he'd exerted over the preceding twenty-four hours. As for the mental costs, she could only guess.

Refreshed and revived, MacLeod clasped Christine's hands across the table. After recent events he needed her contact even if a café was not the most romantic setting. For several minutes they sat admiring each other, their intertwined fingers caressing. Then he demolished pleasantries as he stated his need to disappear.

".....but that would be impossible in a place like Tor'buie."

"I know."

A heavy silence followed as Christine's eyes quizzed his. His set features showed his resolve and hid his inner conflict. Christine was thinking through the implications. Realisation dawned slowly. Her reluctance to accept his decision was evident.

"No, George. You can't leave. What about us? How can you even consider that?"

"I'm sorry ... it's the only way. What's more, you mustn't confide in anyone, not even Hector. Believe me Christine, these thugs will stop at nothing. They've killed at least once and were only thwarted a second time by my good luck."

"But ..." Inwardly she also knew. Her expression reflected her reluctant acceptance of the dramatic changes that were imminent. "Perhaps you're right but ... *surely* not *complete* separation without *any* contact?" The frown, the pained expression, her questioning and pleading eyes, spoke loudly.

"Christine. They'll check and double check and believe I must have escaped when their dogs find no body. The crash will have made them even more suspicious. They'll believe I played a part. So you can expect them to follow you and watch the croft."

"What about Dad? They could be ...."

"No. As long as they believe there's been no contact with me, they'll not harm others. There's a limit to what the police can ignore, even if the Judge does have powerful contacts, but you'll need to act the part of the distraught lover, overcome with grief at your loss." The hurt look on Christine's face mirrored his emotions. "I'm sorry, but there's no other way. Even this plan with all our sacrifices will take a long time to convince them that I'm truly history, and that their secrets are safe. Eventually they'll *have* to accept that I crawled off and died somewhere."

A fleeting smile from Christine, but her watery eyes and lack of words reflected her true feelings. Their fingers interlocked firmly.

"Just remember to stay strong and remain alert. Don't arouse their suspicions. Okay?" Christine nodded, but the imploring look in her eyes showed her hurt. He resisted his urge to comfort her. "I love you but part we must, and *no* contact for a fortnight when they'll be most vigilant. Only in an extreme emergency can you phone, and then *only* from a public box. I'll not be able to phone you in case your phone's tapped but I intend to stay in Edinburgh at Dougie's."

Knowing where he'd be and that he'd be safe removed some of her worries and helped relax her.

"He'll be the only other person, apart from you, who'll hear this story ... understand?" Christine nodded. "They've too much to lose, but not as much as us. Remember ... our future depends on you keeping all this to yourself; absolutely *no* confiding in *anybody*. Okay?" Raising his eyebrows, he waited for Christine's acceptance of everything he'd stipulated.

"Okay. Exactly as you say. I understand." Christine had accepted the inevitable.

They spent the remaining time together anticipating and discussing as many scenarios as they could imagine, and how best to manage each one. Christine did not even suggest the police: she realised that they'd altered evidence to misrepresent the circumstances surrounding the death of the waitress whose body had been discovered by the river after a party at the lodge. MacLeod, supported by Bob's account, believed she'd taken drugs and would have contained semen from several sources in blatant contradiction of the coroner's verdict of 'death by misadventure' on her death certificate. Whichever police and forensics were involved, the Judge owned them. How far his army of corrupt officials extended was a major unknown.

MacLeod asked Christine to raise the waitress' death, albeit in a circuitous manner, in conversations with locals to test their opinions on the unusual circumstances surrounding the poor girl's fate. MacLeod needed to guage villagers' feelings about estate activities and police integrity.

Christine considered matters then aired her intentions to resume her course as soon as the search for MacLeod had ended: her work would be her reason to keep her mind occupied and help her recover. MacLeod admired her ability to accommodate so much so quickly and in such a practical manner.

With the time approaching four pm Christine needed to catch the bus home. MacLeod chose to drop his final bombshell as he explained his need to observe the lodge's Saturday night party. Christine protested but agreed he needed more information and the chance to see adversaries' faces. MacLeod's reassurances that he'd be ultra cautious helped appease Christine, and, to confirm his safe return, he'd leave a jacket button at the back gatepost to Jessie's and Maggie's.

Before parting, MacLeod told Christine where to find his diary with Dougie's details.

"And remember ....."

"I know... don't phone for at least a fortnight, unless it's of the utmost importance," Christine retorted, lowering her voice to the gruffest tones she could manage. Both burst out laughing at her mimicry and mockery of MacLeod's warnings. "I love you, Seoras MacLeod." That pleading look was in her eyes once more. Their imminent separation hit hard.

They left the café, their hands gripped tightly. Privacy was found in the anonymity of the multi-storey car park. They embraced, exchanged a gentle parting kiss, then Christine walked, never once looking back. MacLeod felt gutted. Isolated, he faced the intimidating appointment at the lion's den the following night.

Christine had given him all her money; added to Bob's 'contribution' his total wealth amounted to eighteen pounds and thirty two pence.

Disposable shaving blades were a necessary expense. In the Eastgate Centre toilets he washed and shaved: when thumbing a lift a presentable appearance was an asset. Again he restricted his request to lorry drivers and hoped the fading light would protect his anonymity from Tor'buie residents who had visited Inverness that day.

He got a lift to Borve and then another to River Bridge, only two miles from Tor'buie. The rations purchased in Inverness would suffice to lie low for two days if something went drastically wrong. Leaving the road he headed into the forest and fashioned a shelter from some branches propped against an outcrop of rock. Pine needles were his mattress, but sleep evaded him. Most of Saturday was spent dozing below the summit of Cnoc a' Caoirich, a prime vantage point that lay within two hours' walk of the lodge. Around seven pm he moved, believing there would still be enough light to monitor the guests' activity by the time he reached the lodge. Later, under cover of darkness a more intrusive inspection would be possible.

By nine pm he occupied a position overlooking the lodge. Shortly afterwards the heavens opened. A car arrived, the shrill voices indicating excited, nervous girls; presumably the evening's entertainment. The light flooding through the open door showed three women; two were young and giggling, but the third who ushered the other two, emanated masculinity, further emphasised by her business-like stride.

Stuck in a ditch that skirted a plantation of young conifers, MacLeod remained well hidden. The trees were too small to offer adequate cover and so he was obliged to cower in a sunken quagmire. Rain ran down his neck and was initially absorbed by his cotton shirt, but, before long, the shirt resembled a cold, saturated sponge. Ground water seeped into the hollow and MacLeod's boots became submerged. It was a relieved MacLeod who squelched out of that wallow and headed towards the glow of the lodge windows.

'Like a moth,' he reflected: just as long as he could leave the light when he chose.

Chat and laughter from male and female voices drifted out. In the background, the noise of rushing water was a reminder of the rising river. Nearer the lodge the diffusing light revealed a strip of bare ground about twenty metres wide. The risk of being seen was negligible, but a cautious MacLeod detoured to cross the private road thirty metres below the lodge: there he headed for the river and the cover offered by the birch and alder trees that bordered its banks. Under their shelter, he moved upstream. The roar of the waterfall became deafening, its raw power obliterating most other sounds. The lodge lay directly opposite.

He was relaxed, confident of remaining unseen. The fine spray from the waterfall refreshed his face, in sharp contrast to the large raindrops that had pelted him as he shivered in the ditch. So deep and impenetrable had the cloud cover become that moon and stars were almost extinguished. The sheltering trees became faint silhouettes; discernible only as charcoal outlines in the growing darkness.

99

MacLeod listened carefully but heard nothing except the roar of the waterfall. The frothing mass of water spewed and fought its way through the constricted passage of the gorge before it vented its seething rage on the battered rocks below. In the dark pool the troubled water swirled, before spilling out to wreak further wrath as it churned and cut its way through the boulder strewn river course.

The turbulent water stirred memories of a kayaking nightmare when he'd resembled a leaf in an emptying sink as his kayak was swallowed by the swollen waters of the River Spean. Its deep gorge had vanished under the foaming water that spluttered over its lip. The nightmare of that trip remained so vivid that fear blocked further recall, and his attention returned to the task.

There appeared to be no guards outside. Cautiously, he approached, avoiding the shafts of light that spread through three windows; two at ground level and one upstairs. Pressing close to a wall, he passed below a noisy upstairs room. Around the corner a glare of light blazed through a small fixed pane. Standing on tiptoe he looked inside.

The interior of a walk-in pantry, generously supplied with bottles, was revealed. With the cold penetrating to his very bones, the sight of the alcohol fuelled his craving for a dram. Through the next window the pock-marked 'Pimp' was pouring himself a generous measure of 'The Famous Grouse'.

"Well, Cyril, I guess you'll be gittin' pissed as usual?"

The broad Scots accent named the wan specimen, but its source remained hidden. MacLeod was about to cross beneath the window to view the speaker when 'Red Hair' moved towards Cyril and clamped a strong hand around the bottleneck.

"Christ min, have ye no feelins fur Bob 'n Jim? There ye are behavin' jist the same as ony ither Setterday while oor mates are frazzled embers."

Hand shaking, Cyril downed the large whisky, instantly gaining the courage to counter. "Look Donnie, nothing's going to change what happened. Anyway you said yourself that Jim's driving would be the death of him some day.

What do you expect? Bob must have been out of his senses to let Jim drive that track. He could hardly take the bend at Ardlui never mind that hairpin."

"Aye, I guess ye're richt, but ye could shaw a bit mair respect an' gie the drink a miss, or cut doon a bit instead o' knockin' it back like ye're daein'."

"Away and look upstairs," retorted Cyril. "Go and see if they're acting any differently from their usual Saturday night of pill popping and gang banging. Me? ... I prefer whisky."

"Listen mate, you're the guy that gits maist o' the drugs fur them bliddy yuppies frae the sooth. You an' thon Helga bitch, so dinnae cum righteous wi' me, Cyril boyo." The menacing tone of Donnie's sneer dissipated Cyril's Dutch courage. 'Pimp' resumed his pitiful, cringing manner.

Two names and two faces: plus the bonus revelation that Jim's and Bob's deaths were accepted as accidental. MacLeod hoped the Judge would also accept that the twisting track and Jim's notorious driving had resulted in the inevitable. Despite the unavailability of that dram, MacLeod felt better.

His impression of Cyril as a sleaze and an alcoholic was strengthened. Cyril was definitely worth saving. He'd squeal confessions louder than the proverbial spit pig after ten minutes with MacLeod. If he dealt drugs there was a good chance that he sampled them, making him even more fragile under duress. Donnie's contempt for Cyril caused MacLeod some conflict. The red-haired Scot appeared to have some moral fibre, an attribute sorely lacking in the others; further in 'Red Hair's' favour was the fact that Jim and Bob had not mentioned him when they'd recounted Stuart's murder. Either Donnie had not been there or hadn't played a part.

Perhaps Donnie might contribute incriminating evidence should the Judge be brought to trial? Wishful thinking, but at that stage MacLeod could only view Donnie as a dangerous opponent. As MacLeod watched, the exchanges between Donnie and Cyril became more heated until Cyril fled the room. With no more to be gained, MacLeod moved to the next window, but the small cloakroom was empty.

From the upper window the raucous sounds of a swinging party grew louder. Retracing his steps, MacLeod glanced into the room where Cyril and Donnie had been. Donnie sat, a glare like thunder, ready to wreak his repressed anger on any legitimate target. The dour Scots streak was manifestly obvious. MacLeod was glad he wasn't Cyril, for yet another reason.

The actual party needed investigation. With the rain hammering into his eyes, it was difficult to look up, but light from the upper window reflected off something that caught MacLeod's attention. Shielding his eyes, he identified a horizontal pipe passing below the window: it fed into a down-pipe that he'd passed twice without having noticed it, so dark was the night and so unrelenting the rain. The down pipe appeared to run close to the top window. Running his hands along the wall he made contact and felt water trickling down it. A firm pull ensured the pipe was secure enough before he prepared to climb.

Feet slipping and arms straining, MacLeod gained the top of the first section. Its swollen head provided a small platform to stand on; temporary respite. The ribald laughter from the room was louder. He shook his head to remove water that trickled down his hair, over his forehead and into his eyes. Squinting he sighted the head of the next section; about a metre below and a third of a metre left of the window. It looked a promising position to inspect the revelry.

Braving the blinding rain he stole a glance skywards to discover water spilling directly onto his down-pipe. The gutters were failing to contain the deluge that cascaded off the eaves. Also the overspill had soaked the stone on either side of the down-pipe reducing its friction. He tried to clean mud from the cleats of his soles before tackling the next two-metre stretch. Arms pulling on the pipe were opposed by his toes and knees pushing against the wall to gain grip. Fear of slipping was balanced by a dread of wrenching the pipe off the stone.

Good fortune and secure pipe fixtures received

MacLeod's thanks as he stood on the bulbous top of the second section. His chest was level with the window. If he leaned to his right, he might see into the room, but the distance proved too far. Stretching his right leg, he placed a boot on the cross pipe that ran below the window. He could now lean further, and his right hand grasped the wooden window frame. Balanced precariously, he would not manage to hold that position for long. Also he worried that his hand might be noticed if anyone looked out to inspect the weather.

Suddenly he lost all contact on his right and swung away from the wall. Fortunately his left hand held and his left boot remained on the bulbous pipe head. His right hand grabbed the down-pipe, his right foot scrambling frantically before it secured the pipe head. His heart was in his mouth. It had happened so quickly that he'd no recollection. At that moment his overwhelming urge was to descend and escape before the revellers investigated, but there was no change of tempo from within. The window remained closed. His near mishap had passed unnoticed. Angry wasps had not emerged from their disturbed byke. His imagination had raced too far and too quickly, and yet he still felt vulnerable on his perch.

As he rested he noticed why he'd suddenly lost contact. The wooden window was rotten. There was a space, where his hand had gripped minutes earlier. A repeat performance might produce the coronary attack that would do the Judge's job for him. Next inspection he'd pull against the stone window surround rather than test the wooden frame again.

His right palm pulled against the window's nearest stone upright to hold his body position. Leaning further while craning his neck, he saw past the red velvet curtain and into the room. The two girls he'd seen arriving were seated on the far side, giggling, apparently in response to remarks from a square set man. From Bob's description, MacLeod decided he must be Colin.

Colin appeared to be about five foot ten; broad back and powerful shoulders; weight around thirteen stone, mainly solid muscle. Colin held a glass in his left hand and wore a watch on his right wrist, leading MacLeod to conclude that Colin was left-handed; always awkward customers in a fight. Colin's misshaped nose and cauliflower ears indicated such experience. Definitely one for an early bullet, MacLeod decided.

Switching his drink to his right hand, Colin reached for the blonde's necklace, letting his left hand drop to her medallion, then onto her breast. Just then the door opened, and Cyril and Helga entered. The blonde shrunk away from Colin's contact. Colin spoke to Helga who lit a couple of roll ups, passing one to each girl. Several drags later and the blonde appeared receptive to Colin's renewed advances. She offered no resistance despite her left breast receiving vigorous attention.

MacLeod's right leg started to tremble, and his forearms protested. He was forced to return to his rest station. He shook out each limb in turn, trying to revive fatigued muscle before resuming his perilous position.

Under Helga's supervision the girls were led from the room. Before departing, Helga passed some remark that released a belly-roar from Colin.

Another figure moved into vision. With his fair hair and dark glasses, MacLeod decided he must be Luke. His swagger and general demeanour as he sauntered over to Colin, produced an overwhelming urge in MacLeod to damage that low life. Colin gripped and squeezed Luke's buttock. Jim's diagnosis of Luke being queer and Colin perverse appeared to be confirmed.

Again MacLeod's forearm muscles tightened with cramp. Suddenly there was movement from the chair that had its back to the window: a chair MacLeod had believed to be unoccupied. A heavy hand sporting an enormous gold ring grasped the chair arm as the occupant stood up, at the same time shouting to Colin who immediately removed his hand from Luke's backside. A bald head showed above the high backed chair, but MacLeod's acute discomfort forced him back to the pipe head.

He cursed his bad luck at such timing but knew that to

ignore the pain would have been reckless. His arms needed to relax to reduce the tight bulging forearm muscles that threatened to burst the skin.

As he rested, the Judge's ring preyed on his mind. He'd seen similar adornment before, but where? He'd ponder that later but now he needed to see the Judge's face.

The sight that greeted MacLeod's return was not what he wanted. Luke had moved from Colin and stood beside the Judge's chair viewing the antics. Luke's body restricted MacLeod's view, but he could see partly clothed females being groped by different hands. Despite the intimacy of the probing fingers, the females appeared senseless to the physical attention; probably a consequence of their consumption of drink and drugs. The guests seemed intent on getting their money's worth: two were simultaneously attempting to mount the brunette, one from the front, the other from the rear, the girl seemingly oblivious to the degradations.

Seated and drawing on a cheroot, Helga checked constantly to see if her girls were performing adequately. Her short cropped blond hair and sour, angry features gave the potent impression of one who'd been reared on a diet of hatred. A twisted smile crossed her cruel, thin lips as she watched Colin repeatedly slap the bare buttocks of a discarded victim, then lying prostrate over the couch. Colin rose and indulged in anal sex on the unconscious victim while Helga snapped photos.

MacLeod was forced to retreat again. Cramp was returning sooner to shorten the periods of observation. He decided on one final attempt to view the Judge.

His attention was focussed on a solid stance on the cross pipe; that secured he raised his eyes. His heart skipped a beat as time stopped. MacLeod was staring into pink eyes, cupped between hands pressed against the window pane; a pair of shaded specs dangled from one set of fingers.

MacLeod and Luke remained mesmerised, disbelieving what their eyes stated. MacLeod broke the spell first. The horrendous implications of having been discovered fueled his actions.

Sliding down the vertical pipe, he remained oblivious to knuckles scraping against stone. His legs running immediately his feet contacted the ground as he headed for a wall without lit windows. Darkness should conceal his escape.

He sprinted, jinking occasionally to reduce the chance of being shot. Soon he melted into the night. Near the gorge he rested and watched. Figures, illuminated by the open door, turned one way, then the other; one carried a rifle and ventured into the darkness. MacLeod sank deeper into cover, the natural response of any hunted animal, but the enthusiasm of the searchers was soon dampened by the inclement weather.

"That peeping Tom will be well gone by now," said a voice, and the searchers retreated indoors. MacLeod felt safe enough to leave his hiding place and head for Tor'buie. He avoided the estate road and kept to the hillside and its shadows.

As he squelched and plodded over saturated ground, pictures of the party churned over and over in his mind. That briefest sighting of the Judge, occupied his thoughts. 'If only he'd kept his grip longer; if only ...' he thought, but the devil took care of his own.

On the plus side he'd recognise Colin, evil Helga, queer Luke, pimp Cyril and fiery Donnie and he knew more about them. Also he'd knowledge of the building. Many party revellers would leave for home and could be discounted. The evening had proved fruitful.

He shivered; cold, fear, or their combination? He'd had a bad fright. That stare haunted him. Another shiver, and then a smile as he recalled the pet albino rat from his childhood.

MacLeod hoped he'd be dismissed as an opportunist peeping Tom with no sinister intentions. He harboured serious concerns that Luke might recognise him. To lose the advantage of anonymity would be serious, but he considered that improbable, given the poor visibility of the evening together with the inherent eyesight problems of albinos. His confidence returned. He'd walked a tightrope and almost paid dearly. That pipe descent: so wild it was mental. What if he'd slipped: twisted an ankle? The consequences didn't bear thinking about.

Preoccupied with his newly gained knowledge and its potential uses, his journey passed quickly. The glow of Torbuie's street lights beckoned. His stride lengthened.

On that atrocious night and in the wee small hours, it was not surprising that he didn't meet a soul as he approached Jessie's and Maggie's garden. Ripping a button from his jacket he laid it next to their gatepost. It was inconspicuous enough to escape detection unless you expected to find it. Christine would know he'd returned safely. One final nostalgic look at the elderly sisters' cottage and then he made for the pier.

A lorry was being loaded, ice slipping down the chute to deposit its glassy layer over the boxed fish. He found the driver in the comfort of his warm cab enjoying a flask of hot coffee as he listened to country and western music and thumbed a girlie magazine. Finding that the driver was going south and flanking Edinburgh, MacLeod pleaded for a lift. At first the driver was reluctant but relented when MacLeod offered to buy him breakfast along the way. A weary MacLeod climbed into the cab. With a contract agreed, MacLeod felt no obligation to indulge in trivial conversation and fell asleep, allowing the driver to resume his fantasies.

All too soon MacLeod was wakened. Confused and disorientated, several minutes passed before he remembered how he came to be in a lorry. The musty aroma of his damp clothes was enhanced by the cabin's warmth. He was grateful for the heat despite the temptation the driver must have felt to switch it off to dull the smell. Surprised that he'd slept the entire journey to Edinburgh, he apologised for his lack of manners.

"I owe you that breakfast I promised."

The driver's eye travelled over MacLeod. "Na, na. I'm no needin' breakfast the noo," he said with a kindly smile.

With a pang of guilt MacLeod realised that he'd made an unjustified connection between the magazine reader and the perverts at the lodge.

"I'm really sorry."

The driver's eyebrows shot up in query.

"I'm sorry you had such poor company." Then he stepped down from the cab and waved goodbye. The lorry chugged through first gear, the revs increasing before it faded in a fog of exhaust fumes as second gear was engaged. Soon it had disappeared in that mêlée of traffic that trundles bumper to bumper along Ferry Road.

Suddenly alone, but in the midst of such activity: how ironic that, surrounded by strangers, he was safe, a speck amongst specks, diluted by the masses, whereas in Tor'buie, surrounded by caring friends, he was in mortal danger, his very presence jeopardising those friends' lives; ironic, indeed.

As he considered that contradiction, he started the long march towards the foot of Leith Walk, then along Duke Street to Easter Road where he sought directions for Restalrig Terrace. He knew Dougie lived in an old sandstone house with a partially glazed front door that sported the tartan crest of the clan 'Cameron'. Food and a hot bath were required. MacLeod prayed that Dougie was in residence.

FIVE

It was about nine am when the doorbell rang.

"Jist a minute, I'm comin'." The door opened. His support gone, MacLeod moved from the perpendicular through an increasingly acute angle. His gentle lean accelerated to a fall as he crashed onto the hall carpet. Slowly his vision cleared to identify the bizarre spectacle of floral patterned slippers.

"Dod! Whit the hell?" (Dod is slang for George)

He must have lost consciousness for several minutes. Clouds billowed with a darker object closer but out of focus. The picture cleared slowly, Dougie's head materialising against the background of a white ceiling. Dougie's concern was apparent as he cradled MacLeod's head in the crook of his right arm. His left hand rested firmly on MacLeod's forehead, ready to restrain any sudden movement. Mumbling his thanks to Dougie, MacLeod slipped once more into unconsciousness.

Security and the inner comfort it generates is a strange sensation; taken for granted until removed. Before his eyes opened he felt the pressure of Dougie's rough hands on either side of his head. Dougie was seated, supporting MacLeod who lay in the steaming bath.

"Dinnae pass oot on me again, my friend."

"I'll try not to Dougie, but don't tell anybody about me being here."

"Whit on earth happened? Ye're sufferin' frae exposure."

"Dougie, promise me you'll not speak a word to anybody; *no* contacts, *not even* a call to Christine. I'll explain later."

Dougie's look of disbelief drew MacLeod further.

"No I'm not exaggerating, Dougie. It's that bad. Believe me."

Dougie's grudging assent allayed MacLeod's concerns lest phone calls were monitored.

"I need sleep, Dougie, and then I'll talk."

Sinking into a real bed was MacLeod's last recollection.

He woke to the muffled sounds of machines. It was dark, and he was in completely unfamiliar settings. Lying immobile, he listened, trying to understand where he was. A warm orange glow on the wall did not help. Slowly the puzzle unravelled. The orange glow came from the street lamp. Engine noises were cars and buses in distant streets. He recalled his recent history. With no further need for caution he swung his legs out of the bed. There, he balanced for several minutes, expecting a reaction from his beaten body, but none came. His hollow stomach demanded sustenance. Finding some of Dougie's clothes, he left the bedroom, fumbling the landing walls for a switch. The 'wag at the wall' told him it was ten o'clock. He'd slept more than twelve hours.

In the kitchen Dougie had left a note giving an estimated time of return of eleven pm. A footnote added 'food + cold beer in fridge'.

Dougie returned to find MacLeod replete and seated at the kitchen table. A plateful of bacon and eggs and most of a loaf of bread had been washed down with piping hot tea. MacLeod declared himself fit to answer questions.

Events were graphically described, Dougie listening in sheer amazement. Frowning occasionally, eyebrows raised and mouth agape, he listened aghast, interjecting a rare, "Weel I nivver ...the *bastards*."

As MacLeod concluded his incredible tale, Dougie remained seated, staring into space as he grappled with his friend's revelations.

The pronounced click of his tongue on the roof of his mouth was followed by a pensive grimace. "Ye're richt sure? Nae Doots?" Largely rhetorical, the questions required only a nod from MacLeod. "Weel, Georgie boy, whit ur we tae dae noo? Naebody's gaun tae believe thon story withoot a lot o' evidence. It sounds mair like yi'v dreamed up the hale bliddy loat."

MacLeod agreed but emphasised the veracity of his story stating that he'd played *down* incidents and *not exaggerated* them.

"*I* believe ye. *Nae* doots fur *me*, my friend, but *nae sane* person's gaun tae accept thon: it sounds mair like the feckin' Wild West wi' an ootlaw masqueradin' as a jidge. Feckin' unusual, wid ye no say?"

A resigned shrug of MacLeod's shoulders accepted Dougie's point.

"Neither police nor lawyers will take me seriously, and so...."

Dougie agreed to do as MacLeod insisted: no contact with Christine for the next two to three weeks. Thereafter, Dougie would drive MacLeod to Tor'buie for a reunion. Then their talk covered what had happened since their outing on the Ben before turning to the practicalities of life. MacLeod needed work to pay his way, although Dougie sought nothing apart from being MacLeod's minder.

MacLeod welcomed Dougie's enthusiasm for a fight but regretted not bringing the steel thermos flask to temper the man's fiery spirit.

A cough prompted Dougie to administer the water of life.

"Uisge beatha, my friend."

The copious dram aided recovery, and, if one drink did so much good, then the guaranteed cure was obvious. It was three in the morning before two well oiled mates collapsed into their beds to enjoy sound, untroubled sleep.

Late afternoon and MacLeod awoke courting a very sore head and dry throat and assumed a hangover to be the cause. However his entire body felt sore, his underwear was damp, and his body temperature alternated from hot to cold. He drew the bedclothes closer and waited.

When Dougie checked why his friend had not surfaced for breakfast and saw MacLeod's damp hair and grey face, he realised all was not well. The involvement of a Doctor was rejected as Dougie realised that MacLeod would need to be registered locally: that would require his previous practice to be contacted for his medical records which, in turn, would trigger multi-agency checks, and the Judge had contacts everywhere.

Dougie doubled as a doctor, the witch type. His sole remedy was whisky, as much as the patient could consume. MacLeod's forehead temperature was monitored by thermoreceptors, (Dougie's fingertips), while his body temperature was controled by Dougie alternately removing and replacing the bedcovers according to the patient's changing colour. How MacLeod survived was a miracle. He'd never be ill again in Dougie's incapable hands.

Five days later MacLeod felt strong enough to saunter along Duke Street and the foot of Leith Walk. On the way back, the steak in a butcher's window caught his eye; being so cheap he bought some in appreciation of Dougie's hospitality.

He'd seen no suitable jobs advertised on shop doors, the main reason for his sortie, but he felt so much better. The meat would make a welcome change from Dougie's convenience foods.

Dougie returned and commented on the good smell. A couple of beers were opened, and they sat down to enjoy the meal, proudly served by MacLeod. When their teeth didn't meet, Dougie swore and asked what he'd done to deserve the fried leather. MacLeod commented that the beast must have been as old as Methuselah. Dougie's disbelief at the steak's toughness changed to hilarious uproar when he learned where MacLeod had made his purchase.

Had MacLeod troubled to look above the doorway, he'd have noticed that the butcher was the 'offal' butcher, or, as Dougie called him, 'the feckin' awful butcher'. MacLeod countered that the quality of the meal was a suitable 'thank you' to reflect the quality of the medical care he'd so recently experienced.

"Piss off. If a'd pampered ye too mich, ye'd ne'er hae goatin' better!"

Both enjoyed the banter. MacLeod's enforced exile would bring benefits.

Dougie had considered MacLeod's desire to work, mainly because it would distract his friend from the Tor'buie business. The area was impoverished, and shops, such as the offal butcher, reflected the local wealth, but its people were resilient and adapted to changing circumstances. 'Ad hoc' jobs did not need 'stuff' like insurance cards: 'no questions' for the willing and able.

The next day MacLeod strolled into a fruit warehouse in Leith and was told 'five am Monday and twenty notes would be his at seven thirty'. More searching and a meat haulier gave him an eight am start and a noon finish with a further thirty notes promised: again no questions.

Finances addressed, he needed facilities to maintain his fitness. Meadowbank sports complex and the Commonwealth pool were inspected. He intended to be in peak condition when he confronted the shooting party again but decided to delay training for a week to see how his body reacted to the work which involved moving heavy loads. After his noon finish on day one, the rest of the day was spent recovering. By day three he managed to stay awake until five in the evening, and by the fourth day the soreness was leaving his body. Noon on Saturday found him enjoying a swim in the Commonwealth pool. Work and training helped to occupy his mind, but that night he was overcome with homesickness and the need to see Christine. Also he'd concerns lest rust formed on his rifle. A decision was taken to visit Tor'buie the following weekend. While MacLeod collected the rifle, Dougie would visit the Crown hotel to glean Christine's news and update her about MacLeod as well as arrange a future meeting.

The week dragged, and MacLeod trained more at Meadowbank to ease his frustrations. A notice advertising karate caught his attention. Enrolling at intermediate level, he committed to Tuesday and Thursday evening sessions. He'd practised karate years ago, but Flossie complained so much and so often about the time it consumed, that his enjoyment had waned. Honing his combat skills might prove useful.

At his first session he impressed the instructor who moved him through basic techniques to combinations. Kicks became his speciality especially the roundhouse kick striking with the bridge of the foot; the snapping sidekick delivered enormous power using a foot's outside edge, but it was difficult to time; the front kick using the ball of the foot was easy but more predictable.

Skills returned rapidly. Soon MacLeod thirsted for competition fighting, his appetite whetted by contests amongst club members. Two competitions had been arranged; one at Kirkaldy in a fortnight, but the contest that generated excitement was the national Wado Kai championships at Meadowbank the following month.

Third level green belt qualified MacLeod to compete at 'junior' level. His natural balance, speed of reaction and clean scoring maintained his undefeated status in his bouts to date; MacLeod was confident of selection by his club, but first he had a visit to anticipate.

Some of his pay purchased a gold chain and pendant containing a deep purple amethyst. Saturday involved an early lunch and then off to Tor'buie in a Ford Capri that Dougie had borrowed from work so the car was not traceable; a precaution that impressed MacLeod.

The Capri gobbled the miles with Langhabhat dam reached after only three hours. At that point MacLeod moved into the greater privacy of the rear seats and also donned dark glasses to the comment, 'bliddy poser'. Forty minutes later they drove through Tor'buie.

They'd decided to collect the rifle first, reasoning that Dougie's hotel visit could attract attention if Christine was under surveillance. The subsequent risk of Dougie being followed would be disastrous if it led to the discovery of MacLeod. However, if the rifle was in their possession, and Dougie *was* followed, Edinburgh would be their next stop. How far would a tailing car follow?

Dougie dropped MacLeod at the top of the brae that overlooked the croft. MacLeod followed a gully to the adjacent hill's summit where Dougie and he would rendezvous. Dougie parked beside the bay then took a circuitous route along the shore before heading to the gully and then the summit. It was almost an hour before Dougie arrived, quite haggard looking.

"Its bin too lang since I wis oan the hill. Jist goes tae show ye how easy it is tae git oot o' condition. Anyway, hoo mich fairther?"

It was uncharacteristic of Dougie to complain or feel unfit. Then MacLeod remembered Dougie had not returned the previous evening. Amorous liaisons had costs.

"Well, tom cats sleep during the day, Dougie. Perhaps you'd be wise to follow their example, especially at your age."

"Bliddy ungratefu' wretch: I'm fecked wi' lookin' efter you."

The exchanges continued as they strolled to a position that overlooked Hector's cottage. Grey, curling smoke drifted skywards. MacLeod scanned the area but detected no watchers.

At the crag MacLeod was reassured to find the rifle's protective case dry. Inspecting the rifle's surface revealed a few flecks of rust, the consequence of condensation inside the cover, but the barrel interior was clean due to the anti-corrosive deposits of gunpowder.

"Ye ken, I reckin that ye luv thon thing mair than the lass!"

The taunting remarks interrupted MacLeod's examination of his favourite toy.

"Almost, Dougie. This lady fox is the second significant female in my life!"

Retracing their route they saw the adjacent croft's collie visit Hector's. Its master, old Tom, would be wandering the hillside, sweeping the land with his 'scope in his search for ewes but allowing his glass to settle longer on the cottage. In that neck of the woods your neighbours knew as much about you as you did. It was comforting to know that Tom kept a watchful eye.

Above the road MacLeod waited while Dougie drove to 'The Crown' to contact Christine. Dougie had the pendant plus a button from MacLeod's jacket to prove he was a genuine friend. MacLeod could only wait. He rested against a huge pillar of gneiss as he watched the sun set behind the Gannet Isles; its deep crimson glow half circled those outposts while its rays lit Eolaire rock; the grand finalé before the fire ball sank below the horizon.

All too soon the glow went; colours faded, replaced by shades of grey, and the cool night air penetrated, but the stalwart rock radiated warmth and comfort.

Cars passed with dipped headlights. Soon it became impossible to distinguish one car from another as the darkness swallowed them. MacLeod moved down to the road.

It had passed ten o'clock before the Capri drew into the agreed layby.

In the back, the rifle covered, MacLeod fired questions.

"What kept you? Was everything ok? How's Christine? What did she say? How did she look?"

"Slow doon an' listen. She's fine an' sends her love an' misses ye summit despirate. Indeed I hud a hellish job stoppin' her frae comin'. Hoo ye found sic' a crackin' lass, I'll ne'er ken. Some people hiv a' the luck. Oh aye and here ye are. Christine asked me tae gie' ye this." Rummaging in a jacket pocket, Dougie proffered his clenched fist. MacLeod fielded its content: a circle … a ring? "We didna hae much time tae talk, but she luvs ye, Dod, an' I'm envious as hell."

By the car's internal light MacLeod examined the delicate band of gold, itself graced with a meandering line of platinum. He recalled it adorning the third finger on Christine's right hand. It had been her mother's wedding band and her most valued possession. MacLeod wanted to go straight to the hotel and to hell with the consequences. He'd waste those who got in his way, but Dougie was unimpressed.

"An' run the risk o' blowin' everythin'? Hiv some bloody sense, an' be gratefu' things seem tae be gaun weel. At least, I can see yir feelin's for thon bonny lass. Come tae think o' it, maybe she'll be daein' ok as weel when she gits ye, e'en if ye're a hotheaded bastard! If ye'd hae seen the surprise in her e'en when she passed the table, an' I tell't her she'd drapped this," nodding to the button. "Weel she almost cut aff the circulation in ma airm wi' thon grip'.

Thankfilly naebody seemed tae notice. Later, when I gave her yir present, there were tears in her e'en. That wis when she tak aff the ring, clutched it firmly in both hands afore gi'ing it tae me, sayin' that you'd understan'."

MacLeod resolved to return her ring to the same finger but on her left hand.

"Did she say anything else, Dougie?"

"We didna hae much time since she wis servin' drinks to the tables, an' wi her attention bein' commanded by mysel', ane or twa impatient glances wir bein' directed oor way. However she did say that hir shadow hid gaun noo for twa days, so it looks as if they've swallowed the set-up. I hid tae tell her tae git on wi' hir job, although I could hiv enjoyed her company a' evenin'. She's a gem an' I'm glad for ye baith. Nothin' can stop ye frae concluding this business, an' I'll be wi' ye a' the way."

"Thanks Dougie. You're a true friend."

The Capri set off on its long journey south.

"Anyway it's a' set up fir a rendezvous in a month's time wi' me the matchmaker," teased Dougie.

The first Saturday in September had been arranged. Curled on the back seat MacLeod resembled the cat that got the cream before he slipped into a deep, contented sleep.

"Weel, I wis wonderin' when the sleeping beauty wid surfis," but Dougie's sarcasm was ignored. MacLeod remained bemused at their 'sudden' return to 'Auld Reekie' then cloaked in dense fog. The hazy glow of streetlights diffused through the airborne droplets reminding MacLeod of mist shrouded moors, and he shuddered.

"Dreich an' dank; nae better Scots words tae describe it."

MacLeod agreed. After the clean west coast air MacLeod felt claustrophobic in that smothering fog.

As the car rattled over the cobbles the security of every nut and bolt was tested. Soon they'd be home. MacLeod whimpered some lame excuse for having slept the entire journey.

"Glad o' the break. Great tae no hiv ye rantin' on aboot that lass, only makin' me mair jealous than I am a'ready.

Nae way, mate. I prefer my ain company an' the sweet purr o' the engine."

MacLeod's first task was to clean and oil the rifle, *then* breakfast and another sleep.

The next fortnight passed quickly as MacLeod trained intensively; the competition against Kircaldy was seen as the final chance to impress selectors before the Meadowbank tournament.

MacLeod's Kircaldy opponent was nicknamed the 'boxer' because he dodged and dived, always moving, nervously punching air. MacLeod stood motionless; leaning most of his weight back onto his right leg, his leading left primed to strike; constantly searching his opponent's face for signs of tightening lips or narrowing eyes to warn of immediate 'attack'.

MacLeod's left foot touched the floor but lightly in anticipation; a coiled spring about to unleash. At the moment the 'boxer' rushed, MacLeod's left foot swung up sideways, his body swivelling on the ball of his right foot. The solid thud of left foot contacting the 'boxer's' right cheek raised a cheer. The 'boxer' lay unconscious for a long minute.

MacLeod was worried that he'd struck too hard, but the referee awarded him 'Ippon', and that full point secured the match. MacLeod revelled in the attention and anticipated more bouts.

Meadowbank hosted the national championships with teams from the Lothians, Fife and Borders and Edinburgh. Penicuik was considered *the* team; its reputation probably worth a wazare or half point start in most competitions, but MacLeod did not respect reputations: rather the opposite. He'd trained many hours to attain razor sharp reactions, his counter strikes approaching the speed of reflex responses.

A large crowd attended the competition which was run on a knock out basis, with Penicuik and Meadowbank seeded one and two respectively. Against Livingston, Meadowbank won every bout and won their next three matches to take them into the final against Penicuik. The final required each contestant to fight twice against different opponents.

MacLeod was pleased with his personal performance

with three wins and a draw, but he'd collected several bruises and a burst lip on the way.

Brian, their captain, had followed Penicuik's progress carefully, and, as for previous rounds, he'd chosen an opponent whose style best suited his selected team member. To ensure his choices met in each bout he'd forbidden any of his team to stand until the selected opponent had risen. Contestants sat cross-legged facing the opposition across the floor. The Penicuik team was playing the same waiting game, and continued to sit despite the referee's command. The referee fired a warning, and the Penicuik member cracked first. Brian had won the tactical game.

The captains competed first with Brian winning a close-fought bout by a half point. Graham, their vice-captain, was next: likeable but cocky, he winked as he strutted across the floor. The customary bow and his contest began, but the formbook was turned inside out as Graham walked onto a right fist that left him on the mat, blood oozing from a broken nose.

First aid administered, and Graham's senses regained, the referee awarded 'Ippon' to the Penicuik opponent, a former paratrooper. After that spectacle none of the Meadowbank lads savoured drawing the para in the second round.

MacLeod's first bout proved uneventful. His opponent had a similar style, preferring counter to attack. Evenly matched, neither scored, and the referee awarded a draw: honours even.

At the end of the first round, Meadowbank were two points behind. MacLeod second-guessed his captain as Brian drew them together at the break.

"Gee thanks, Brian."

Brian smiled.

"He's tailor-made for a roundhouse kick, Dod. Just watch his short punches. Ask Graham!"

With those 'reassuring' words ringing in his ears, MacLeod wondered how Christine might appreciate a fiancé with a squashed nose. His state of alertness was raised significantly.

In the final round Brian won but scored only a half

point, the overall deficit reducing to one and a half points. Graham fought again despite his broken nose and swollen eyes and scored 'Ippon', the advantage to Penicuik now a mere 'Wazare'. The pressure was building with only three fights remaining: the next two were drawn; only MacLeod and the ex-para left.

The former red beret glared at MacLeod and nodded approval as if he'd already won. If wild looks counted, he was well ahead. His sparse hair was tousled and unkempt while his squashed nose and misshaped ears bore testimony to past encounters that were not held under the Marquis of Queensberry rules. The ventral slit of his jacket was open to show a hairy chest and the tattoo of a dragon. MacLeod would not wish to meet him in a dark alley, but this was a supervised bout, and MacLeod returned the glare with unflinching eyes: *not* what military man expected.

Called to the floor, the cheering and goading rose as the crowd anticipated more blood. MacLeod concentrated, blocking out everything except his opponent.

The soldier squared up as a confident and accomplished fighter. Both stood their ground, only a couple of feet apart. MacLeod leant back firmly on his right foot while his left foot, slightly forward, remained lightly poised on the ball of its sole, like a squeezed trigger primed to explode. His fists were ready to block. His body was wound up; tensed like a coiled spring.

Immediately the soldier stepped forward, MacLeod reacted; feinting with his left hand to raise the para's right arm, MacLeod's left foot rose rapidly. The vicious roundhouse kick landed with a deep thump, its power absorbed by the soldier's abdomen. MacLeod stood over his opponent, then bent double on the floor.

Vaguely aware of congratulatory comments from his team, MacLeod retreated to the central mark; there he knelt waiting for his opponent to recover and also for the referee's decision. MacLeod hoped for 'Ippon'. To his dismay, 'Wazare' was called: teams then evenly scored and another chance to collect a broken nose.

Having checked his abdomen, the para cast malevolent

glances at MacLeod before the referee called them together to resume the bout. MacLeod detected greater respect from a less assured soldier. The trooper felt his way back into the contest moving one way and then the other. MacLeod responded, revolving his body, weight on rear right foot, always maintaining a tight defensive posture, alert and ready to counter any attack.

The soldier sprang, his right fist aiming for MacLeod's head, a move which exposed his nether regions. MacLeod repeated his left foot roundhouse kick. The fist never reached its target. MacLeod looked down at the bent figure gasping on the floor. They'd won. The Penicuik lads took defeat well and promised to reverse the result at their next encounter. As he took the acclaim MacLeod's stature and self-belief grew. He'd gained confidence in raw combat if that need ever arose.

Many pints were consumed by the team that evening. The alcohol encouraged their feeling of invincibility. They'd gone onto the streets as vigilantes looking for thugs, and had frightened a group of yobs who'd grown used to dishing out intimidation rather than being its recipients. Afterwards the Meadowbank lads had separated with Wilf and MacLeod heading down Leith Walk. Suddenly the same five yobs stepped from an alley immediately in front of them.

"Not so fuckin' brave now, are we boys?"

The shaven-headed leader's face carried the tattoo of a coiled serpent on his left cheek. Both hands had every finger armed with a chunky ring: knuckledusters being illegal, such adornments made substitute weaponry. The right hand entered the leather jacket.

"Think a lesson's needed, boys. Nobody messes with us and leaves fuckin' happy."

While the leader ranted abuse the other four surrounded Wilf and MacLeod who then stood back to back. Suddenly the leader screamed and jumped, his right arm extended over his head. The street lights glinted off the object's blade.

Instinctively MacLeod stepped left drawing his right knee up to his stomach. As he pivoted on the ball of his left foot his right leg snapped out to drive the outer shoe edge under the assailant's raised arm. The crack left no doubts; only the number of broken ribs was in question.

With their leader writhing and screaming on the pavement to the accompaniment of a metal cleaver rattling into the gutter, the remaining four thugs stood rooted to the spot. Their jaws gawked wide as they gazed in awe at the pair who remained in defensive postures. Their open-mouthed disbelief at the summary cancellation of their leader was a memory to be treasured. Several seconds of indecision and then the gang fled leaving their idol groaning on the pavement.

MacLeod needed to disappear lest the disturbance had stimulated a public spirited person to call the police, but his conscience dictated that he considered his 'victim'. Wilf called for an ambulance from a public phone to retain anonymity. Six minutes later it arrived. From the shade of a doorway the pair slipped away confident in the abilities of the paramedics. MacLeod considered it unlikely that any gang member would be filing a police complaint.

The next morning with his head cleared, MacLeod realised that his judgment had been severely impaired. He daren't risk publicity of any type. With his fight successes attracting attention and his name appearing in a paper's sport section, he decided to leave the club.

The Tor'buie trip was only two days away, and he had much to prepare.

Saturday couldn't arrive quickly enough. Christine had phoned from a call box and arranged to rendezvous in the car park at Coire na Poite, a favourite tourist spot. Dougie was looking forward to the tranquility of Ross-shire after the bustle of city life.

After a fine start to the day the weather deteriorated turning to heavy rain after Borve, but Dougie continued to make good progress on the quiet roads and pulled into the empty car park half an hour ahead of the prearranged time. The foul weather had discouraged sightseers for the Coire na Poite gorge. The deluge battered the windscreen and hammered the roof like drumming fingers.

The downpour continued unabated. Trickles spread over the tarmacadam and converged into rivulets and then channels at the sides of the road. With the incessant rain, those channels gained in volume and momentum to carry leaves and twigs down the steep brae. A car passed, its wheels hissing as they cut the surface water; spray glistened as it flew to the verges.

Another car approached, coming *up* the brae. Its engine slowed, lower gears were engaged. MacLeod's heart pounded: could it be Christine? He slid out of sight, relying on Dougie, but his anger grew at the clandestine behaviour forced on him while murderers strutted around with apparent impunity.

"I spy wi' my little e'e a beautiful damsel."

MacLeod was up and out the car, cutting short Dougie's torment.

A long kiss and hug; only afterwards did they appreciate their sodden state and that Dougie had gone. Christine had the minivan. They slipped through the rear doors and lay on the carpeted floor. With the rain continuing to teem down their privacy was guaranteed.

"You'll need to get out of those wet .... " Her soft, velvet lips pressed his mouth and quelled further talk. His tongue probed, pushing against her's. His mouth moved down, nibbling her neck. Deftly his hands opened her blouse and cupped her firm breasts. Unfastening the black lace, his mouth teased and nibbled the firm nipples that stood proud on milky domes. His hands explored and caressed, their excitements reaching a level of frenzy. Christine's nails dug into his back. Emotions gushed like water flooding through a breached dam.

Later, bodies still entwined, they lay content, oblivious to everything except each other. Fond exchanges were murmured. Gentle caresses, missed so badly for so long, enjoyed. A car entered the car park, but the driver left on seeing the toilets closed. Their peace disturbed, they realised that their time together was limited, and that Dougie must soon return.

They laughed as they tried to dress in a space that was

inadequate, their difficulty compounded by their attempts to avoid contact with the cold van sides down which heavy condensation ran. Clothed they moved into the front and talked about themselves and their future after this ordeal was over. When MacLeod asked Christine to marry him, she agreed instantly with uncontained glee. They hugged, kissed and behaved like excited children full of hopes and enthusiasm. They had extra reason to persevere.

They agreed Hector should be the first to be told of their commitment; Dougie later; impossible for others until this business was concluded, and then everyone could know.

Dougie found them occupying front seats, talking animatedly, smiling, joyful at being together. They moved into Dougie's car, and Christine rewarded him with a kiss for looking after MacLeod and for bringing him north to see her. With pleasantries and small talk out of the way, Christine recounted what had happened, and what she'd learned of the Judge and his estate.

She described the strain of acting the role of grieving lover. Barely a day passed without someone arriving with some baking or offer of help, typical of the caring community.

"I cried, mainly from anger and frustration at the grief we're causing. It's wrong, but what can we do?"

All three were victims of circumstance. MacLeod felt shame that he'd abandoned Christine to manage an extremely awkward situation. At the same time he was proud of the way she'd handled matters.

"Our shadows lost interest quite quickly," she recalled. "I suppose I wasn't the most intriguing character to follow. For three weeks they surveilled the cottage, and then that stopped as abruptly as their visits to check on me and my contacts at the hotel. Once I approached the red haired chap to ask if he'd like to order anything, much to his embarrassment. I think that was the final nail with no surveillance since. You were right, George, but it's been tough. Then I asked about Jane, the waitress drowned near the lodge."

MacLeod leaned forward.

"There's a porter called Ricky. Appears he had a crush on Jane, according to the other waitresses. He took her death very badly, but, and here's the interesting thing, he believes she *didn't* drown but he always clams up when he's asked to explain. However he's taken me into his confidence. Here I feel such a traitor."

"Christine, there's too much rolling on this for pangs of conscience. Come on. What did he say?" MacLeod's impatience upset them, but lives were at stake; hurt feelings repair.

Christine frowned but continued. Ricky recounted occasions when Jane had been collected by 'The Führer', the nickname Jane had given the blond with the short-cropped hair. After the lodge parties it was not unusual for Jane to stay in her bed for most of the day. When she did surface, she was pallid and empty of emotion; like a zombie. Ricky reckoned she'd been drugged and abused, although Jane denied it. Whatever happened, Jane seemed unable to remember.

As Christine paused, MacLeod confirmed Ricky's suspicions, relating brief details of events he'd witnessed at the lodge, omitting to mention that he'd had to flee for his life.

Christine continued. "Ricky had been adamant that Jane wouldn't go near a river. She'd watched her sister drown and had a deep fear of water ever since. He thinks she must have stumbled that way in a drugged state or else been carried over. When he'd gone to identify her body she had bruises on her face, but they weren't consistent with a fall onto rocks when you'd see broken skin. Ricky believes the marks were more consistent with fists and a beating."

MacLeod recalled the perverse pleasures of Colin. Had Jane threatened to contact a newspaper? Also possible, if her mind was disturbed by a cocktail of drugs and abuse, was that she may have taken her own life. Whatever the truth, murder, suicide or the coroner's convenient 'death by misadventure', MacLeod believed that the lodge debauchers had played a major part in her death.

Christine shrugged her shoulders. "It seems our Judge

has influence."

"Correct: our evidence has to be flawless, although I doubt we'd survive if we collected enough to incriminate him". Eyebrows were raised all round. "That's right. The rot goes right to the top. We need to adopt their rules." MacLeod omitted that he'd already exercised such standards when he'd torched the land rover.

Christine protested that she'd not sink to that level which confirmed MacLeod's intent to keep her sidelined. Keeping Christine from danger accounted for ninety percent of his decision: the final ten had just been cemented by her disapproval of his 'no rules / regardless' mentality.

Conversation about the lodge had been guillotined. Updates followed on family and friends, and how village gossip emphasised the uncanny similarities between MacLeod's and Stuart's disappearances with some black humour injected by certain bizarre connections. Christine chose that lighter moment to confide her breach of MacLeod's trust, revealing that she'd told Hector that MacLeod was not dead, hastily adding that her father would never divulge that knowledge to a living soul.

"I'm sorry, but I couldn't continue the deceit. Dad's grown so fond of you that his health was suffering." Those dark eyes, tears welling, conveyed some of the hurt she'd been experiencing.

"I'm glad you did. The surveillance seems to have stopped, which should mean less risk."

More snippets of news brought them up to date on intervening events.

"And he's not been seeing other women, I hope. Is that right, Dougie?" teased Christine.

"I'd hae thocht the experience o' a deprived man cravin' for his wumman wid hae rendered sic' a view untenable ... or wis his welcome sae poor that yi'v' furgoaten a'ready?"

Christine's blush was laughed away.

The sombre mood returned when MacLeod explained his intentions to book himself into Loch Aoil for the same course as the Judge's group. He tried to lessen their concerns by stating that nobody would suspect, and it'd be an excellent opportunity to gain information on the group and the Judge.

"Well, I'll pray that it's fully booked, and you can't go."

Christine's statement caused MacLeod to change tack. With their time together running short, MacLeod invited her to Edinburgh for a weekend that would take in a concert and give her a credible reason for visiting the capital.

Christine was keen but worried about how Hector might manage during her absence. She'd call from the public phone in a couple of days; by then she'd know if the trip was possible. They kissed and exchanged commitments and then Christine turned to go. MacLeod remained stationary, oblivious of the continuing deluge.

Christine's car coughed and spluttered into life. She stopped, looked back, waved, and then the minivan disappeared in a cloud of spray. Dougie headed south, away from Loch Breac and its lingering associations.

Memories comforted MacLeod on the long haul south. With Dougie driving in his customary 'foot to the floorboard' fashion, the car ate up the miles. All too soon they'd returned to the city with no more than half a dozen sentences exchanged during the entire journey. MacLeod's despondency continued until they reached Dougie's place. Then he took the bull by the horns and phoned Loch Aoil.

"Commander Brandt," boomed the voice. MacLeod held the phone at arms length. That guy didn't need a phone. MacLeod imagined some old seadog, pensioned off, earning a crust in some dreary office while reminiscing the day away.

"I was wondering if you had two places on your January/February kayaking and ice climbing courses?" Dougie had decided that MacLeod needed company, and MacLeod was grateful.

"Hold the line please while I check." A minute dragged into five. MacLeod was about to replace the receiver when his eardrum was blasted again. "Sorry sir, there's only a fortnight's course starting the third week in January. It covers kayaking and ice climbing, but there's only the single vacancy. A party from the north-west booked all places bar two, and one of those was taken yesterday. We're unable to exceed our instructor to student ratio for safety reasons which, I'm sure, you'll appreciate."

Although disappointed at Dougie's omission, MacLeod was delighted by the confirmation, unwittingly provided, that the Judge's party had booked the same course.

"Okay, please add my name. A deposit? Certainly."

Fifty pounds seemed steep, until he learned another three hundred and fifty were needed to guarantee his place.

Dougie considered the venture too dangerous for one person alone. Following discussion it was agreed that Dougie would stay in the area, probably renting some freezing caravan for that fortnight. Dougie's presence would also reassure Christine. Also MacLeod intended to adopt the name 'Horace' which sounded similar to his Gaelic name 'Seoras' to which he'd grown accustomed. He'd a good chance of responding to 'Horace' without revealing his true identity.

MacLeod practised responding to his new name, but only when Dougie remembered to call him 'Horace' without the prefix 'Horrible'. A Loch Aoil form arrived together with literature outlining the courses and the minimum standards expected. He signed and returned the application enclosing a cheque signed by Dougie to protect MacLeod's identity. Confirmation of his place arrived together with a programme that was adaptable to the weather conditions prevailing at the time. Dougie arranged accommodation in the Lochy caravan site. It only remained to keep fit and arrange some kayaking and climbing to maintain skills and confidence.

Christine phoned, her tone intimating disappointment even before the words confirmed her inability to leave Hector and travel south. With MacLeod 'dead' Christine had once again become Hector's sole carer. MacLeod's enrolment on the outdoor courses did not unduly surprise her but did cause her concern until she learned that Dougie would never be far away. Also MacLeod made Christine aware that she was forbidden to make contact, but would be kept in touch by text messages to confirm his safety.

MacLeod kept fit by working and doing circuits in the gym. Surplus money purchased equipment in Tiso's for the outdoor course. By January he owned a varied selection of quality gear, some tested on a couple of ice climbs with Dougie in Glen Coe.

Immediately prior to the course MacLeod checked all the gear he'd need and went over communications with Dougie. They agreed that MacLeod would text Dougie to update him with changes to the original programme since Dougie intended never to be far from the course activities. The final item to be prepared was the rifle which received a light coating of oil to prevent corrosion during storage in the car boot: having it available was reassuring.

Hours were spent fine-tuning plans and considering alternatives if circumstances changed. Eventually MacLeod could prepare no more. Lady Luck would play her part. He hoped she continued to smile on him.

Despite his meticulous preparations, he lay awake for long spells, considering and reconsidering, unable to relax. Eventually he slept but only in fits and starts, and only after his nervous energies, fuelled by a racing brain and vivid imagination, had subsided.

On the late morning of Friday, the fifteenth of January, Dougie and MacLeod stepped from the warmth of the house into a cold easterly wind that sliced through their clothing. Both had second thoughts on the wisdom of their decision to sup with the wolves.

Perhaps the west coast would be more inviting? Doubtful, but the die was cast. The course contained dangers, but none would compare with the threat from the Judge's party, *should* MacLeod arouse suspicions. The magnitude of that threat was starting to be appreciated. The next fortnight would decide if MacLeod had a future, and how Fate might influence its direction.

SIX

Deep in thought about Loch Aoil and the uncertainties surrounding the outdoor course, MacLeod noticed nothing unusual until they passed Crianlarich. Why were they so far north and still an hour of the morning left?

"Well micht ye ask, my friend." A knowing smile creased a wrinkled face. "Perhaps an early arrival micht settle ye better, an' let ye see the lie o' the land? Perhaps, we micht drive past an' dae some exploration o' oor ain? We micht even change oor minds at this late stage." Dougie's frown emphasised serious consideration of that last option until his eyes contacted MacLeod's. "On second thoughts, maybe no. Ne'er mind. We'll probably dae summit entirely different."

His curiosity aroused, MacLeod inquired, "What do you mean, Dougie? You never said anything before."

"Weel then, sunny Jim, ye hivnae been listenin' or communicatin' for some time noo. I came tae a joint decision, but on my ain – we're goin' tae break oor trip in the Coe, an' hae a quick crack at Agag's Groove."

"Why ... you sly, old bastard. You'd planned this right from the word 'go', hadn't you?"

"Flattery'll git ye naewhere, an' I reckon it's the best way tae tak' yir mind off matters an' relax. Yir too tense. Ye'll only draw the type o' attention ye're tryin' tae avoid. Anyway it's ane o' the classic climbs, an' it's no' richt that ye hivnae enjoyed it at a'. We'll no' tak' lang tae breeze up it. Jist remember whaur ye are!"

MacLeod relaxed as Agag's occupied his thoughts. The mist shrouded the mountain tops in a foreboding way: typical weather for the Coe that still wept for the MacDonalds.

The proximity of mountains and road gave those rock buttresses altitude *and* attitude. Above towered Buachaille

130

Etive Mor with Stob Dearg, the start for Agag's. They picked their way amongst the boulder-strewn heather to reach the foot of the climb. There they were dwarfed by the magnificent Rannoch Wall; six hundred feet of vertical rock craned their necks back.

"Right, Dod, we'll climb through an' I reckon four pitches should dae it. I'll lead off. ..Ok?"

The first pitch led into the groove, its shelter generating a feeling of security, and progress was rapid. MacLeod's turn arrived, and he set off, soon passing Dougie as he led through until he ran out a full rope's length, and then it was Dougie's turn.

Dougie's second pitch was much shorter, and MacLeod soon received the 'taking in' call and then climbed. Passing Dougie, MacLeod received a nod and a wink and soon understood why. The comfort and security of the groove ended abruptly with MacLeod confronting the sheer vertical exposure of the Rannoch Wall. Gazing down, MacLeod appreciated just how high they'd climbed; a long drop.

"I spared the final pitch fir yirsel'!" A mischievous smile creased Dougie's face. "I firgoat tae mention the Wa', an' it bein' straight up. Let's see if it'll waken yir senses afore bliddy Loch Aoil kills ye!"

The holds seemed *very* thin. MacLeod's boot tip engaged a fissure, the metal plate in the boot's sole creating an artificial ledge as it perched over space. Relief followed when his right hand discovered a jug hold. Hauling his body up and off the climb released controlled emotions, and he enjoyed the exhilaration of achievement. When Dougie arrived, they shared their excitement and a snack before heading down Curved Ridge to the car.

Once again they headed for the Fort, a Mecca for climbers whose numbers increased annually, swollen by posers in pristine climbing gear; or, as Dougie called them, 'feckin fairies'.

Through Fort Bill and north, turning left at the filling station to pass over the River Lochy and through Corpach with its pulp mill and mountain of wood chips that resembled a gigantic bowl of cornflakes: onto the single track Mallaig road and Loch Aoil soon materialised, its ominous, dark waters reflecting MacLeod's mood.

"Richt. Snap oot o' it. Ye're too deep, an' remember no' tae let emotion clood yir jidgment. Try tae act natirally or ye're goin' tae fa' aff the seat, ne'er min' some bliddy ice pitch. In short git yir feckin' act thegither an' yir arse intae gear because soon we'll be pertin'!" The bite of Dougie's reprimands worked. MacLeod prepared himself mentally for the demanding unknown.

In the remaining light a few dinghies were visible, undulating gently on the tidal swell. A track led to the lodge: it was bordered by a dense stand of rhododendrons which intensified the darkness. The car headlights reflected the sheen of their evergreen leaves.

The track opened into a large, circular courtyard from which rose a magnificent sandstone building. Its turrets towered high, their stepped outline resembling a staircase that disappeared into the black night. A dim outside light directed the new arrivals to the vestibule. Dougie passed MacLeod his gear and left quickly to avoid attention.

Inside, MacLeod heard voices from behind a door, second on his right. Facing him was a large, ornate fireplace: in its hearth a couple of rucksacks, each sporting an ice axe. To the left the knurled banister of a stairway peeped around the corner. A couple of paces revealed the extravagent staircase that would comfortably accommodate three adults moving abreast.

The door on his right opened. It was filled by a bear like figure that sported a mop of red hair groomed by fingers rather than comb. Square at the shoulders and tapering to a slim waist emphasised the frame's upper body development. The high cheekbones, red with recent exposure to the elements, complemented the other features. The figure looked as if he'd been chiselled from granite. Dark eyes fixed MacLeod, silently challenging him.

MacLeod introduced himself and was then cut short.

"You'll be for the kayaking and ice climbing"; statement more than question. Without awaiting confirmation, the giant shouted, "Alan, another for the course. I'm off to shower." Passing MacLeod, he commented. "We've been expecting you. The others are all here. Alan will show you to your dorm. I'll see you tomorrow." Pausing briefly at the foot of the stairs, he turned. "By the way, I'm Trimble."

"Nice to meet you," MacLeod heard himself say, "and I'm Ge. Eh, Horace." Damn, he'd almost revealed his real name. The hulk showed no interest, the prospect of a hot shower more attractive than humouring another greenhorn.

"Horace? Hi, I'm Alan."

A small, thin chap had emerged from the same room. At first sight he looked like a boy: closer inspection revealed the creases of age and character. His eyes sparkled with a lively intelligence; their crow's feet giving the impression of a constant smile. His gaze was direct but non-threatening and complemented his relaxed manner: he conveyed the ambience of quiet confidence and inner strength. Elflike, his features contradicted the macho image of the outward bound instructor. Trimble, on the other hand, was type cast. There was no doubting his vocation. MacLeod felt comfortable in Alan's presence.

"Well, we'd better get you settled in your dorm before the evening meal."

The dormitory contained two double bunks. One had bedding made up, the contents of a rucksack spread neatly across its upper tier.

"There's a German student called Jurgen. He arrived much earlier and may be in the common room at the moment. You'll meet him over the meal ... say," glancing at his watch, "... half an hour? There are only the two of you in here so there's plenty room. A party of four's in the next again dorm. They insisted on staying together, but you'll get a chance to meet them over the meal. Anything I've missed?"

MacLeod thanked Alan and asked what he did. In his quiet unassuming manner he stated that he and Trimble ran the winter mountaineering courses. He excused himself and returned to his duties. So much for prejudices: MacLeod had stereotyped Alan as the indoor type. A number of things at this centre appeared to contradict what was predictable in civilian life.

He'd just unpacked his rucksack when he realised it was six o'clock, and the meal would be waiting. Abandoning everything except his valuables and his diary, he followed his nose, the smell of food leading him to a double glass door on the other side of which the clatter of cutlery and the sound of voices were clearly audible.

He joined the queue at the serving hatch and stood behind a short, curly haired chap: the fresh face smiled a greeting before turning to choose his meal. The hard, abrupt voice left little doubt of his Germanic origin. An attractive cook served generous helpings. Balancing a large plateful of steak pie, boiled potatoes and peas, MacLeod moved to sit opposite the stranger.

"Hi. I'm Horace. I believe we're sharing a dorm. Jurgen, unless I'm mistaken?" MacLeod's offered hand was grasped firmly.

"My accent must be very apparent to identify me so quickly," he smiled. "Ja, I'm Jurgen. I'm studying Physics at Edinburgh University. This is my extravagance for the vacation. I've good snow and ice skills, but my canoeing has room for improvement. And you?"

An Edinburgh connection provided common ground for discussion and helped to cement a friendship. They resolved to pair up whenever possible. MacLeod warmed to the open, friendly nature of Jurgen who might prove to be a valuable confidante and intermediary, if contact with Dougie was severed.

As well as the kayaking/climbing course there was one for sailors. MacLeod observed the clientele to identify the yellow wellie brigade, but his attention came to centre on a group of four at the furthest table. The red hair identified Donnie. One, only his back visible, had such a muscular frame that he had to be Colin. Opposite Colin sat Luke, tinted glasses perched astride the bridge of a hooked nose, a permanent sneer twisting his features. He looked arrogant and disdainful. MacLeod felt loathing for Luke: 'He'd make a feckin' fox look stupid'; a 'Dougie' comment seemed apt until MacLeod considered the comparison did the fox an injustice.

The fourth person was a complete stranger. His features appeared soft and gentle, strangely incongruous in that company. With short hair and a pink complexion, a boyish innocence was conveyed, but MacLeod had already made one error in character assessment that evening. He'd reserve judgment.

"Horace?" MacLeod started and then turned to look at Jurgen quizzically. "You were in a different world."

"Sorry, Jurgen. My mind was elsewhere, thinking of somebody special."

"A girl, ja?" The wide grin on Jurgen's face was too honest and expectant for MacLeod to disappoint.

"Ja," mimicking Jurgen in a genial way, "but her name and telephone number are confidential." Jurgen laughed, simultaneously slapping MacLeod's shoulder. They were going to get on well together, of that MacLeod was sure.

Over the meal they discussed their expectations and concerns, their friendship strengthening through refreshingly honest revelations. Jurgen commented that the other four course members had ignored his earlier greeting and that they seemed intent on remaining distant. Both agreed to implement a buddy system to look out for each other which negated the sense of isolation created by the four.

Jurgen was astute. MacLeod was pleased, not only by Jurgen's friendship, but also by the albino's failure to recognise him. The meal over, Jurgen and MacLeod retired to the common room to pass the half hour before all course members met. Trimble and Alan arrived, followed by the four who sat on the opposite side of the room without a greeting or acknowledgement which created an awkward atmosphere for an introductory session.

Jurgen asked MacLeod if either of them used the wrong soap. His chance remark was overheard by Trimble who smiled, then beckoned the others over, assuring them that nothing infectious had shown in anybody's medical form. Grudgingly the four complied.

"For starters, some self-introductions," commanded

Trimble. Nobody questioned his authority as he scanned faces. "I'm Trimble, senior mountaineering and kayak instructor. Alan and I share equal responsibility for the course. We expect you *all* to function as a *single* unit while retaining your individual style and identity. Those styles and techniques are for scrutiny by us. We'll develop and improve them."

Alan introduced himself as having spent eight years at Loch Aoil during which time he'd organised and run such specialist courses. Then, it was Jurgen's turn with MacLeod following. 'Horace' reeled easily off MacLeod's tongue although he played down his skill levels and attracted no interest from the others.

Colin introduced himself in a confident and self-assured manner as the factor of a sporting estate; a rôle requiring outdoor skills. He explained the estate was considering canoeing as an activity to diversify into and so boost its earnings. His arrogant manner was characteristic of the privately educated and privileged few. In MacLeod's limited contacts with the rich, he'd found their abilities did not match their assertions, but conceded that his working class background and envy might have coloured his attitude. Certainly his childhood would have benefitted from 'having' rather than from 'doing without'.

The others reinforced Colin's points to assert a group identity. Red haired Donnie Ross confirmed his present position as the estate's stalker. Attired in plus-four tweeds with woollen knee-length socks and richly polished brogues, he was a caricature of the traditional ghillie.

"Billy MacLean," was said slightly nervously. "I'm the general handyman around the estate although I'm a joiner to trade. I have to admit I'm happier working indoors than this macho stuff." Those remarks brought looks of stern reproach from the other three. Billy appeared to be the weak link.

Then Luke was in full swing, extolling his kayaking skills and questioning whether he'd get much out of the course, although he did concede he lacked mountaineering experience.

With such introductions they were flung together. Next, Trimble and Alan unpacked their rucksacks to reveal the gear of real mountaineers. While MacLeod possessed most of the major items displayed, he decided to sign out a pair of Yeti gaiters in case deep, soft snow was encountered. Interestingly, all the estate party, except Colin, expected to sign out several items from the Centre's store.

With good weather forecast for the next day, Alan decided on their programme; "Breakfast's at six thirty, one and a half hours before other courses, to allow us an early start on the Ben. Meet at the main entrance, seven fifteen sharp. Make sure you have *all* the kit for a long winter's day to include emergency rations, spare clothing plus sleeping *and* survival bags, just in case. A special packed lunch with extra rations is ordered. We intend returning by five thirty, giving us time to clean up and get wet gear into the drying room before feeding at six. Questions?"

The effectiveness of his delivery covered everything.

"None? Okay. Gear can be signed out over the next hour. Also the canteen will open at eight o'clock for twenty minutes to let you buy chocolate, ciggies and anything else you need. Tonight we'll read your skill statements. Tomorrow will be a fact finding exercise to see if your actual performance justifies your claims."

Trimble informed them that the town swimming pool was booked the next day for a canoeing session from eight till ten pm. It looked as if they were going to get value for money if every day had such a full itinerary. Whether they'd appreciate the evening schedules after a day's strenuous activities was debateable. MacLeod's initial impressions of the Centre were of a very professional organisation with highly qualified instructors.

Retiring to their dorm, they packed all their gear for the next day and decided on an early night in anticipation of a demanding assessment. After his exertions on 'Agag's Groove', MacLeod slept like a log. Only Jurgen's firm shaking wakened him.

"Better be smart, Horace. It's six twenty; breakfast's in ten minutes. I'm heading down. Don't fall asleep again, will you?"

Twenty minutes later and MacLeod joined Jurgen. The group of four were two tables away. They ignored MacLeod as much as they'd ignored Jurgen.

"Guess we're not the tweed and tackle brigade, Jurgen."

"Ja. What makes them like that?" However MacLeod was interrupted by the arrival of Trimble and Alan who sat at their table.

"Morning" greeted Trimble. "I see you've still made no impression on your companions. Queer bastards."

Jurgen and MacLeod exchanged looks of disbelief, amazed at Trimble's comment, but pleased to know their instructors were not happy with the four.

MacLeod asked about the other group's background, but there was little that either Trimble or Alan could offer, except that a portly gentleman driving a Range Rover had delivered them, the driver resembling someone from an Arthur Conan Doyle novel.

His curiosity unable to be contained, MacLeod asked. "Did he wear a velvet smoking jacket?"

Trimble stopped eating and looked straight at MacLeod. "How did you know that?"

Another faux pas, but MacLeod recovered quickly without heightening Trimble's suspicions. "I didn't," he grinned. "It just seemed to fit the Conan Doyle remark."

"Ugh." Trimble's attention returned to his bacon and eggs. MacLeod's nerves calmed. There appeared to be no lasting damage.

"Interesting lump of ring the old buzzard was wearing," continued Trimble and paused. MacLeod stifled his urge to ask more questions, but Alan, intrigued, posed the question MacLeod had contained.

"So what made it so interesting?"

"Well, for one thing, its size. It had a massive head with some pattern like a picture and writing in reverse, so the office ladies said. One thought it might be a family seal … you know, for pressing onto wax to secure letters. Anyway it makes him even weirder."

Feeling himself on safe ground, MacLeod probed. "It'd be interesting to know the name. He may be from an old established family."

"Oh, that's no problem," replied Trimble. "Francis said she read 'Whinfie...' something or other. Seems he's a judge wanting us to instil skills as well as discipline and character into some employees. Think we'll do well if they learn some manners. Anyway gents, entrance hall in ten minutes, please." Trimble rose to return his dishes to the hatch.

In the transit van the four continued to ignore Jurgen and MacLeod, which made conditions difficult for everybody, especially the instructors.

Leaving the transit at the distillery they zig-zagged up the heather-clad slope, slowly approaching the snowline. Another mile and the snow had a frosted crust that crunched under their boots. An invigorated MacLeod anticipated what lay ahead. The feeling was infectious as Jurgen winked and smiled. Entering the amphitheatre of Coire Leis, their eyes feasted on the Ben's gigantic cliffs, its snow gullies and the green mantle of thick ice that coated the rock.

Like the mermaid who lured ships onto rocks, the beauty of the virginal white snow beguiled most climbers. That Arctic environment commanded MacLeod's attention until its hypnotic spell was broken by a call from the instructors.

The students demonstrated individual skills in different situations. Trimble's and Alan's advice was put into practice to improve techniques. Feedback was provided in mid-afternoon.

The instructors' comments proved flattering for Jurgen, MacLeod, Colin, and, to a lesser extent, Donnie. Billy was criticised for being too cautious and lacking self-belief, while Luke was told, in front of everybody, that he lacked drive and commitment; comments which further soured his sullen look.

The day had been physically demanding but interesting and worthwhile, and it had given MacLeod greater knowledge of the four, helped by an observation from Jurgen who'd observed Luke *inhale* from a neatly folded

139

handkerchief. At first Jurgen believed Luke was going to blow his nose, but the care to unroll the handkerchief had intrigued Jurgen who noted the marked improvement in Luke's mood *and* performance: too much of a coincidence.

MacLeod considered the possibility of drug dependence which could limit Luke's abilities but might, on occasions, produce a power surge and greater unpredictability: pluses and minuses.

On the return to Loch Aoil the chat was, predictably, amongst Trimble, Alan, Jurgen and MacLeod. All were glad to leave the claustrophobic confines of the van. A hot shower followed by a meal restored some energy and set them up for the evening pool session.

"Have you chaps canoed much?" The question came as a shock, rendering Jurgen and MacLeod speechless. Billy, away from his friends, was making contact. They replied that they had, but Luke appeared and Billy returned to the fold, undoubtedly to be reprimanded.

The pool session intended to assess individual's techniques. Alan asked them to pair up while Trimble questioned if skills, about to be demonstrated in the warmth and safety of a pool, could transfer to raging, ice-cold rivers.

Colin had shown himself to be competent but could roll effectively using only the 'Pawlata' technique, failing every time with the 'Screw' roll favoured by accomplished kayakers. (The 'Screw' maintained normal hand position on the paddles and produced a fast roll to reduce the risk of injury in dangerous rapids.)

Luke revelled in the kayak showing off his mastery of advanced techniques. He'd be as comfortable on the river as he was in the pool.

MacLeod decided to underplay his skills since it might pay dividends later and encourage even greater dismissal by the four. His sculling and support strokes lacked commitment, and he failed to roll on several attempts, Jurgen hauling him up after every failed attempt, but MacLeod overplayed his hand. His antics had amusement value and caught others' attention. When MacLeod executed a successful roll, Jurgen's applause directed everybody's gaze.

As he blinked and looked through the trickle of water that ran from his hair his gaze met that of Luke. Recognition impacted as both players stepped back in time: MacLeod, rain streaming down his face and clinging to his precarious perch looked in on a party, only to find the gaunt face of the albino peering back. That zombie stare was as vivid to MacLeod as was the startled appearance of the rain-drenched 'peeping Tom' to Luke.

MacLeod's cover was blown and with it his safety. Jurgen would also be at risk since the four must assume that he was MacLeod's accomplice. In the transit MacLeod sensed Luke's furtive glances. He could only hope that Luke had doubts. Jurgen assumed that MacLeod's despondency followed his weak pool performance.

Luke would inform the others, but would they believe the highly unlikely coincidence that the peeping Tom was on *this* course without more evidence? Regardless, MacLeod would need to be on his guard. An attack could be imminent.

Jurgen asked about the next day's programme to draw MacLeod out of his sombre mood. Trimble answered that the morning indoor session would consider dangerous river scenarios while the afternoon would be spent on the River Lochy where the aluminium smelter outflow entered. There they'd experience a large stopper and feel the holding power of the vertical wall of circulating water. Trimble prolonged their anxieties before informing them that the outflow stopper did not *usually* hold kayakists *for too long*. Jurgen found himself holding his breath.

Before supper a slide show presented the fierce, recirculating stopper. Their apprehension increased when Trimble allowed an appreciation of scale as he pointed out a red paddle blade. Until then all attention had been on the frothing wave with nobody noticing the immersed kayakist. If the picture was designed to scare, it succeeded. Fatigued they retired to bed, but sleep was delayed by the charge of adrenalin the slides had generated.

MacLeod had problems sleeping for other reasons,

although he doubted there'd be any treachery that night. He decided against confiding in Jurgen at that stage. Better to seek Dougie's advice first. He woke up feeling more tired than he'd been before going to bed. Jurgen confirmed MacLeod's troubled sleep by asking what his nightmare had been, describing how MacLeod had tossed and turned and mumbled, but Jurgen had been unable to make out what was said. MacLeod dismissed it as an unpleasant water incident from his boyhood years, and that the slideshow must have triggered its recall.

Saved from further scrutiny by breakfast, Macleod yearned for the tranquillity and sanctuary of the croft: the Loch Aoil venture, sound in theory, no longer seemed a good idea.

The morning session was held in the common room and involved more slides and diagrams for risk assessments and students' considered responses to each situation. The session concluded with first aid and cardio-pulmonary resuscitation on manikins. A short break allowed them to check their gear. Lunch consumed, they proceeded to the boathouse to choose their kayaks.

MacLeod chose a short kayak that would be manoeuverable and easy to roll. His paddle was designed for comfort and energy efficiency with its tailored shaft and curved aluminium blades. They loaded the trailer and waited for Trimble and Alan. Only then did MacLeod notice Luke's absence and begin to suspect skullduggery.

"Okay, here they come. Better hook up the trailer."

"Check the indicators." shouted Alan. "Fine, now the brake lights. Okay. So let's go."

MacLeod interrupted. "One of us is missing."

Only then did Donnie explain that Luke had felt sick and had reluctantly withdrawn.

"Thanks for the advance warning," commented Trimble sarcastically. "We'll manage."

Donnie's eyes avoided MacLeod's. His body language contradicted his words and confirmed MacLeod's suspicions.

At the River Lochy they unhitched the trailer in a lay-by

and unloaded the kayaks. The white water section would allow Trimble to assess each individual's skills and plan for future outings. Alan had errands to run in the Fort and would return to collect them later.

Jurgen read MacLeod's thoughts. "Perhaps it'll not happen," he commented.

"Capsize simulation, my arse. Truth is we're all for a trashing some time today."

Trimble smiled knowingly on hearing his recently stated phrase repeated.

"Right, a quick warm up and then the rapid, but we'll inspect before we commit."

Three minutes of river descent brought them closer to the growing noise of approaching rapids. They beached their kayaks on a shingle bar that overlooked the main rapid and inspected the surging water to identify dangers and a good line of descent.

A large rock occupied an almost central position in the rapid: a line to the left lipped the outflow torrent and risked the stopper; the line to the right was boulder strewn and narrowly missed the outflow but led into a powerful eddy, where, with no orderly escape of water, a maelstrom of swirling energy had formed; this whirlpool could prove as hazardous as the stopper.

A catch twenty two: line left and hit the outflow and stopper; line right to be sucked into the downward spiralling vortex.

"I know where I'm going. Watch and learn." Trimble chose the left line.

MacLeod observed, noting a position on the bank where Trimble leaned and braced in anticipation of the outflow surge - there, at that bush, Trimble leaned his kayak before he was catapulted sideways into the stopper. Only his red helmet showed. The stopper held him for thirty seconds before it spat him out. He paddled to the riverbank where he raised his paddle: the gauntlet to challenge the first lemming.

Colin went first. Back-paddling to reduce speed, he steered away from the main surge and just lipped the stopper. His kayak shuddered, but he executed a support stroke to avoid capsizing before paddling behind Trimble. His relief was apparent; he leaned back, exhaling and looking skywards.

Trimble raised his paddle again. Out of the corner of his eye MacLeod saw Donnie break into the current like a bolted rabbit. Donnie was heedless of the hazards in his desire to get the business over as quickly as possible.

Jurgen disrupted the other group's order of descent as he shouted, "I'm next" and moved off the shingle.

Billy was too busy concentrating on Donnie's progress to notice Jurgen. Donnie had successfully ridden the cross flow but, on skirting the eddy, he capsized. Only his head was visible as he went round and round. Also he'd lost contact with both kayak and paddle.

Jurgen and MacLeod heard Billy's groan. He sought reassurance. "What's easiest? I'll not manage." The tone was querulous, and Jurgen took pity.

"Watch me. Horace will talk it through."

Jurgen broke into the mainstream to surf a standing wave to keep warm while he awaited Trimble's signal, but it took five minutes to retrieve Donnie, kayak and paddle to the safety of the banking. Leaving Donnie coughing up water Trimble shook his paddle angrily. They watched Jurgen pick a line through the rocky channel, and then he reached the whirlpool where he used a support stroke while leaning into the vortex. When Jurgen's kayak was circling at the same speed as the whirlpool, he sat upright and paddled at an angle out of the eddy and over to the opposite bank from the others.

Billy seemed buoyed by Jurgen's success and MacLeod's running commentary, and MacLeod took the chance to ask why he'd enroled on a course alien to his interests.

"I had no choice. The Judge tells.." Billy stopped. His unease was apparent. "There's Trimble's paddle." Billy cast his fetters and cut into the current to escape MacLeod's attention. Colin and Donnie would have seen MacLeod speaking to Billy and would not allow another opportunity. Then Jurgen appeared, dragging his kayak on the opposite bank.

"I'm taking the top run this time. I saw you talking to Billy. His friends were agitated. So what's the problem? I know more than you think because you *did* talk in your sleep."

"What did I say?"

"You called the names of 'Stuart', 'Colin', and some judge, and then shouted out 'murderers'. I thought it none of my business but I'm involved now and need to know."

"I'll speak later, Jurgen. Just watch your back, although I don't think you're in danger."

"Who's this judge? Is the law after you?"

Jurgen required some explanation; otherwise, perplexed and confused, he might approach the others who'd spin a plausible yarn to lure him on board. Then Billy capsized which allowed MacLeod enough time to deliver a version of the truth.

"Jurgen, the others are drug traffickers, possibly involved in murders. I work for the drugs squad, but my cover's been blown, and I'm now in grave danger. I'm sorry our friendship might make you a target." Jurgen's eyes were wide with disbelief. "No time now: explain later." Jurgen nodded, the enormity of MacLeod's words slowly being absorbed. "Right, there's the signal. You're safe enough for now. We'll talk tonight." MacLeod felt relief at having kept Jurgen contained; that extra pair of eyes would watch MacLeod's back.

Paddling into the flow MacLeod executed a sweep stroke that spun the kayak half circle to face immediately downstream. He chose the left line. The roar increased as the creaming crest of the stopper loomed large above MacLeod's head. A good timely lean exposed the maximum amount of smooth keel to spill the side channel's racing water, and then he was thrown sideways into the buffeting stopper. He'd entered the outflow higher than he should, but Trimble shouted encouragement. Like a rodeo cowboy MacLeod rode the surging wave. Suddenly freed, he automatically leant in the opposite direction as he entered the swirling vortex of the eddy.

"Well done, Horace. Keep leaning into the eye. Work your way towards me when you feel happy." Trimble's approval was uncontained.

Concerned in case others reviewed their opinion of his kayaking abilities, MacLeod wobbled and slapped the surface clumsily before struggling out of the eddy in an unconvincing manner.

"Well done, Horace. You handled the difficult part well but made an arse of the finish."

Jurgen's second descent was as masterful as his first. Then Trimble invited them to tackle the stopper from its downstream side when the weaker left arm would be used for control and support. With Colin being left handed, the challenge would suit his favoured side. They watched Trimble paddle to the side of the outflow before he launched into it immediately above the stopper. Tilted at an acute angle downstream, his kayak was held. The stopper's surging power bucked Trimble, like a terrier worrying a rat, but he kept sculling to remain upright. As he bubbled near the crest of the stopper his expression showed he was working hard to control his position. After an exhausting two minutes, he was spat out to a loud cheer from everybody. His delight at having mastered the challenge could not be hidden. His desire to impose his superiority followed.

"Who's game?" There was no rush of volunteers. Only those who did not shake their head had their names called. "Colin?"

"Possibly next time." Colin tried to save face, but his bluff was challenged.

"There won't be another time. We've other rivers, like the Spean." Trimble disliked Colin and rubbed his nose in it. "No? Okay, just admit you've bottled it. What about you, Horace?"

"In for a penny, in for a pound: what the hell. You will save me, won't you?"

MacLeod had no trouble entering the outflow and remained upright. In the stopper he leaned inadequately and executed a swift, short backstroke that angled the stern of his kayak upstream. The kayak's tail caught the stopper and was driven down, the main torrent forcing the bow up. The opposing forces twisted the kayak. Now upside down he saw a cloud of bubbles as light was reflected off the foaming top of the standing wave. His trained reaction was to stretch his arms to catch the undertow that would pull him out of the stopper; then he'd roll upright but he daren't demonstrate such skill and decided to abandon his kayak and paddle. Feigning panic, he surfaced, hoping the escapade would convince the others that his previous success was pure luck and that he was a rather average kayakist after all.

"Grab my tail and I'll have you out, Horace: brave try but a bit above your level."

His performance had convinced Trimble.

With MacLeod safe, Trimble went after the kayak and paddle. Coughing and spluttering, MacLeod took several minutes before he could respond to Jurgen's concerns.

"Tenderised, is a good description, Jurgen. Thanks, but I'll be fine once I've returned some of this water to the river."

Jurgen's smile was reassuring. "You're okay, Horace." The accompanying nod and wink confirmed his acceptance of MacLeod. MacLeod sat down and then noticed the spectator on the opposite bank. Despite the balaclava and upturned hood there was no mistaking Dougie.

"Everythin' fine?"

"Aye," responded Trimble. "Just a swim, nothing to worry about."

"Nice of you to ask," MacLeod shouted. "Tempo's been increasing; recent shock but surviving. For how long, who knows?"

MacLeod's weak humour with the spectator drew no undue attention except from Jurgen who analysed everything MacLeod now did.

"Okay, we'll call it a day. Your attempt, Horace, appears to have killed the others' enthusiasm. Must admit I'm grateful. My arms are tired with all the fishing out."

For those who'd taken a swim their energy reserves had not only been sapped by effort and emotion but also by the chilling effect of the cold water. It proved difficult to drag kayaks up the banking and secure them to the trailer. Twenty minutes later they'd returned to the Centre with its promise of a warm shower and a hot meal.

"Leave the boats on. We'll be using them again."

Grateful for Trimble's summary dismissal, Jurgen and MacLeod went to their dormitory.

The bunk looked so inviting. It would have been easy to lie down and sleep, but a hot shower was needed. Jurgen stopped MacLeod in his tracks.

"Horace?"

"No, Jurgen. I'm too tired. Shower first: *then* I'll explain."

"Horace. Have you been in my rucksack?"

Initial disbelief turned to anger that Jurgen would consider MacLeod capable of searching his friend's belongings. Hurt and resentment were soon forgotten as the truth dawned.

"Shit. My diary."

Ignoring Jurgen, he searched his own rucksack. His diary lay on top of his clothing, *not* down the side where he'd pushed it. Their possessions had been searched, but nothing taken.

Holding his diary aloft to command Jurgen's attention, MacLeod began, "Time to explain."

The diary contained a summary of events that MacLeod had witnessed at the lodge, plus a note on the Judge and each member of his group. Luke had the necessary evidence to convince his team that MacLeod had been the prowler that evening and was more than a peeping Tom.

It was inevitable they'd try to eliminate MacLeod as soon as the opportunity arose. Winter climbing and white water kayaking were dangerous sports. There would be no surprise should a client have an accident; fatal, of course. The problem for the four would be the accident's design.

Jurgen listened for almost half an hour.

"... and all because Luke went sick. I have to let Dougie know but don't want Dougie's identity and involvement revealed lest he becomes a target as well. Don't know what to do for the best."

The efficient Hanoverian brain suggested the simple but ingenious proposal. "No problem. If one of them can go sick, then I do not see why one of us cannot do likewise. Ja?"

"You mean you'd contact Dougie?"

"I'm a bit confused but I know when somebody's telling the truth. I'll keep quiet unless things turn ugly. *Then,* Trimble and Alan *must* be told."

MacLeod had struck oil when he'd met Jurgen.

Small signs, each insignificant on its own but ominous when grouped, made Jurgen and MacLeod sense they were being observed differently from before. At the evening meal the four cast frequent glances in their direction. Previously they'd shown no interest. Something was brewing.

In the evening's debriefing session Trimble identified important points for each kayakist to address before the River Spean outing, programmed for three days later. Immediate attention turned to the next two days of winter survival on the mountains, and the gear needed.

"Remember to carry *all* your extra gear. A night in a snow-hole is not the ideal way to pass an evening. We'll issue snow-shovels as standard and an extra sleeping bag for those who think their own is inadequate." Trimble drawled on, but he kept looking at Luke who seemed, to Trimble's sceptical eye, to be in the best of health. Once, when their eyes met, Trimble's glare spoke volumes.

MacLeod considered the best defence involved pre-emptive attack, but he had also to consider Jurgen. While packing their gear Jurgen and MacLeod discussed accident scenarios and decided the best safety precaution was simply to stay clear of the four in any high risk situation.

Two days mountaineering to include a night of snowholing would be a long time to remain alert. They retired to bed early. A good sleep was needed to preserve their energies for whatever the expedition might throw at them, but first they took the very necessary precaution to lock the door and check that all the windows were secured.

149

SEVEN

Something woke them. A quick examination of the room confirmed it remained secure. Jurgen reacted in a similar manner. It was a comfort to MacLeod to know that they were on the same wavelength.

"How are you, Horace?"

Strange how he hadn't revealed his true identity to Jurgen despite telling him so many other things: better to remain 'Horace' to avoid further complications.

"Fine. Wonder if someone trying the door handle spooked us?"

They listened, but the only sounds were parts of the building contracting in the cool night. It was just after six am, and they couldn't settle so decided to go to the canteen to make tea and pass the time. They were in luck since the cooks had already started breakfast with bacon and sausages cooked; only eggs to fry. They enjoyed a feast of calories and protein.

MacLeod doubted if cholesterol merited a mention in the cooks' training, but the instructors had greater dangers than diet. Alan had lost two friends in separate climbing accidents on the Ben which claimed more lives than the Eiger: a sobering thought since its cliffs would soon welcome them.

Eventually the four plus Alan and Trimble arrived. The instructors sat beside Jurgen and MacLeod, but, after an initial greeting, the instructors said little. They appeared pensive. Between mouthfuls Trimble stated, with an air of resignation, "Just my luck to draw the short straw."

Their puzzled expressions prompted Alan to explain. Normally ice climbing involved splitting students into teams of three students, but the unpleasant circumstances had caused a review, and another instructor had been included to produce a ratio of one instructor per two students. A coin had been tossed "to see who would end up with *them*" as Trimble stated, nodding at the four. Alan had called correctly and chosen MacLeod and Jurgen. Another instructor, Tony, would take the two rejected by Trimble.

With the forecast good for the following five days the programme would run as planned ie the two day snow-holing expedition first, then a day on the River Spean, followed by another two days of snow and ice climbing. A final check of gear and then they gathered in the foyer and waited for the minibus.

Again little was said during the drive to the distillery car park. They separated into two groups; the three instructors plus Jurgen and MacLeod while the four skulked behind. Slowly all progressed up the lower slopes of the Ben.

The imposing spectacle of ice coated cliffs and snow filled gullies loomed on their right. They headed for the abseil posts and a direct route onto the Carn Dearg arête. Their destination was the northwest slope of Aonach Beag where they expected drifts deep enough to take snow-holes. The air was crisp and clean. Despite the sun shining brightly on the crest of the arête, they shivered in the shade of the corrie.

Trimble's voice called out. "Better get the crampons on."

Securing crampons in cold conditions was always a bit tricky. Invariably gloves were removed to thread the crampon straps; fingers, exposed to the low temperature, soon numbed and lost their dexterity as well as their skin which stuck to the ice-cold crampon metal. They followed Trimble and climbed up the steep slope to escape the frost hollow, stopping often to tap crampons to dislodge compacted snow; that prevented 'balling up' of the tines to maintain their ability to pierce and grip the ice.

MacLeod marvelled at the untainted beauty of that Arctic desert. Its cold clean air frosted the insides of his nostrils and marked each breath with a cloud of condensation. The frictionless surface of the crisp snow was so firm that it hardly yielded to the sharp crampon tines. Snow and ice was his favourite environment, but, in that world of pristine purity, there existed the risk of serious injury. As the arête wound upwards it appeared to meet blue sky. Faint cirrus clouds wisped subtle patterns on the blue canvas. The beautiful picture hid dangers; the predictable risks of the climb itself; the unpredictable and most treacherous by human design.

The ridge was gained. Its narrowness screamed 'accident'. The arete inclined sharply to the summit of the Ben, but they would leave it earlier. The view of range after range of mountains was stunning. The sharp features of the 'Grey Corries' and the adjacent Mamores stretched immediately before them with the flat plateaux of the Cairngorms due south.

They spent time examining the cliffs, considering routes for the final two days' of climbing that would conclude their course. Jurgen and MacLeod assumed the position of backmarkers to avoid a trip or other designed incident to send them flying onto sharp rocks which would flay their carcasses of flesh. Leaving the arête a steep descent separated them from Aonach Beag.

The instructors fanned everybody into an arrowhead formation to minimise the casualty toll of a fall. In single file descent any uphill faller would fell those below like skittles. The gentle lower slopes were reached without mishap. The lack of interest by the four towards Jurgen and MacLeod made MacLeod uneasy. Something was planned. Jurgen's shrug of the shoulders and furrowed forehead indicated similar unease.

"There, gentlemen, is your hotel for tonight." Trimble's finger pointed to the corrie and its snow drifts. "Enjoy your sandwiches here or stake your spot. I'm off to claim mine."

Colin reaching into his rucksack for a flask stated the intentions of the four: that decided Jurgen and MacLeod to follow the instructors.

"What do you make of it so far, Horace?"

"I'm at a loss. Something's planned. I feel it."

Trimble and Alan staked their spot where the greatest

depth of snow would be found. Jurgen and MacLeod settled next door, hoping the instructors' proximity would avoid designed danger. Sandwiches and contents of flasks were ravenously dispatched while Alan demonstrated snow-hole excavation.

"Dig horizontally for a good metre, then *angle* sixty degrees up for half a metre before digging horizontally again. Excavate a big cave but keep a safe thickness of roof." Mindful of that advice, the pair set about the task and took alternate turns at digging.

The four walked past to take up residence on the other side of the instructors.

"I guess your property value has dived." Jurgen's quip brought a chortle.

Soon only Jurgen's bottom was visible as he cut snow and pushed it backwards. The arduous work continued with MacLeod shunting the loosed snow backwards out of the tunnel. As Jurgen threw down more snow from the growing chamber, MacLeod grew hot and impatient.

"Jurgen, I'm buggered, your turn down here."

The emergence of Jurgen's wiggling backside was evidence he'd got the message.

"Be careful of that manoeuvre, my friend, in case it's taken as an invitation. I'm straight but who knows the effects of a prolonged spell in a snow-hole." Jurgen's startled expression on a beetroot complexion released a fit of laughter from MacLeod. "Back to the grind but now *you* clear the avalanche. I'm for the cosy chambre."

Jurgen bowed graciously with out-swept hand in mock derision, but both hoped their snow-hole would become an impregnable fortress offering physical and psychological security.

MacLeod completed the sleeping chamber and then cut ledges for bunks. Final preparations involved Jurgen and MacLeod smoothing the ceiling to remove condensation points. They expected to be cold but not to waken up soaking wet from drips. Finally an ice axe was pushed through the roof to admit air. To provide light and to show there was adequate ventilation as it continued to burn, a candle was lit. The instructors were impressed by the finished item.

In the limited space Jurgen arranged his sleeping quarters first and then called MacLeod. Jurgen looked very comfortable inside his down sleeping bag, itself on top of a 'campamat' to insulate body from snow ledge. Inside the snow cave all was quiet and peaceful.

"Comfy?" MacLeod asked.

"You bet. This could be very relaxing."

"Don't relax too much. Something's planned."

"We'll be fine. What about a brew?"

MacLeod was worried. How could Jurgen fully appreciate the dangers? MacLeod was wiser only as a consequence of his attempted execution.

MacLeod looked out stove, paraffin, meths and the largest pot before he snuggled into his own sleeping bag on the hewn ledge. As each batch of snow melted more was added until the pot was almost full. Eventually, it boiled, and Jurgen added tea. Its strong aroma was comforting. Generous doses of sugar and condensed milk replenished their energy reserves.

There was little to do apart from chat, rest and make a brew every hour or so which meant a regular need to empty the bladder. With the rising wind whipping snow into every crevice of clothing, the first outside toilet visit became the last. The small hole that took their warm contributions widened and deepened to become a yellow pit.

The candle flame flickered on the grey interior reminding MacLeod of Halloween. Ghostly, gyrating forms animated the cave walls. He tossed and turned in a fruitless search for greater comfort. Finally sleep arrived; a welcome release from the discomfort and the penetrating cold.

What wakened him, he'd never know, but the brow of his head was throbbing. He felt giddy. Something was wrong, but dulled senses couldn't identify the problem: complete *darkness*; the *candle*. MacLeod sat upright, swayed, and almost fainted. Barely conscious, he slid off his shelf. Completely dark … *no* candle flame …*no* oxygen.

His head leaned over space. Then he slid, seal like, down, ever down. Crawling along that endless tunnel, he met a solid wall of snow. His last recollection before passing out was one of thumping an unyielding barrier that sealed their sarcophagus.

Uunconscious he drifted on a cloud to look down on his empty shell. Detached from the ugly confines of the tangible world, he was a weightless spectre witnessing two bodies in a snowy crypt; both looked peaceful as they slept.

The icy wind on his face revived him. He felt pain. He withdrew a frozen, bleeding hand from the hole in the entombing snow door. "Jurgen." His head was clearing fast. "*Jurgen*." He twisted round and headed back, up the chute and into the suffocating atmosphere. Grabbing Jurgen's collar, he hauled with all his might and dragged the limp form. The journey seemed interminable. A fine line existed between life and death, and speed was of the essence. His punched ventilation hole regained, MacLeod investigated the crumpled form of Jurgen lying behind him.

He listened intently for faint sounds of breathing and cursed the noise of his own heartbeat. That cold air smelt so sweet. He felt shame indulging his own needs when Jurgen's were so pressing. Placing his ear close to Jurgen's mouth and, with a hand on Jurgen's chest, he waited. Time seemed endless before he discerned movement. *Yes - there* it was; he *hadn't* imagined it. Jurgen *was* breathing. He almost broke down in tears. They'd survived, but how close had it been?

His fingers found a strong neck pulse. He felt confident that Jurgen would recover. Turning Jurgen into the recovery position proved difficult in the confines of the tunnel, but he managed and continued to monitor Jurgen's pulse and breathing; only briefly abandoning Jurgen in order to collect a sleeping bag and campamat. In the chamber he also worked the ice axe to clear the vent, itself as firmly blocked as the snow-hole.

As MacLeod worked Jurgen into the sleeping bag, Jurgen emitted a deep throated groan which sounded like music to MacLeod's ears. Another two minutes and Jurgen stirred and tried to push imagined obstructions from his face. MacLeod coaxed him awake, praying he'd suffered no brain damage.

Jurgen improved until he was able to sit without support. Progress looked good.

"I'm frozen, and my head aches.Where are we?"

"Someone tried to smother us and almost succeeded"

Slowly MacLeod's statement and its implications dawned, and Jurgen's eyes widened.

"*Smother*? How?"

"Pure speculation, but I expect to find footprints around our snowhole and near the air vent, and they'll not be ours. The compacted snow to entrance and vent is too hard to be caused by wind blow.

MacLeod knew snow changes quickly, and any evidence would soon disappear. He'd anticipate a coroner recording 'death by misadventure': that convenient phrase again.

Jurgen had remained quiet, struggling with the enormity of the 'almost' syndrome.

"You saved my life, Horace. What can I say?"

"Bugger all. Just remember, I got you into this mess. Never forget *that* before you go all sentimental. *Now* you know what's at stake. Lose and we're history. I'm going outside to check. You crawl back to your pit and rest. We should be okay, now they think we're dead."

Having helped Jurgen back, MacLeod donned boots, fleece and jacket and then ventured out. The breeze was slight, the faint morning light greatly enhanced by the reflecting snow. His watch showed three twenty am. They couldn't have been asleep more than two hours when their visitors had tucked them up for the night.

Inspection outside the entrance revealed pat marks of gloved hands. In the vicinity were hollows covered by soft snow. Blowing out the spindrift revealed two sets of boot prints. MacLeod's attention turned to the vent; again hand patted snow to choke the air supply, the footprints identical to those about the entrance. Hollows led past the instructors towards the antisocial neighbours.

"Well?" Jurgen quizzed.

"Spot on. Two visitors. Come morning, we'll find out who."

"How?"

"When you feel ok, poke your head outside and memorise those boot prints. When you discover whose they are, don't let on. Say nothing. Understand - verstehst du?"

"Ja, mein freund."

"Now forget your mother tongue. I was merely checking, in case your old brain hadn't fully recovered and ... well, to be truthful, that's about the *limit* of *my* German!"

Jurgen laughed. In the absence of liquor, it was time for a celebration brew. Having courted the big sleep neither wished sleep so soon again.

Trimble's shout up the tunnel to get breakfast going and be ready to move in approximately one hour was welcomed. MacLeod poked his head outside. Colin and Luke appeared to be taking an unusual interest in Trimble's visit. Their upraised palms and shrugged shoulders suggested confusion at Trimble's lack of concern. They continued to stare at MacLeod's snow hole, but MacLeod kept them guessing for another forty minutes before venturing out for a stretch. He wished he could see their expressions.

The sunshine rose above the mountains, its warmth steadily increasing. Before long it would bathe the corrie and its occupants with yellow heat. The morning promised much, especially for those who were not meant to see it.

Only MacLeod and Jurgen knew how close to success the murder attempt had been. Both were shaken by their vulnerability. Perhaps they needed to change tactics, but the first task was to identify the passing 'angels of death'.

"Gather round," shouted Trimble.

The boot prints identified Colin and Luke as the night walkers.

"Sleep well?" asked Alan.

"Almost the sleep of the dead," replied MacLeod glaring at the four.

"Good. The plan is ..."

MacLeod half listened as he mulled matters over. He thought he knew how Jurgen and he had survived. Large flakes of snow trap air which is why some avoid suffocation when buried in avalanches. MacLeod's attention returned to Alan's briefing. Alan had decided on map and compass work in make-believe, white-out conditions. Each would take the lead rôle at some time. Everybody checked the leader's calculations while the back-marker lined up the single file of bodies against the compass reading to monitor the leader's bearing in case he strayed.

Jurgen had easy terrain to cross during his spell as leader. MacLeod led the descent of a curving ridge with precipitous drops on his left. Billy was immediately behind him, and MacLeod felt quite composed. On checking again he found Colin. MacLeod responded by walking a couple of feet off the ridge on the right side.

His sixth sense registered the fast approaching shadow. Instinctively MacLeod side-stepped, a move which avoided the full force of Colin's 'stumble' that would have sent him head over heels down the slope and over the hundred foot drop; but his evasive action failed to avoid Colin's legs taking out his own. MacLeod fell but automatically dug his ice axe into the snow to arrest his slide.

Without full contact on MacLeod's body to check him, Colin's momentum gathered pace. Spinning out of control he rocketed downhill, feet first and on his belly, the ice axe following on a cord attached to his wrist. Colin attempted to slow himself by lowering his feet to scrape the snow with the crampons' front points, but he went too deep and was catapulted three feet into space. The impact of his plummeting body winded Colin and also broke the compacted top snow which helped to slow him. Before his momentum picked up, Colin grabbed his ice axe, angled it under his chest and used his upper body weight to press its point into the snow. He slowed to a halt, only thirty feet from the drop he'd intended for MacLeod.

"Are you all right, Horace?" An anxious Jurgen grasped MacLeod's arm.

"I'd feel better had the bastard gone over" was MacLeod's curt reply.

Everyone else had gone to check Colin who remained face down, clinging to his axe for dear life. That sight made

MacLeod grin.

"Did you see what he did?" but Jurgen had been too far back and had only witnessed Colin's spectacular show. "Well, Colin was meant to be here and me there, only a bit further down."

"A push?"

"A body check. If I hadn't sensed the shadow, I'd be gone and no mistake."

"Better tell Alan and Trimble."

"Don't you dare," MacLeod growled, "schh, here's Alan."

"That could have been nasty."

"Tell me about it. So how's Colin?" MacLeod appeared solicitous although he secretly hoped that the ape had broken his bloody neck or, at the very least, some ribs; but no such luck.

"A bit bruised and shaken, otherwise fine. Quite an escape: I was impressed."

Yet again the devil took care of its own. The sight of Colin being helped to his feet dismayed MacLeod, but, at the very least, Colin would not pose any further threat that day.

Although Colin was limping he appeared in good shape considering what he'd experienced. MacLeod had to admire the man's resilience. Colin was, indeed, a dangerous enemy.

The expedition was abandoned although its targets had been met. Colin required assistance until his stiffness waned and his confidence returned: he'd think again before tackling MacLeod.

MacLeod considered his own charmed existence. He'd survived three attempts on his life. His ration of good luck had to be exhausted. To survive, a more ruthless mentality of 'strike first, ask questions later' was required. Bob's and Jim's fates bore testimony to that capability. In such modus operandi MacLeod was as willing as the enemy to employ any tactic. The four had yet to experience the dark side of his character.

Torlundy forest reached and only a mile along a track

to the collection point and the transit. Alan and Trimble described the snow-holing to the driver, but made no reference to the incident.

MacLeod had a shower and a shave. After spreading his wet gear in the drying room, he lay on his bunk and mulled over events. The aroma of the evening meal drifting along the corridors reminded him how hungry he was. Two hours later, the lingering tastes of the hot curry spices were still smarting their tongues as Jurgen and MacLeod waited in the drawing room for the instructors. Colin appeared although he'd missed the evening meal, apparently because he'd fallen asleep.

The post mortem on the snow-holing expedition was remarkable for its brevity. Apart from the 'accident', the instructors commented on how everyone had responded *like a team*. If only they'd known the truth, the Lochaber constabulary would have had the room surrounded. Attention turned to white water kayaking. Starting on the lower section of the River Roy they'd continue into the River Spean. Trimble had slides to prepare them for the following day. Nothing caused concern until Trimble showed the 'Shelf'. Then everybody felt anxious.

Billy broke the silence first. "We won't be canoeing *that* ... will we?"

Trimble prolonged the pause, enjoying the apprehension before replying. "Not unless you ignore me. See that drop?" pointing to the waterfall. "It's about twelve feet to the pool below. Not difficult to go over but problems start when you hit the pool. Anybody know why?"

Luke suggested the narrowness of the stopper's slot had such fierce recycling water that it would not only have a tenacious hold on objects but also a long tow-back that would pull adjacent objects into its circling spout.

Trimble was impressed, stating he'd little to add except to stay clear. Pausing, he added that they'd inspect the chicken run from the safety of the bank and then decide if they'd paddle it. A slide showed the chicken chute to be a grade three twisting rapid that propelled the kayakist into the pool near the stopper. The 'Shelf' *had* been kayaked, but that carried high risks. Slides of other rapids were shown, but they paled into insignificance after the spectacle of the 'Shelf'.

Another early bed was needed after the expedition's demands; physical and emotional. The good news was a late breakfast at nine o'clock with a ten o'clock rendezvous at the boat shed. It wasn't long after their heads touched the pillow that both were sound asleep.

It was the soundest sleep MacLeod had enjoyed. He was reluctant to rise but pleasantly surprised at how good he felt after such an arduous expedition. Jurgen also declared himself fit. Given the urgent need to contact Dougie, Jurgen decided to go 'sick', miss the day's kayaking and visit the caravan site. MacLeod disliked the plan but had little choice. He needed Dougie to monitor the remaining activities and prepare for sinister developments.

MacLeod breakfasted alone, but the cooks prepared a tray of bacon and eggs for him to take to Jurgen. Jurgen would lie in bed for another hour before declaring himself fit for a constitutional walk. MacLeod asked Jurgen to check if any programme changes were planned and to let Dougie know, and then MacLeod took his leave.

Clad in a wet-suit, MacLeod headed for the boathouse: ahead lay a day of unknown dangers to be faced on his own.

EIGHT

The kayaks were still on the trailer from the Lochy trip. The instructors knew about Jurgen and had assumed MacLeod's lateness to be a direct consequence. MacLeod apologised for delaying them and boarded the transit: he felt abandoned, exposed and *very* isolated. If the four had designed an opportunity to eliminate MacLeod then *this* was *it*: MacLeod at his most vulnerable. Seeing Colin compounded that fragility. He'd have bet against Colin making the trip, but the man's resilience was something else.

MacLeod felt like a mouse sharing a cage with four weasels. Alan drove through Corpach, then Caol, across the River Lochy to arrive at the junction with the A82. Fort William looked inviting, but they headed in the opposite direction, away from public attention and the safety it might have offered.

Slowly the transit wound its way up the twisting hill. They passed Torlundy and into the Great Glen; the snow covered peaks of Aonach Mhor and Ben Nevis gazing down on them. MacLeod was aware of frequent glances from the pack. He was relieved when they reached Roy Bridge and stopped to inspect the River Roy. It offered escape from the claustrophobic confines of the vehicle and the malignant atmosphere generated by the four.

From the bridge a surf wave on the river looked inviting, and MacLeod's interest rose.

The kayaks were unloaded and roped to be lowered down the steep gully to the river. To warm up they ferry glided from bank to bank, but only Trimble, Alan, Luke and MacLeod surfed the standing wave. MacLeod hoped Colin's unwillingness to surf indicated damage that might

162

reduce his capabilities. At least MacLeod could enjoy the moment and steered from side to side on the wave's crest. Then Luke showed off his skills as he commandeered the curling wave until Trimble reminded him that others might like an opportunity. On water Luke would pose the greatest threat. MacLeod intended to stay clear of him and as near the instructors as possible.

Warmed up, they set off. Each took it in turn to lead, reading the water to decide the best line for each rapid. Trimble remained close to the leader while Alan brought up the rear; an arrangement considered safe. Progress was good, and the River Roy soon drained into the River Spean. The further they descended meant less river for an 'accident'. As a consequence the threat factor increased all the time. MacLeod felt strain and pressure.

"A short, grade three's approaching. The Shelf's another four hundred metres." Trimble sensed the tension and hyped their anticipation and anxieties before adding. "There are a couple of pools above the fall. We'll get out there and inspect the chicken run."

The grade three rapid involved a tight, technical bend that led into a narrow, fast flowing chute which opened into a pool; there a rescue would salvage any capsize.

Trimble led, signalling his readiness for the next descent by raising the green blade of his paddle. Nobody seemed keen so MacLeod drove the kayak up and into the current. Using a sweep stroke he turned the kayak half circle to face down river. Paddling away from the twist's outer bend where a massive wall of water piled up, MacLeod passed the first obstacle safely. The kayak was responding well, and MacLeod negotiated the remaining twists to gain the narrow chute and its fast, concentrated flow. He was bulleted forward with so much speed that he skimmed across the pool's surface.

"Nice one, Horace. Hell of a speed down the channel and no problems. Well done."

MacLeod was pleased by his own polished descent and by Trimble's comment. Trimble raised the green blade. Luke made the descent look simple, but Trimble voiced no approval.

"Better wait in the eddy around the corner to make room for the others."

Luke and MacLeod moved around the bend and out of Trimble's sight. MacLeod maintained a healthy distance between Luke and himself. No words were exchanged as they waited.

Next to arrive was Colin. He nodded to Luke, completely ignoring MacLeod but stating loudly for MacLeod's benefit, "Trimble says to head to the next pool and wait. He'll join us."

"Okay, let's go." Luke started to move, as did Colin. MacLeod's immobility stopped them short. Luke challenged MacLeod. "Didn't you hear?"

"I thought I'd wait in case help's needed," MacLeod added feebly.

"I see," responded Luke cynically. "*That'll* reassure Trimble, but he *did* say the next pool and *no* further. Maybe you're not happy *that far* from Mr Instructor?"

The sneering challenge questioning MacLeod's bottle was too great to ignore. MacLeod followed but at a healthy distance. He felt uneasy but not unduly worried.

When MacLeod rounded the next bend he found himself at the top of a narrow race. It dropped straight into the pool, alleged by Luke and Colin to be the agreed waiting place. Warning bells began to ring. The sudden appearance of the rapid caught MacLeod unawares. He managed to align his kayak before the plunge.

Half way down he noticed the pair skulking behind a rock to his right. They occupied a small eddy, the first safe position any good kayakist would choose after negotiating the rapid. MacLeod had no option except to paddle past.

A blurred movement caught the corner of his eye. Instinctively he ducked and tilted his head away. The pain, nausea and dizziness arrived simultaneously; then darkness.

Jurgen had waited an hour before visiting the kitchen, ostensibly to return the tray and dishes. He'd left most of the fried food to confirm a squeamish stomach. In a couple of minutes he'd charmed the domestic staff and learned that the programme remained intact with the next two days devoted to ice climbing on the Ben.

Jurgen talked himself onto the shopping trip. As staff headed into shops Jurgen hot footed it to the caravans and was out of breath when he reached Dougie's. The door opened before his knuckles contacted.

Dougie glowered. "Well?" Jurgen was practically hauled inside before he managed to gasp Horace's name. "Whit's happened? Come on: oot wi' it an' quick."

To Dougie's annoyance, Jurgen recounted events slowly and carefully. Despite his frustration, Dougie listened without interruption, but the hardening of his jawline and narrowing of his eyes said much.

MacLeod was drifting slowly to the pool outlet. There the current's speed increased, the water accelerating towards the waterfall named 'The Shelf'. By some miracle the kayak remained upright; its unconscious cargo was slumped forward on its deck, an arm either side, the water lapping at elbows.

At that time Trimble was helping Billy back into his canoe. "How the hell did you capsize there? You were past the difficult bit." Trimble hadn't waited for Billy's reply before signaling Donnie down. At exactly the same spot Donnie capsized. "Shit!" Trimble was annoyed at capsizes that prolonged his stay. Colin and Luke gained more time; and no witnesses.

Badly dazed, MacLeod stirred, slowly regaining consciousness. 'The rumbling sound of a train ... a train? What the hell's a train doing here?' The question nags while concussion continues to bewilder and confuse. Cool water sprays his face. He feels the sudden surge in speed. 'Train rumbling ... water ... movement.' Suddenly he recalls the last rapid. The change from befuddled brain to one of clarity is electric. His body snaps upright. He processes the array of information being fed by his surroundings. The noise is now a roar of deafening proportions.

The danger now understood, MacLeod resigns himself to circumstances outwith his control. He looks for his paddle: it lags three metres upstream. Further back two spectators enjoy the unfolding spectacle of a kayakist about to become history and so solve many of their problems.

With no escape from the powerful current, MacLeod back paddles with his hands to slow himself and let the paddle catch up, but the Shelf rapidly approaches. He accepts the inevitable.

The river disappears before his eyes. Spray shoots skywards. Tons of water rolling over the abyss creates a boiling cauldron of destructive force: at the base of the waterfall angry torrents curl back to tear and erode the cold black rock. Centuries of attrition have scraped away a large undercut which forces water up and round to produce a fierce stopper where objects are trapped fast in its looping water.

Helpless, mesmerised, being drawn closer to the edge and the deafening roar: billowing spray refracts light to produce a beautiful rainbow, a bizarre contradiction as alluring colour and magic mask such a dire and evil setting. Perhaps he's entering another world with a choice between heaven and hell? He'll fight both.

Steering with the palms of his hands, he keeps the kayak in the fastest current. With the bow leading, he hopes for enough momentum to blast through the stopper. Ravenously it waits. Can he breach its grasp and reach the pool? He paddles furiously with both hands to drive the kayak *outwards before* it falls in order to clear as much of the swirling maelstrom as possible.

The bow of his kayak crosses the lip. For a brief moment he remains suspended until the kayak's fulcrum passes over the divide. He plunges *vertically*, his stomach moving to his mouth. Then everything is in slow motion. A metre high wall of white foaming water looms to swallow the bows of his kayak, literally in his face before rising up his body to envelop him. *Still* his kayak moves *forwards*, and, *still upright*. His hopes rise of clearing the stopper. The kayak's nose kisses the pool where its forward momentum halts. The stopper's tow-back reels it in.

MacLeod feels the backwards pull; slow at first, then faster. The kayak's tail re-enters the stopper: with pile-driving power the waterfall crashes onto the rear deck plunging the stern down; the bow shoots skywards before the kayak crashes sideways, caught and held in the swirling water. He sees a dancing mosaic of sparkling lights that remind him of a drunken stupor, lying supine on a hall floor looking at the bright ceiling lights ... becoming hazy ... ever fainter. MacLeod realises he's churning around in nature's washing machine. He's less lucid, his consciousness drifting. Still he's being turned over and over, without respite, without escape.

Despite running out of breath he's fascinated, almost hypnotised, hallucinating on those shimmering lights, their intensity magnified by millions of trapped air bubbles and all the time he's being tossed in a perpetual roll.

The searing chest pain breaks the trance. 'Damn it, you're drowning; dive for the undertow to be swept clear.' He reaches to pull the spray-deck off his cockpit when a bump knocks his helmet. Fumbling, his hand contacts the paddle.

His lungs are close to bursting. No time for a second chance as his left hand holds the curved blade next to his left hip. His right hand grips the paddle shaft near the same blade. He cocks his right wrist away and pushes the free blade up near the surface, his preparation painstakingly deliberate. He can afford no errors. To abandon the kayak would mean remaining in the stopper. Fighting panic, MacLeod prepares for the controlled release of his few remaining energies.

Sweeping the paddle over his head, he moves his upper body backwards. The power of his triggered torso is unleashed from its forward angled position. With his body still unwinding and his eyes fixed on the furthest blade, he maintains the pull over his head. A slight flick of his hips assists the sequence to complete a classic Eskimo roll.

The smart of air ... clean fresh air is gulped voraciously

… breathing is restored … bliss … followed by a horrendous hacking cough from deep within his lungs. Gasping and wheezing, MacLeod forgets his predicament until he feels the tow-back drawing him into the stopper *again*.

Luck had played her part. After rolling, the tailrace of a through jet had caught the front of the kayak to sweep it into the pool and clear of immediate danger, but the kayak had *just* cleared the stopper. With the 'replay' button activated the nightmare was about to return.

Adrenalin pumped, and his paddle blades bit deep. Shoulder muscles strain as he labours forward, inch-by-inch moving from the churning rage and into calm water. A few more strokes brought him to the other side of the pool where he rests beneath an overhanging branch.

The coughing and retching continue, accompanied by stabbing chest pains. Gradually the coughing eases and with it his discomfort. Physically exhausted, emotionally drained, he slumps forward, his arms dangling in the water, the roar of the fall a mere background noise.

He'd been lucky. The big sleep had been close; too close. Gazing through the spray above the fall, he imagines the motionless form of the Grim Reaper. The spectre moves! Turning away it's swallowed by the hanging mist. MacLeod cringes under the branch; its shelter is inadequate.

The figure reappears on the opposite bank, staring intently at the stopper for a sight of MacLeod's corpse. Despite the waterfall's noise, MacLeod hardly dares to breathe, willing the branch lower. With nothing to be seen Luke descends to the rocks abutting the pool to inspect more closely. It's only a matter of time. Raising his gaze, his attention rests on the opposite bank.

Luke's jaw drops open, his eyes widen, his arms hang limply. For fully a minute he remains in that awed state. Then his face contorts with rage. Turning, he scrambles back up the rocks.

MacLeod draws in air in ever deepening breaths. His brain has cleared. His survival instinct is stronger having so recently courted permanent darkness. Believing there will be a death, he resolves it will not be his.

A cursory self-inspection assesses damage. Touching his tender brow he feels a weal across his forehead. The dilute blood on his fingertips causes no concern. The rest of his body seems fine. His violent coughing explains the slight taste of blood; again, no cause for anxiety.

The thought of Luke about to run the chicken chute is the catalyst to get MacLeod moving. Feet pushing on the footrest give extra purchase to arm and shoulder muscles. He powers across the pool to its outflow. Ahead are unknown hazards. He's no plan except to paddle until cornered.

Downstream, a section of moderate rapids is visible: still no sign of Luke. At the outflow, MacLeod pauses considering a ruse. Luke's the superior kayakist. Guile is needed: the element of surprise might tilt the odds in MacLeod's favour. His simple plan resembles the mother grouse dragging a wing to lead the predator away from her chicks.

At that moment Luke believes MacLeod is in a bad way: battered by the blow to the head; tenderised by the stopper; energy levels low; ripe and ready for the coup-de-grâce.

Feigning injury, MacLeod supports himself against a rock, his left hand nursing his side. His head is tilted and his face shows pain.

Luke, at the top of the chicken chute, sees his injured victim and is spurred on. He launches down the chicken chute. Concentrating so much on MacLeod he fails to correct his entry to the pool. To MacLeod's amazement Luke capsizes but immediately executes a screw roll to right himself. MacLeod pushes 'painfully' off the rock. His kayak limps forwards. The chase is 'on', MacLeod once more the prey.

A series of short drops and twists through a boulder field follow. MacLeod swings the kayak to avoid rocks. Safely through the rapid he turns into the next eddy to see Luke start his descent.

MacLeod bends forwards, arms holding his sides; the abject spectacle. In his excitement Luke grounds on a submerged rock but avoids capsizing. Frantically he works to free himself, his frustration and rage showing as he snarls at his bedraggled prey.

169

Teasing the predator, MacLeod struggles into the main channel. Out of Luke's sight he drives the kayak hard to maintain a safe distance between them while searching for the right opportunity. Rumbling sounds warn of an approaching rapid that needs inspected. Gingerly, he advances, back paddling to slow his progress to allow a cursory inspection. The cost is time with Luke rounding the corner at any moment.

The fleeting examination reveals a sharp right turn half-way down. On the bend water piles up, a capsize trap for the unsuspecting kayakist. Below that hazard MacLeod can only guess, but the unabated speed of flow suggests further drops. Just before the turn stands a large rock. Behind it an eddy should offer shelter and avoid running the uninspected section blind: it'll also hide him from Luke *if* he reaches *before* Luke shows. The final uncertainty reflects his depleted energies; will he manage the demanding manoeuvres?

He edges over the drop and into the rapid. A fleeting backward glance glimpses the nose of Luke's kayak before MacLeod is thrust by the rushing water. Gritting his teeth he attacks the channel and drives hard for the target rock behind which lies the promise of shelter. There is no room for error. Shoulder wrenching actions power his kayak's nose over the eddy line behind the rock. With the main body of his kayak still in the racing torrent, he digs his right blade in at the bow and pushes forwards while opening the blade to maximise its grip. The kayak spins on its nose to draw its body into the eddy.

Hidden by the crag MacLeod waits; breath held; heart pounding.

With Luke searching for MacLeod's body, Colin returns to 'raise the alarm'. He knows that the 'capsizes' will occupy the instructors' time and attention. Twenty metres from the group Colin starts to run, shouting loudly at the same time. "Accident; there's been a terrible accident."

Trimble needs answers, and fast. "What's happened? Spit it out."

Colin slumps on the riverbank, his head held in his

170

hands; a picture of concern and distress.

Out of his kayak, Trimble rushes forwards and hauls Colin to his feet. "Tell," he menaces. Colin's unused to such treatment. Shock, coupled with his need to cooperate, produces the rapid explanation. With no further interest, Trimble pushes Colin to the ground. "Alan, look after this shower of incompetent shits." With that parting order, Trimble fixes his spray-deck on the kayak and sets off, gobbling up the distance to the Shelf. He fears finding two bodies swirling around in the stopper.

He curses the sheer stupidity. 'Imagine daring each other to run the Shelf? And that stupid bastard letting them.' With those recriminations echoing, he reaches the waterfall and shoots the chicken run blind to save time although he considers it to be already too late.

Luke has just seen the stern of MacLeod's kayak dip over the drop and into the rapids. Luke goads himself to greater speed, his limping prey no more than fifteen metres away. Without pausing, Luke launches his kayak over the edge. He sees the water piling up at the bend on his left and paddles hard away from it and towards the large rock. He imagines MacLeod to have been upended and to be floundering helplessly around the corner. He'd show no mercy for the pleading, submissive figure, as he pictures himself clubbing MacLeod unconscious with the paddle. With the judge's influence the coroner would deem such injuries to be consistent with those sustained in dangerous rapids. The recorded 'drowning; death by misadventure' would satisfy legal requirements and please the Judge who might reward Luke with a small boy. Luke licks his lips in anticipation. Suddenly his twisted smile turns to sheer amazement, immediately replaced by horror as MacLeod shows from behind the rock.

As Luke's right blade bites the water and drives him forwards it leaves his upper body exposed. From a position starting well behind his hip, MacLeod surges his right paddle blade upwards, its aluminium edge slicing the air. Luke's eyes bulge. The clean cutting sound of Luke's throat is followed by the splintering crack of bone.

MacLeod capsizes, knocked backwards by Luke impaled on his paddle. Luke is exacting revenge as his dead weight drags MacLeod towards the rapids. Jerking the paddle twice, thrice; MacLeod succeeds on his fourth attempt to free Luke's body. A good screw roll and he regains the eddy in time to see Luke's upturned kayak bounce off the corner and disappear over a drop.

Drained, MacLeod rests. Several minutes lapse before he struggles from his kayak to drag it up the banking. He has no wish to inspect, but it's necessary.

Luke's upturned kayak rests in a pool. MacLeod wades over, apprehensive at what he'll find. To his surprise the kayak flips easily upright: no Luke.

The nudge on his hip causes him to spin around, instinctively raising his arm in a blocking action, but the expected blow does not materialise. The slight pressure on his thigh persists. Looking down, he gazes on the corpse floating just below the water: face up, its forehead, bumps against MacLeod. The head's tilted back at a peculiar angle; its haunting eyes fix MacLeod's with a stare of horror. The unnatural head position is grotesque, a consequence of it no longer being firmly attached to the torso. It lolls back, attached by a sliver of rear neck muscle. Throat, trachea and spine have been severed. A faint pink stream seeps from the gape which opens as MacLeod lifts the body. No longer buoyed, Luke's head falls back and gurgling noises escape the severed windpipe. Dropping the corpse on the bank, MacLeod retches before collapsing on his knees. Only the thought of Colin's arrival encourages him to move.

Later, following MacLeod's appearance but not the discovery of Luke, there'd be searches near the river. MacLeod needs time before Luke's body is discovered, and foul play confirmed. He drags Luke away from the river and through trees to find a steep slope with bushy undergrowth at its foot. Pushing the body he watches it roll down the slope: the head moves slower than the torso as muscle strands twist and stretch and threaten to tear and separate skull from torso, but the thicket's reached with the corpse settling under brambles.

A few branches are used to cover the flattened brambles where the body has trundled through. Leaf litter over the branches hides the body from cursory inspection. With luck, Luke could remain undetected for some time. MacLeod hurries back to the river and inverts Luke's canoe: pushed into the current it rounds a bend and disappears. He rams Luke's paddle under the overhanging riverbank and stamps to collapse the undercut but is careful to avoid exposing fresh brown earth which could be noticed by an alert searcher.

He hopes the searchers' inability to recover a paddle will suggest it was trapped under a rock, and that a similar assumption will explain the inability to find Luke's body. His own paddle has a cracked blade with a missing piece the size of a fifty pence coin. An autopsy will reveal that fragment in Luke's vertebrae. Paddle damage is common in white water kayaking and, in the absence of Luke's body, will attract little attention.

MacLeod drags his kayak upstream, intent on reaching the Shelf pool to give the impression that neither Luke nor he have gone further and so limit the initial search area. The delayed discovery of Luke will give MacLeod more time but, in his exhausted state he collapses, unable to reach the Shelf, unable to defend himself.

In his kayak Trimble zigzags the pool below the Shelf. Stopping several times, and with hands cupped, his eyes attempt to pierce the depths for any sign of Horace and Luke but without success. Puzzled, Trimble wonders if Colin *imagined* seeing them go over the drop? He widens his search and moves downstream.

"Horace." The call seems distant. In his soporific state MacLeod ignores the call, preferring the peacefulness of sleep. Suddenly sleep is violated. His body is forcefully shaken.

"Horace. Snap out of it. Don't give up on me."

Unresponsive to the command, MacLeod experiences a

searing pain across the side of his face. He groans and opens his eyes. Trimble's craggy features come slowly into focus, anxiety written all over his face, but MacLeod's eyes are so heavy he can't stop them closing.

"Listen, mate. If you don't fancy another slap across the kisser, stay awake."

MacLeod props himself on one arm to convince Trimble another slap is unnecessary.

"Where's Luke?"

"Don't know. Sleep. Need sleep."

"Not until I get answers." Another sharp slap and MacLeod's face smarts, but his eyes keep closing. Alan's arrival, along with the others, interrupts the treatment.

Alan's ecstatic at seeing Horace alive but horrified by Trimble's rough attention. Alan places MacLeod in the recovery position in case MacLeod loses consciousness and vomits and then checks his pulse. MacLeod, the patient, is a distant, near comatose spectator.

"You're not going to get anything out of him in that state. Be thankful he's alive and make sure we keep him that way." MacLeod's grateful for Alan's advice.

"Right Colin, you're at fault as much as those stupid bastards. I told you to wait around the corner with them, didn't I?" Trimble's anger is redirected.

"I did wait. I did, but they wouldn't listen. They were determined to test each other's bottle to see who'd back out first. I never thought that either would go for it. There was nothing I could do. Honest. That's when I high-tailed it back to you. I'm only grateful Horace survived."

Those lies did more than Trimble's slaps to get the adrenalin coursing through MacLeod's veins. His leaden eyelids flicker open. Trimble notices and resumes his interrogation but minus the 'encouragement'. MacLeod states that he's no recollection after the Shelf and is grateful for Alan's mumbled advice to Trimble.

"Shock. Best let him be. I'll stay and keep an eye on him. The rest of you search for Luke." Reassured by Alan's presence, MacLeod lapsed into a deep sleep.

The experience of the 'Shelf' and the haunting stare of Luke occupy MacLeod's nightmare. The anguish of the churning cauldron reaches such unmanageable levels, it breaks MacLeod's trauma: MacLeod sits bolt upright; soaked in warm sweat. The gentle but firm grip and the calm female voice placate him during those moments of fear and uncertainty while he determines where he is.

"You're safe after a *very* nasty shock, but no more harm will come to you."

The nurse coaxes him to lie down, to close his eyes and think of a warm colour. A muted ringing precedes the arrival of a doctor, and MacLeod undegoes tests: a light on his eyes to check the pupil's reflex contraction, followed by pictures for his considered response to each. MacLeod tells them he's fine and to take their recognition tests back to the nursery.

After his outburst a discussion takes place outside the ward. 'Traumatised' is the angelic nurse's opinion. She doesn't understand MacLeod's hatred of games. Odd snippets of talk filter round the partially closed door; the doctor seems happy with MacLeod's condition.

The nurse returns and reassures him that she'll not be far away and will check him often. Any problems and he only needs to press the buzzer beside his bed. With that parting information she leaves MacLeod who dozes, only to have his rest interrupted within a short space of time.

"Somebody wishing to speak to you, Mr MacLeod."

The constable is accompanied by a plain clothes colleague. The doctor must have summoned them after deciding MacLeod was fit to answer questions.

"Mr. MacLeod?" The nodded acknowledgement and the detective continues. "Perhaps you could answer a few questions, sir?" The uniform prepares to take notes.

The doctor and nurse remain during the interview which starts by confirming MacLeod's details: name, age, address. MacLeod decides he'll only corroborate Colin's fictitious account concerning Luke, himself and the Shelf. Colin, in his desire not to incriminate himself, has unwittingly provided MacLeod with an alibi. MacLeod reinforces Colin's version of events but plays the amnesia card and claims no recall of other incidents.

"I'm sorry officer, but I can not permit further questioning. It should be apparent that my patient has no recall of the horrors that he experienced. Amnesia is the brain's reaction to events too unpleasant to relive. Perhaps time will heal, but you may have to face the possibility that events will remain as much a mystery to Mr. MacLeod as they are to you. Now, I'd be grateful if you'll leave and allow my patient some rest."

Some mild grumbling conveys police dissatisfaction at the interview's forced curtailment, but they remain courteous and thank MacLeod for his cooperation and wish him a speedy recovery. Pausing at the door the detective asks MacLeod to contact them if he recalls anything that might help the police discover his friend's body.

"Body?"

"Haven't they told you? We ... ", but the doctor interrupts.

"We were biding our time; waiting for the correct moment, officer. Now, thanks to your indiscretion, we'll need to deal with that matter. Again I'd appreciate you leaving."

Such strong support comforts MacLeod. Protected by his medical minders, he intends to maintain the amnesia condition to avoid answering awkward questions. With no further distractions he realises how hungry he's become. His request for food pleases the doctor who declares he's no further worries about MacLeod's *physical* health.

Twenty minutes later MacLeod's enjoying meatballs, carrots and boiled potatoes with rice pudding to follow. His cheeky request for beer is greeted by a cool response from the nurse who informs him that he'll soon be out of hospital if he maintains such progress. How soon MacLeod intends to leave she can't guess.

Time drags. How people survive long-term hospitalisation is incomprehensible to MacLeod, but, of course, he doesn't have medical problems. The sound of Jurgen's and Dougie's voices is like sweet music. Their entrance with a nurse in their wake is a sight for sore eyes.

"It's okay nurse. I'll keep them under control. I promise."

Against her better judgment the nurse agrees to leave them with MacLeod, but states, "only twenty minutes." MacLeod needs less than two minutes to communicate his intentions.

"How's Dod, .. eh, sorry, Horace?" Dougie's faux pas goes unnoticed by Jurgen. Both friends seek reassurances about MacLeod's health before asking him about the Spean.

"Just get me out of here and back to your caravan, Dougie. A few drinks will help me remember." Their puzzled expressions tell MacLeod they're unaware of his 'condition', and so it's possible they've no knowledge of other events. He intends to remedy those matters soon. "It's my amnesia. Now get my clothes before I spend more time in here and really do go gaga."

Dougie returns with the mother of all matrons, a caricature of the 'Iron Lady'. MacLeod refuses to be cowed by her domineering manner. She tells MacLeod he'll stay another night for continued observation. MacLeod is equally adamant that he'll be discharging himself. Finally, matron relents and hands him a form to sign to acknowledge that he's leaving contrary to the hospital's medical advice. He waits for his clothes. Whether it's her spite or genuine time needed to complete the formalities, but two hours pass before his clothing arrives.

"Wish I was half the man she is," declares MacLeod as they head to the off-licence for beer and a bottle of 'The Famous Grouse'. Then Dougie drives them to the caravan.

Over a beer and a dram MacLeod recounts events but reserves the worst details until he's savoured another dram. The liquor helps, but reliving matters isn't without distress. Describing Luke's near decapitation caused Jurgen and Dougie to 'need' more whisky.

It was almost midnight before the taxi returned Jurgen and MacLeod to the outdoor centre. Several staff and course participants had returned from an unsuccessful river search that was coordinated by the police. They were chatting in the entrance hall and greeted the pair's return. Trimble apologised for his rough treatment of MacLeod but blamed MacLeod's rash behaviour. When MacLeod stated his intention to continue with the course, Trimble warned against future recklessness, but his wink indicated implicit approval of spirited responses to challenges.

Talk returned to the search. The consensus of feeling was that Luke had drowned and that his body lay trapped under a ledge with the Shelf stopper considered to be the most likely place. The following morning another search was planned with police frogmen involved while more police, assisted by volunteers, would cover river bank areas.

Then interest focussed on the prospect of the course continuing. It seemed likely that it would be curtailed, but a decision had yet to be taken. Trimble was making an announcement to that effect when Colin's voice came from the back of the group.

"We know Luke would have wanted the course to continue. While hope that Luke could have survived appears forlorn, there remains the possibility that he could be in a state of shock, suffering from exposure, even memory loss and might have wandered off somewhere. Given Horace's miraculous survival we have to remain positive about Luke's chances."

Knowing the truth, MacLeod never considered such possibilities but wondered if those options had occurred to the police. The prospect of an intensive search near the riverbanks made his heart flutter. If dogs were used, there was a high chance that Luke's body would be discovered quickly. It would not require Sherlock Holmes to find the weapon that killed Luke.

Colin continued. "If the river search is fruitless tomorrow, I expect a land search and hope for a radio announcement with a description of Luke to be conveyed to alert the public."

You had to hand it to Colin: he knew that MacLeod had accounted for Luke but he needed another chance to eliminate MacLeod.

Trimble agreed to delay a decision to consider Colin's

announcement and the wishes of other participants. Those gathered voted unanimously for the course to continue. Trimble thanked them for their support and confirmed that those views would influence Alan's and his decision which he'd announce next morning.

As they headed for their dormitories, MacLeod considered how they'd shown group unity for the first time, although its reasoning would have shocked the instructors, had they known. The competition had evened up numerically with three (including Dougie) on each side, and all at a stroke, grimaced MacLeod, as he recalled the cutting sweep to Luke's neck.

Jurgen secured their dormitory. MacLeod expected no problems until the three had licked their wounds and appreciated that the game had become *equally* deadly for *both* sides.

Early next morning Trimble confirmed the programme would continue, but that the present day would be a rest day; snow and ice climbing on the Ben would conclude the course as originally planned. Jurgen and MacLeod did not volunteer for the day's search but researched number three gully buttress, their chosen climb. The route involved a steep snow ramp classed as a high avalanche risk in certain conditions. The crux move came below the ramp and involved a traverse over ice-covered rock: below that delicate move was a vertical drop of a thousand feet. Above the ramp a vertical wall led to a large cornice, the final barrier to the summit.

Their homework done they retired to their bunks, grateful for that rest day.

The group searching the river banks returned mid-afternoon having had no success. The river search had been limited since safety equipment had been delayed by a day. Fates were smiling on Colin and MacLeod.

In the evening briefing Trimble explained that the routes chosen by each group had been considered suitable for that group's ability. Alan had allocated instructors; Jurgen and MacLeod teamed with Alan while the other three were under Trimble's umbrella. The others' choice of

Tower Scoop was straightforward enough to allow Trimble to manage three on his own. There was no further need for the other instructor, Tony.

After parting company, Jurgen and MacLeod went to prepare their gear when Alan arrived to inform MacLeod of a phone call. The caller had left a number requesting MacLeod to call back within ten minutes. Dialling from the public phone in the foyer, MacLeod heard Dougie's voice. The call was short but long enough for MacLeod to impart information of their routes. Dougie intended to be in the vicinity in case he was needed.

Content that Jurgen and he would have a guardian angel looking over them, sleep was deep and untroubled.

NINE

The next morning they were wakened by Alan's call. Their anticipation and excitement were tempered by the unknown dangers posed by the others.

After the River Spean episode an oppressive atmosphere pervaded the Centre: the professionalism of its outdoor instructors, especially Alan and Trimble, was in question following the disappearance of a student in circumstances that suggested inadequate supervision. The local newspaper reported on the missing canoeist. Soon national papers would show interest. Health and safety standards at outdoor centres would be questioned and risks exaggerated to increase newspapers' circulation.

Alan joined Jurgen and MacLeod at breakfast to inform them that there was still no news and that the search had resumed. He asked how they felt, especially with a demanding day ahead.

"Aren't conditions good?" MacLeod asked.

"Yes, but … well."

"You're worried about how *I'll* fare if the going gets difficult?" Embarrassed and caught off-guard, Alan was lost for words. "Please, don't worry about me, Alan. I'll manage."

Having broached the problem and received a positive response, Alan became cheerier and enthused about their route. "When we reach the top of the first slope, and you look around the corner, the exposure will blow your minds."

The two groups' routes were well separated, and so no threat was anticipated by Jurgen and MacLeod who looked forward to a challenging climb.

They parked the transit at the distillery. Alan, Jurgen and

MacLeod put distance between themselves and Trimble's group, arriving at the foot of Number Three Gully twenty minutes before the others reached Tower Scoop.

Hot sweet tea washed down chocolate as they gazed at their route. Also MacLeod scanned the slopes of Carn Dearg looking for a lone walker but saw no sign of Dougie.

"Mmm, wonder what gives with Trimble's group?" Alan stared back along the path. Jurgen and MacLeod followed his gaze and understood. Trimble's group had dwindled to three. Colin appeared to be missing. Intrigued, Alan went to investigate.

He returned with the news that Colin had slipped on the icy path and had suffered a muscle strain. Reduced to hobbling, Colin had been unable to continue. Trimble had advised him to return to the transit, relieved to be rid of the person he most disliked.

MacLeod and Jurgen shared similar concerns. Was Colin's injury genuine or the excuse to let him pursue another plan?

Having uncoiled one rope, Alan advised them to get prepared while he busied himself with the second rope.

Crampons were tightly strapped to rigid soled boots, ice axe and hammer looped to separate wrists. MacLeod roped up and led first, keen to prove that he was suffering no ill effects from the Spean saga. Jurgen, belayed to the ice wall, paid out the rope as MacLeod made steady progress. An ice bulge slowed him, but then he climbed quickly again. Jurgen was soon calling, "Twenty ... Ten feet left." MacLeod belayed and brought up Jurgen and Alan. Jurgen led the steepening snow slope where a horizontal crack warned of avalanche. Jurgen heeded the warning and belayed on two separate anchor points before bringing up his colleagues. Each secured himself to a separate point to maximise protection.

The horizontal crack was a concern. They were climbing on wind slab over consolidated snow so there was a risk of the entire surface slipping; that risk increasing below the crack. Alan decided they'd continue to climb but *above* the ominous looking fissure.

Alan invited MacLeod to lead up the precipitous slope for another forty metres to a vertical wall. Bolstered by Alan's trust, MacLeod set off and climbed about three metres from an edge over which nothing except space was visible. Another hundred feet using the crampons' front points and he reached the foot of the wall where he found a piton hammered into exposed rock: it would provide a bomb-proof belay.

The overwhelming peace and purity captivated them as they watched a figure on the opposite buttress. Like a spider on a white wall, the stranger progressed; the clean, cuts of his ice axe and hammer sliced through the crisp, clear air. The sounds were reassuringly solid: the lone figure no longer a stranger.

Alan broke the spell as he prepared for the crux pitch. He checked Jurgen's and MacLeod's belays to assure him they'd have a reasonable chance of being held if he peeled during the perilous traverse; then he moved onto the vertical ice, climbing steadily until he encountered a shelf. Progress was possible only below the overhang. Alan spent time threading an ice screw using the pick end of his axe as a torque drive. Jurgen and Macleod watched the core of ice extrude from the screw's hollow centre as its metal thread twisted deeper. Alan attached his rope. That 'protection' gave him psychological comfort, despite the knowledge that most vertical falls greater than two metres removed such fragile resistance. Alan added another ice screw a metre to his right, immediately before the critical step around the corner. He spent considerable time positioning and repositioning his feet before committing himself to the delicate move. Step taken, he disappeared, the rope paying out steadily. Thereafter 'contact' relied on sound clues. They heard the pick ends of Alan's axe and hammer slice cleanly into solid ice with the fainter 'zip ... zip' of lobster points biting and guessed Alan's progress.

Alan stood perfectly balanced on four downward curving, lobster points, his hands holding the shafts of ice axe and hammer, their curved noses imbedded in the sheer ice sheet. Below was several hundred feet of space, the nearest sensation to flight without attempting the impossible. Despite the exposure, Alan felt secure, his destiny in his own hands; his emotions inexplicable to those with no spirit of extreme adventure.

The tiring manoeuvre of axe, then hammer, followed by right then left crampon cutting into the ice, was repeated again and again. Alan gained height steadily.

"Rock and a piton, thank Christ." The reassuring information drifted around the corner.

The crisp cutting and chipping sounds continued for another fifteen minutes, then stopped. Perfect peace pervaded. Either Alan was taking a breather or else he was making himself secure for Jurgen's and MacLeod's ascents. Several minutes later came the call, 'Taking in': the unused rope was pulled up.

"That's me," responded Jurgen freeing himself from his belay. "Take in": the remaining slack tautened. On a tight rope Jurgen prepared to move. "That's me." Jurgen alerted Alan to his state of readiness.

"Climb when you're ready."

"Climbing." Jurgen set off, reeled in by Alan and paid out by MacLeod who cast an occasional glance to the top of the Ben, but still no sign of Dougie. Something was wrong, and where was Colin? The sharp call, 'Taking in', returned his attention to the immediate setting and to the fact that it was his turn.

At the corner he appreciated why Jurgen had hesitated. Below him the faint, wispy clouds blurred the drop, effectively blending tangible and ethereal. A dark spike of rock breaking through its white snow cover threatened to impale any faller. It waited patiently, its sinister presence veiled by swirls of cloud. MacLeod continued. Around the corner, he was greeted by two smiling faces.

"What kept you, Horace?" Jurgen's taunts were ignored. MacLeod moved onto the steep ramp, belayed and cut a ledge for standing. Forget drugs and booze; there could be no buzz like the sensation that environment generated.

MacLeod's character had developed. The discovery of inner strengths had carried him through situations where previously doubts and fears had limited his personal growth. Opening the curtains of his Johari window had answered many questions about life. He was operating at a higher level. Who needed God? Controlled adrenalin was his drug, but where, he wondered, did his abilites peak? Perhaps the mist hid and confused the finite pinnacle until that ultimate challenge was attempted. Failure would bring release from his voyage of self-exploration and replace it with everlasting and weightless darkness. Failure had some attraction to the suicidal element of MacLeod's psyche. He'd no need to boast, no wish to gain a rung in society's artificial hierarchy; a game for the blinkered, the dissatisfied and the insecure that equate strength with finance and materialism and become victims of that perception.

"Ok, gents, time to move." Alan interrupted MacLeod's musings.

Having checked that Jurgen and MacLeod were secured as well as their situation allowed Alan started the final pitch to the summit.

"Remember. *If* I come off use *dynamic* braking to slow me. *Avoid abrupt* braking at *all* cost." Alan had no wish to test the strength of their belays.

Above the ramp a cornice projected, but it was small compared to the gully's cornice which curled over the edge like a gigantic surf wave; tons of snow waiting to avalanche. Previous climbers had cut a hole through that huge cornice, gambling against it breaking.

MacLeod's attention returned to Alan, then at the top of the ramp. All was going well, the small cornice the final obstacle to the summit and the roof of their world. Suddenly Alan slipped. MacLeod remembered Alan's instructions: 'Dynamic belay'. He'd let Alan shoot past before applying the brakes gradually.

MacLeod's mind raced. Alan slithered past him and off the ramp, his body falling through space. The interminable wait that, in reality, actually lasted only seconds before the rope ran out. He waited for the violent jerk that would wrench out belays and pluck Jurgen and himself from their stations. MacLeod 'saw' that frightening chain of events.

Then Alan stood, only a metre below the point he'd peeled off! MacLeod's imagination had raced wildly ahead of events to prepare him for the worst scenario. Alan was smiling in sharp contrast to the shock and horror that creased Jurgen's and MacLeod's faces.

"Close!" was Alan's sole statement before he resumed his assault on the cornice. Their hearts still in their mouths, afraid of a repeat performance but for *real*, Jurgen and MacLeod remained silent observers. Great relief accompanied Alan's legs disappearing over the top.

"Thank Christ. Underpants need a change, I'm thinking."

Jurgen enjoyed the tension releaser. "Ja, I thought we'd had it. My thoughts were in German - you wouldn't understand."

"Bloody good thing."

Alan was a long time on the summit. MacLeod guessed he'd secure three separate anchors as well as sit with his heels dug into a rut; necessary precautions in case any of his charges fell.

Eventually the call, "Taking in", arrived. Soon Jurgen was moving confidently. Without warning, the rope went slack.

"Tight rope," yelled Jurgen. Still the rope remained slack. Jurgen turned to MacLeod, his face a mixture of fear, worry and puzzlement. Suddenly a hissing noise: the unattached rope snaked in flight as it unwound past them. They held their breaths waiting for the jerk that would test Jurgen's precarious hold. The previously imagined scenario replayed. MacLeod could only watch and wait and pray that Jurgen would not test MacLeod's belay.

Dougie had been ready to leave the caravan when there was a sharp knock on the door. A police sergeant stood, flanked by two constables.

"A few moments of your time sir. Just a few questions. Shouldn't take long."

"Weel, I'd planned tae go oot walkin'."

"I'm sorry, sir, but …."

"The problem is serge that a friend is relyin' on me appearin'. Cannit no wait?"

"Sorry, sir, but *no*. You don't mind if we come in? Ah, climbing gear. Ben Nevis was it?"

Dougie repeated to himself, 'Ben Nevis *was* it?' and smelt a long dead rat.

One constable followed his sergeant in while the other remained outside, ominously guarding the door. The sergeant and the constable's roving eyes missed no detail as some idle chit chat was exchanged during preliminary pleasantries.

Dougie's patience wore thin. "Come on, min. Ye've no' come tae save me frae ootdoor hazards, an' I dinnae regard this as a social visit so whit the hell's yur game?"

The sergeant paused; the convivial impression he'd strived to project, changed. A steely coldness entered his eyes. "You know one Horace MacLeod?" Dougie nodded. "Well, we're pursuing a certain line of enquiry following the disappearance of a canoeist. Your friend was on that canoe outing but has been of little help; hence our visit."

"I'm listenin' tho' I canna see how I can help."

"You visited Mr. MacLeod during his convalescence in the Belford?"

Dougie's mind was racing. 'How the hell had they found that out and then traced him?' Someone must have seen George, a.k.a. Horace, leave hospital and remembered the car to allow a police trace. The visit was no routine enquiry. Some deep shit was being stirred, and Dougie did not like it one little bit. Extreme care with his answers was necessary lest he dropped his friend in the very stuff that was being agitated.

After ten minutes of questioning, Dougie heard a vehicle slow and stop beside the caravan. The sergeant looked out the window. Dougie made to do the same but was told to remain *exactly* where he was as the sergeant stepped outside.

Curious about the visitor but with no wish to upset the police and further prolong his 'assistance with police enquiries', Dougie remained seated but shifted his position slightly to view a grey Range Rover courtesy of the cracked shaving mirror above the sink. Another slight shift brought the driver's area into view, but the driver remained hidden by the sergeant who'd leaned down to talk. Straining his neck for a glimpse of the driver, Dougie's concentration was broken by the constable.

"Sorry, what did you sa ..." Dougie stopped short as he noticed the driver's fingers curled over the open window. Adorning a finger was the largest and most ornate gold ring he'd ever seen. His heart skipped a beat: the Judge.

"I don't think you're listening."

Dougie ignored the warning. The Judge had to be behind the police visit and the 'caravan arrest' that kept Dougie out of action. Treachery was afoot.

As the vehicle departed, the sergeant stepped back, and Dougie glimpsed the driver's face as he turned to wave farewell. There was something familiar about that face, but he needed time and space to recollect. Of immediate concern was the tactics to delay him further. On re-entering the caravan the sergeant's first words provided the answer.

"Okay, sir. We need you to accompany us to the station": a statement, *not* an invitation.

It would be futile to refuse. Dougie could only hope that Jurgen and 'Horace' would experience no difficulties during his enforced absence.

The snaking rope hisses as it gyrates in the air.

"Hold on, Jurgen."

The rope straightens, yanking at Jurgen's waist. Jurgen teeters. MacLeod, heart in mouth, watches, helpless to do anything except stamp his heels deeper, anticipating what seems imminently probable.

Unsteady, on the point of losing contact, Jurgen steps down, that action sinking the hitherto emerging ice axe back into the snow ramp to restore grip and balance. Jurgen froze, remaining motionless for fully a minute before his nerve returned. The immediate drama passed, but they sensed danger all around them: and what about Alan? The rope thrower's identity is no secret: what will Colin attempt next?'

"Down," hisses MacLeod, maintaining a watchful eye on the lip where, only ten minutes earlier, Alan had ascended. If they kept low, Colin would need to venture to the cornice edge to pinpoint their position. The fragility of cornices should discourage him. Their greatest danger is a flailing object to sweep them away. A limp body would be ideal. MacLeod shudders. Alan is either unconscious or dead. If Alan has not seen his assailant then Colin has no need to kill him. MacLeod can only hope.

Moving very tentatively, Jurgen moves next to MacLeod. Both understand what's required. They untie their connecting rope, effectively severing their umbilical cord. Unroped, each has a better chance of survival if one is dislodged. Each coils a separate rope over a shoulder before traversing towards number three gully. Above them the projecting cornices seem less menacing as they obscure the pair from Colin's view.

MacLeod leads with Jurgen ten metres back to deny Colin a single target.

Twenty metres ahead the slope steepens. Another ten metres and it's a vertical barrier. Beyond that perilous wall a benign slope leads to their objective, number three gully.

Tension, emotions and physical demands are taking their toll. MacLeod's arms are sore and tired. He lowers one at a time, shaking it to increase the blood flow and help its recovery before he tackles the ice-veneered rock. If he or Jurgen survive that obstacle, they'll reach safety, and, if Alan's alive, there will be an independent witness to testify.

"Okay, Horace?" Jurgen advanced to within a metre of his friend. Feverishly MacLeod scans the skyline. "I've been watching but no sighting. Perhaps he's gone?"

Both wished it true, but neither believed it probable.

"Jurgen, we'll need to belay each other for this ice wall."

Jurgen nodded. "But without tying on, ja?"

"Ja."

A look upwards: both sense they are being watched.

189

The ice covering the rock is veneer thin, nigh impossible with or without crampons and axes. Eyes meet; their strained expressions acknowledge the risk.

Jurgen will belay, while MacLeod attempts the critical move. Covering the piton head with a glove to muffle the ring of metal on metal MacLeod drives a piton into the rock using his ice hammer. Jurgen ties himself to the piton but not to MacLeod's rope which Jurgen will feed through his hands: in that way he'll be able to release the rope instantly if MacLeod falls and so avoid putting strain on the piton belay. Remaining unroped offers more chance of one surviving. MacLeod's rope serves largely as a psychological prop, but, if MacLeod reaches safe ground Jurgen will tie on. Then, with MacLeod securely anchored, Jurgen will be protected during his traverse.

A final look at Jurgen and MacLeod sets off. Jurgen's eyes mirror the very fear MacLeod faces: falling, his body accelerating earthwards; his scream rising; the jagged rocks hacking off meat, possibly limbs. What on earth's he doing there when he could be in Christine's arms in front of a glowing peat fire? Such thoughts are delusions. Danger will exist until the Judge and his thugs are dead or jailed, or, until he, himself, dies.

"Be careful, Horace."

MacLeod reaches for the glassed rock. Conditions are not fit for climbing either ice or rock.

Gritting his teeth, he takes his first tentative step onto the wall. Crampons scrape rock: turning his foot allows the shorter side tines to 'feel' the thin ice. Progress is painstakingly slow, and then it stops. Unable to move forwards; impossible to look backwards, let alone reverse the move, he clings, feeling his strength sap: it's only a matter of time before the inevitable. A final prod of his right boot, his last kick or, rather, scuff, of defiance searches for an invisible notch.

The ball of his foot feels resistance. Gingerly his foot presses on the 'support', and he commits his weight; a reckless, almost suicidal move, but he's certain to fall if he waits. Then he experiences a sinking sensation and moves forward before his support collapses.

A relieved MacLeod feels his crampons cut into snow deep enough to offer grip and relative security. Life, taken for granted is cherished by those who step back from the brink. Gaining the snow slope, MacLeod examines his right crampon. His heart skips a beat. A front inner tine is *bent* outwards to an almost horizontal position: that explained the sinking sensation.

A few moments are taken to recover before MacLeod crosses the slope to the gully. There he'll monitor Jurgen's progress. At first only Jurgen's legs are visible, the rock hiding his torso. MacLeod calls instructions to direct Jurgen's search for holds. Jurgen turns the corner, pleased not only to see MacLeod belaying him but also the slope not far away. Several moves, each more confident than the last, bring him closer. Above, he notices movement. Relief turns to horror. He faces MacLeod, his mouth wide open, but his warning cry is drowned out.

'C r a c k': the sharp noise resembles a rifle report. Frantically Jurgen's right hand unties the rope while his left grips a thin hold.

MacLeod has turned to look in the direction that startled Jurgen. At first nothing seems amiss; and then a slow, gradual distortion of the skyline as the cornice creaks, groans, *and parts from* the summit's edge.

A v a l a n c h e: the lumbering mass gathers speed; clouds of spindrift fly ahead, creating a wind that soon becomes a gale. Only solid rock will resist the snow torrent.

MacLeod presses his body onto the gully face as he prepares for the onslaught. The cold ice on his left cheek is his last memory before the rush of wind tears at him; a nightmare precursor to the river of snow. The disintegrating cornice mushrooms to resemble an atomic blast.

Jurgen spots Colin above the gully just before the cornice avalanches: too late to alter fate. Freed from the rope he spectates as events unfold. The ever-burgeoning cloud advances; the billowing snow envelops Horace. The rope whips through Jurgen's hand, its end whistling past his face. Events are extreme and rapid: the crashing sound of the avalanche, the sucking velocity of its tail wind as it pulls at Jurgen; finally the powder snow as that white swirl swallows everything in its path and to its sides. Soon all is quiet and calm. The spindrift settles: no sign of life where, only minutes earlier, Horace had stood.

Jurgen looks up. The massive bite out the cornice confirms the nightmare. A figure is silhouetted by the bright light that cascades through the gap. Jurgen presses into the cold cliff.

Staring into the gully Colin sees no sign of life and is pleased. He's removed those two thorns in such a manner that nobody'll question it being anything other than a horrible accident. Alan had been too busy to notice Colin's approach. Colin's slicing blow had knocked Alan out instantly. Colin is confident nothing can link him to events. With a spring in his step he heads towards the tourist trail that leads down into Glen Nevis.

Life is already much better: the poachers are history; his plan has worked. He expects to be rewarded by the Judge, but, more importantly, he anticipates a return to *his* lifestyle of cash, drugs and bimbos. On his mobile he calls the Judge; they'll meet at the youth hostel. He anticipates the return of parties with hostesses who satisfy every dream.

Remembering the death of the drugged waitress, Colin frowns then smiles as he recalls the struggle; she'd been a fiery bitch who'd needed some persuasion, but the river had been blamed for her injuries and death. Now the river was blamed for Luke's death. It was a pity about Luke, but, with so many enticements, Colin anticipates no problem finding an eager replacement.

MacLeod presses hard against the ice face; clinging for dear life. The violent wind threatens to rip the cagoule from his back. Soon he's fighting for breath, sucking against the mighty force that vacuums air from around him. The powder snow arrives. It enters his eyes and ears. In freezing rivulets it trickles inside his clothing, but, worst of all, it gets into his lungs. He fights the instinct to shield his mouth and nose; both hands are needed to hold his perilous position. Ice-cold pin-pricks on his face are forgotten as a force of unimaginable power arrives. His arms feel as if they're being wrenched from their sockets; the searing pain as muscle tissue tears. The cascading mass reaches. Trapped, unable to free his imbedded axe and hammer he's close to passing out with the excruciating pain. It's a merciful release when the snow face to which he's attached is ripped away to swell the burgeoning avalanche.

Relief; no longer are arms being parted from torso. Life is surreal: he's buried in a moving cloud. From afar a deep moan reverberates. The hairs on his back stand on end.

Swept along, rotating, somersaulting with no idea of which way is up: suddenly he's thrown clear; a flash of blue sky shows before he's returned to the boiling mass. Everything is playing in slow motion; time to think. He discards axe and hammer to reduce the risk of puncture wounds while his rucksack is jettisoned in case it traps his arms.

Thrown into the air again allows temporary release and also the opportunity for tons of snow to pass by. 'Swim, Dod'. He knows that powder avalanche victims who do breast stroke remain nearer the surface and increase their chances of discovery. He swirls his arms and legs. The avelanche's momentum slows. All around are creaking and moaning sounds as the snow settles.

He's avoided the crush injuries that twist, distort and mangle victims of slab avalanches. Continuing with wide arm sweeps, he tries to stay afloat in that sea of powder snow. He's almost stopped moving; time to cover nose and mouth to keep his airways clear.

Now pinned in a silent world of greyish white, he's unable to move; unaware of the way he faces. Claustrophobia; suffocation; panic: inexplicable phobias that haunt individuals. MacLeod's fear is of being smothered, a dread he tries to contain. He loses consciousness; a welcome release from his nightmare death of asphyxiation.

It is late afternoon when Dougie makes his third request to phone a lawyer, his previous two having been ignored.

"Now why would you want to do such a thing when you've been as free as a bird on the wing to leave here any time you wish?" The sergeant's gloating face tests Dougie who shows unusual restraint. He's more important business than self-gratification but would still love to smash the bastard's lights out.

"Of course, serge. Perhaps we'll meet again for anither chat, nice an' quiet like, in *different* circumstances?"

Dougie dashes from the station towards the taxi office. So much time's been wasted that Dougie suspects a plan's underway to eliminate his friends. He needs his hill gear and fast.

The taxi waits for the brief time Dougie takes to add a first aid kit, a flask of sweet tea and mint cake to his rucksack. Grabbing his own sleeping bag plus a large nylon survival bag to cover any emergency, Dougie jumps into the taxi and exhorts the driver to speeds he'd never previously considered.

In his snow vault MacLeod regains consciousness. He draws slow, shallow breaths to control his panic and also to conserve oxygen that diffuses through the snow. He's lain unconscious for a long time. The snow around him has melted offering space to move hands and twist his body slightly. Although cold, he's not unduly uncomfortable. It's good to be alive despite his predicament. In his mind he checks his body from head to toe. Remarkably all seems fine.

His limited movement produces further snow compaction and more space. How deep is he? His chance of being found is slim. Can he escape? He decides to scoop the snow but in which direction? Despite the cold he manages to urinate. The warm liquid trickles *up* his abdomen and past his navel before *veering* towards his *right* armpit.

Analysis of the urine's passage tells him that he's face up, but his head is lower than his body which leans to the right.

194

Direction of escape is understood but is exactly *opposite* to his gut feeling. Analysis and science are trusted. He scrapes the slowly yielding snow.

Fatigue interrupts progress. The gruelling task does not achieve as much freedom as he hopes. He realises that he's held fast by a snow-embedded rope. He fumbles with the knot on his climbing belt but without success. Frustrated, he tries to unfasten the belt buckle, but it's iced fast. He returns to the knot. Ten minutes later he's free to move his body into the hard earned space.

The arduous scraping and pushing aside of snow is resumed; precious inches are gained at enormous costs to an energy drained body. With so little progress and no exit, nagging doubts about the chosen direction resurface, but he perseveres.

Several rests later, arms almost incapable of further toil, he craves sleep. Fear of containment keeps him going. If he ever emerges he'll have to fight sleep or die from exposure in the Arctic environment and subzero temperatures.

Again clasped hands push 'up' through the snow. Suddenly his fingers register 'no contact'. Slow to comprehend until cold, *fresh* air reaches his nostrils. His emotional surge is uncontrollable. He lies *inches* from freedom. The euphoria is savoured for several minutes before toil resumes.

It takes another hour to make an opening large enough to exit. His energy level reads almost zero. Labouriously the bedraggled figure pulls itself into the charcoal grey world where twinkling stars are its light. In a sorrowful state he struggles to place one foot in front of the other. Only hatred keeps him going as he staggers downhill, but two hundred metres further and he slumps onto his face. The cool snow is so welcoming; no further need to support his great mass on unresponsive leaden legs; his eyelids so heavy they ignore his weak commands to stay open. Sleep invites. 'Keep awake,' he chides. 'You've so much to live for. Christine, I'm sorry, dear. Please forgive.'

Misted eyes blur the sea of snow and night sky. There are no rescuers; nothing except stars to witness his ebbing existence. The Judge wins.

As the taxi speeds towards the Fort its headlights pick out a lone walker heading in the Mallaig / Loch Aoil direction. There's something familiar about the figure. Twisting around, Dougie sights the shadow in the tail lights. He's certain it's Colin. A grey Range Rover parked in a lay-by confirms that belief. The Judge must have dropped Colin far enough from the centre to avoid being linked to the day's events.

"Hurry, there's no time to lose," but Dougie's words sound despairingly hollow. His gut feeling tells him something dreadful's happened.

It's been an agonising wait for Jurgen. He hopes that Colin'll consider it impossible for anyone to survive and will have left. Jurgen believes Horace to be dead. His concerns turn to Alan. If Colin's knocked him out, then, exposed to the chilling wind, Alan will suffer hypothermia. Frequently checking the ridge Jurgen grows increasingly optimistic that Colin's gone. He crosses the slope to reach the gully without incident.

The remaining snow's secure, the avalanche having swept away the unconsolidated material. Progress up the gully's quick. The remainder of the cornice provides few problems as Jurgen slides over it and onto the summit. Eighty metres away lies the motionless figure of Alan.

Jurgen advances to the limp form. Alan is on his side, one knee bent, maintaining the belay position to protect his colleagues. Jurgen checks him. Alan's pulse is weak and his breathing shallow. Inspection reveals a weal and severe neck bruising that reaches down to Alan's left shoulder. Colin had delivered a solid blow. Had it struck only the neck, it would have killed, but the shoulder has taken much of the impact. Alan needs medical attention and shelter.

Satisfied there are no broken bones, Jurgen drags Alan to the summit hut which projects above the snow. He fits Alan into his sleeping bag talking reassuringly to the unconscious instructor in case Alan can hear.

Popular mountains, even at such advanced hours, have visitors, and it's not long before three walkers appear after a late traverse of the Carn Dearg arête.

Jurgen gives a brief account of the avalanche, explaining away Alan's injuries as rock contacts, and that, with assistance, Alan had managed to ascend to the summit. Jurgen expresses his fears for the third member, Horace.

It's agreed that two walkers will leave for the hostel and phone the police as soon as their mobiles indicate a good reception. The third walker stays and lights his stove to brew up tea.

Another half hour passes before Alan stirs. He mumbles incoherently for several minutes before regaining consciousness. With some encouragement he manages several sips of sweet tea. With Alan improving, and the prospect of help in three to four hours, Jurgen decides he'll search for Horace. The walker points out that Jurgen might be endangering his life for a dead friend but agrees to remain with Alan until help arrives. Jurgen thanks him and takes his leave.

In the failing light Jurgen heads for the 'halfway lochan' and from there to Coire Leis and then back to Number Three Gully. The hollow feeling in his gut is a reminder of the void left by his friend. The harrowing events so preoccupy him that light from an approaching headlamp goes unnoticed until it's very close.

He calls and is surprised to hear Dougie reply. Finding Jurgen alive and unharmed raises Dougie's hopes until Jurgen describes the avalanche. Despite their gloom they must persevere 'in case'. They pass twenty feet from a prostrate body that's as unaware of them as they are of it.

The avalanche debris elicits hope and fear but mainly fear. Systematically they quarter the ground until Dougie shouts excitedly. A length of climbing rope exits the snow.

"Weel let's dig man," commands Dougie as his axe attacks snow adjacent to the rope.

"A moment, my friend." Jurgen, still the analyst, holds Dougie's attention. "Remember the rope is fifty metres long. We may waste valuable time digging where there is nothing."

Without a practical alternative, Dougie's frustrations are aired. "Weel whit the hell are we gonna dae? Wait until the snaw melts? You suit yirsel' but I'm goin' tae find ma mate." Dougie resumes digging.

Jurgen paces uphill, zig-zagging a pathway he's extrapolated using the uncovered rope's exit position together with flow lines in the avalanche debris. Dougie grunts his disapproval as Jurgen continues his methodical search.

"Dougie, Dougie. Hierkommen!"

Dougie rushes over. The excitement in Jurgen's voice and reversion to his native tongue signifies something important. Dougie slows as he nears, frightful of what he might see.

"See, Dougie," pointing to the ground. "Horace is *out*. He's *alive*."

Dougie's eyes shine wildly. That exit hole is proof. MacLeod *has* dug himself out. Dougie's spirits and excitement rise. "Jesus, could it really be? Please God, keep 'im alive."

"Here, Dougie. Follow the marks." Jurgen assumes command. Soon Dougie has usurped the lead, his headlamp lighting the trail. It isn't long before they walk up to the pile of clothes.

"Is ... is he okay?" Dougie fears the worst as Jurgen examines their friend.

"Pulse is very faint, and his breathing is shallow but regular. I'd guess exhaustion plus hypothermia. He's poorly, but we'll see him fine if we get him warm."

Dougie removes the sleeping and bivvy-bags from his rucksack. "I'm glad I picked these up: bliddy feckin' miracle he's alive."

With a struggle they get MacLeod into the sleeping bag; then all three enter the bivvy-bag.

MacLeod hears their talk despite his comatose state. He's no desire, indeed no ability to speak. He's content, enjoying the warmth of being sandwiched between two trusted companions. Safe and secure, he falls into a deep sleep.

"I'm real sorry fur thon ootburst back there. If ye hidnae been sae controlled an' observant, I'd still be kickin' up snaw, an' MacLeod here wid be gettin' beyond savin'."

Jurgen grips Dougie's arm and smiles. "No apologies needed. Emotions confuse, but they also show your concerns. I'd already forgotten the incident: best you do likewise. When the walkers contact the police, there'll be calls to mountain rescue and the centre. Then the news will be out, and the group will know the game's up. My guess is they'll have flown the nest before we return. Setting up their alibi will be getting serious thought, but *we* know the truth. I saw Colin on the summit. Remember?"

Dougie's expression shows he doesn't share Jurgen's optimism.

"Of course it's my word against Colin's, but I've asked the walker who's looking after Alan to insist the police take photos and drawings of footprint patterns plus their measurements and I showed him where we found Alan. When that material's compared with Colin's boots, it should incriminate him."

"Ya beaut! Ye really are cool an' smert the way ye handle yirsel' in a crisis. An' I also saw Colin the nicht nae far frae the Judge's Range Rover." Dougie explained what had happened. The pair analyse evidence to strengthen their case. Occasionally Jurgen checks MacLeod noting a stronger pulse and deeper breathing. Their optimism increases for MacLeod's recovery and also for a prosecution.

MacLeod hears strangers' voices. Cool, rough hands immobilise his neck. The rescue party lift him onto a wheeled stretcher; a bumpy journey follows to disturb his slumber. MacLeod doubts if any severe trauma victim would survive on that contraption. More jolts jarr his body. MacLeod is very relieved to be spared further torture as he's transferred to the ambulance.

MacLeod's next memory recalls harsh lighting that makes him squint despite his eyes being closed. "Very good: he responds to brightness." While MacLeod pleases the paramedic, he himself is not in happy mode having his sleep disturbed. His examination continues until he feels a sharp prick in his upper arm.

'Surely they hadn't given him an injection to make him sleep?' Then *all* lights went out.

Sleeping for almost twelve hours, he wakens in the late afternoon. Physically tired and sore but he's pleased to have denied the angels his company. The nurse is startled by the sight of MacLeod sitting upright.

"Oh, I must get a doctor. How are you?"

He assures her that he's as well as any man who's endured the stretcher trundle. Persuading her to delay summoning the doc, he learns that the police want to interview him regarding his recent accident as well as a canoeing incident. The nurse believes a body has been discovered and is about to say more when an authoritative voice interrupts her.

"*Nurse*, I was to be informed *immediately* of *any* change in the patient's circumstances." The nurse stammers, but MacLeod intervenes.

"Listen, Doc. I'm to blame for delaying this charming young lady and I'm thoroughly pissed off with nobody to talk to after being so near the land of permanent nod. Now don't be so bloody obsessed with your own damned importance and get me a phone so I can contact my friends."

MacLeod's verbal coherence, and its unequivocal message, surprise both doctor and nurse. Never has she heard anybody raise their voice to Dr. Ashby and can only stand, open mouthed, unable to do anything except stare; but she collects herself and responds first.

"I'll get a phone." Remembering her position, she checks, "if that's all right, Dr. Ashby?"

"Well, yes. I guess it's okay, nurse. I'll ask Dr. Naisby if he can inspect our, umm, patient."

MacLeod knows he hasn't amassed brownie points with Ashby, but he is allowed to phone. The caravan site owner answers and tells MacLeod that he'll pass on his message to Dougie.

Further medical inspection pronounces MacLeod remarkably fit for a man so recently avalanched and suffering hypothermia.

"Avalanche? What avalanche?"

MacLeod deems it prudent to revert to the amnesia syndrome, guessing shock will be blamed as its trigger stimulus. How well his 'condition' continues to serve is dubious but worth pursuing, especially if it's true about the discovery of Luke's body. His examination concludes, and the doctors and nurse leave.

Twenty minutes later a red-faced Dougie arrives, an attractive nurse in his slipstream. Once Dougie's hugged MacLeod and the nurse updated him on MacLeod's health, she leaves them alone. Dougie recounts the latest developments.

Alan was in hospital, under observation, the police having left strict instructions that he was to have contact *only* with hospital staff. Apparently the police suspected both Jurgen and MacLeod of foul play towards Alan: those suspicions increased when Jurgen's account did not match other information. As a consequence Jurgen was under arrest and remained in police custody, but better news followed. Alan had described events to a nurse, and his account corroborated much of Jurgen's story, effectively exonerating MacLeod and Jurgen from the foul practice suspected by the police. However, with so many unanswered questions the police continued to detain Jurgen. Also they wanted to interview MacLeod, and, with Dougie confirming the discovery of Luke's body, bad news returned.

The tragedies and dramas surrounding MacLeod were becoming public. Leaked information fuelled speculation and caused the police headaches. MacLeod remained their chief suspect despite Jurgen citing Colin for the avalanche and Alan's assault. Initially the police had dismissed Jurgen's allegations. Only when Jurgen threatened legal action if important evidence was ignored did the police send two specialists to the Ben's summit to record footprint data.

"Oh aye," continued Dougie, "an' Colin, Billy and Donnie checked oot last nicht withoot troublin' tae say 'goodbye', jist as Jurgen predicted. He's a smert cookie, thon Hun."

MacLeod's legs are already over the bed, but a dizzy turn keeps him seated.

"I'll get a nurse, jist wait there."

"Like hell you will. I have to go after them. We've already lost too much time. Once the police question me, I'll be held for weeks and I'll probably get charged with murder. Listen in."

Dougie informs the nurse that his friend's tired and wishes to rest, but omits to tell her that he intends to return within an hour. Dougie leaves Belford hospital to pack all his gear and gather clothes for MacLeod, but Jurgen will have to remain in custody. Dougie hopes Jurgen will understand their apparent abandonment of him. An hour later and Dougie is back in the Belford, a package under his arm. The nurse hovers in the patient's vicinity as he 'sleeps'.

"I'll no disturb him. Jist leave things he wanted," tapping the package. "He's a'richt, apart frae bein' exhausted. He'll be fine once he's slept, an' I'll look in occasionally jist tae mak sure he disnae fa' oot o' bed." Dougie smiles as the nurse sniggers at his banter. He hopes she'll not suffer too much trouble if MacLeod's plan works.

Dougie deposits the package beside the bedside cabinet and glances at the form almost smothered from view below the covers. MacLeod winks before the nurse comes into sight.

"Isn't he marvellous to have come through all that danger?" she comments admiringly.

MacLeod imagines the row she'll receive from Dr. Ashby once MacLeod's absence is discovered. However, if he stays, his next bed will be in a police cell, and his incarceration will not advance the cause of justice.

Dougie departs, followed by the nurse chirping happily after him. As her voice fades, MacLeod slips out of bed, rips open the package and puts on its contents. The trousers and jacket are loose but will do. The inclusion of a cap to hide his face was excellent thinking. The sound of returning footsteps allows him just enough time to stick a pillow and spare bedding below the bed covers before retiring behind a screen. He hopes the shape will pass for a sleeping patient

202

in the dimly lit room. The nurse pops her head around the door for a final check before continuing her ward rounds.

Once her footsteps have grown faint, MacLeod leaves his room to head in the opposite direction. With the cap pulled down tightly over his forehead, he walks past the slumbering foyer porter and out the main exit. His departure was straightforward. Around the corner is Dougie's car. They set off to pick up rations before heading to the lodge at Camusbheag where, MacLeod believes, the gang will gather. In their naive compliance the police will continue to pass information to the Judge. After all, who'd suspect a respected magistrate of masterminding a drugs ring and ordering assassinations? The police have many questions to answer, and *if* justice prevails, the ramifications will be explosive.

MacLeod needed his Sako Vixen. The rifle will offer him a chance of survival if trench warfare breaks out. Also MacLeod's hunger for *raw* justice is growing.

Dougie speeds on, putting as many miles between themselves and the Fort before their departure is rumbled. They hope the police will not anticipate them heading north, and that the search for the fugitives will start with checks on the traffic south bound for Edinburgh.

TEN

The moon reflects off Loch Breac and warms the night sky; normally a spectacle to be enjoyed, but their sole concern is to reach Tor'buie without encountering a roadblock.

Tor'buie approaches. It would be a cruel twist of fate to crest the final hill and be stopped. Dougie's set jaw indicates his resolve to crash any barrier. They'd come too far with too much to lose. Single mindedness excluded compromise, but their concerns do not materialise. Small boats bob in the sea swell, nodding approval of the visitors' return.

They drive along Beach Road. It's late with few people out, but MacLeod pulls his cap down to cover his face. Word travels fast when the dead return, regardless of whether the witness partakes or is teetotal. Dougie turns up King Street, past the church and along Seaforth Lane where he parks in the shadows.

They'd decided that Dougie would prepare Sandy for the revelation that MacLeod was very much alive. They expected Sandy would need to see MacLeod to verify that fact. Afterwards they'd involve Sandy in any plans. A nod of understanding and Dougie leaves MacLeod in the car, only to return much sooner than intended. Mary is not expecting Sandy home until midnight. Hungry and with an hour to kill, Dougie sets off to buy a couple of fish suppers. Their hunger is satiated, but sleep's denied. MacLeod *must* contact Christine, preferably after seeing Sandy.

Midnight arrives, and Dougie phones Mary, but Sandy's not yet returned. It's likely Sandy's involved in an impromptu ceilidh; it'll be mid-morning before he gets home. Dougie thanks Mary and promises to phone again. MacLeod and Dougie consider it's time to head to Christine's and set off for Ardroan. MacLeod feels more relaxed when he sees the welcoming light of the croft house; almost home. The Ford winds its way up the twisting track.

Light floods out the opening door to silhouette Christine's figure. She's apprehensive of unexpected visitors at such a late hour. Uncertainty's replaced by sheer joy as she recognises Dougie, and then MacLeod as he alights from the passenger side. In a flash she's over and embracing him. Her whispers are intense with emotion; her body warm and inviting. The enquiring calls of Hector interrupt their reunion.

"Best not to mention Dougie and me yet. I'll explain, but there's still a lot of trouble. Say it's a lost tourist. We'll back the car behind the outhouse as if we're turning."

Christine's concerned expression requires an explanation.

"We'll see you in the outhouse after Hector's settled. How is he?"

"Good, but he'd be a lot better if he could see you. Remember he'd believed you dead until I couldn't stand his grief any longer and broke my word, but it was only Dad I told."

"Understood. I'm only sorry it's not possible to divulge everything yet. Soon, I hope. Now off you go, and we'll see you soon."

With the car parked out of sight of the road, MacLeod retrieves the rifle from the boot. The Fort William police had not searched the car, a grave oversight on their part. Inside the outhouse Dougie flits through an old newspaper while MacLeod extracts the Sako Vixen from its cover. The smell of gun oil triggers memories of the hill and Stuart. 'Soon,' resolves MacLeod, 'your murder will be avenged my friend.' Carefully he prepares the 223.

Dougie's disturbed, and the attention MacLeod affords the rifle only hypes him more. On a mission already fraught with peril, MacLeod needs no passengers and then has a brainwave.

"Dougie, I need you to stay here tonight and visit Sandy early tomorrow to explain all that's happened. I'll watch the lodge, and you come up as soon as you can. How does that sound?"

"Weel, I dinnae like it. Whit if onythin' should happen tae ye, an' I'm no' aroon'? Whit then?"

MacLeod promises only to *observe*. Only then does a reluctant Dougie agree before returning his attention to the paper.

"Jesus Christ. That's 'im." Dougie's startled exclamation means nothing to MacLeod.

"What are you gabbing on about?"

"The Jidge: ah saw the Jidge at the caravan when the polis wis haudin' me back frae finding you. Ah kent ah'd seen 'im afore but couldna place 'im, but there he is" pointing to the newspaper as he brandishes it before MacLeod's eyes.

"But Dougie, you never said."

"Wi' a' that wis goin' oan, ah scarcely kent ma ain name ne'er mind remembering seein' some slimeball. Remember that you wis near deid an' everythin' else that wis happenin'."

MacLeod looks at the picture of swimmers being presented with medals. His brow furrows. "Which one's the Judge, Dougie?"

"Naw, the *ither* photo o' the Assistant Chief o' Polis; he's a dead ringer fir the Jidge. Or else their pappy splashed his genes aboot."

MacLeod concentrates on the face of the uniform presenting certificates to members of the public. It's clear now how the Judge accessed confidential information. Small wonder 'Mr Big' always escaped. The similarities in appearances between Judge and Assistant Chief of Police suggest blood ties, assuming Dougie was correct.

"Thon bastard must hae gi'en the order tae his lachies tae haud me back. He kent whit wis happenin' a' the time. Him an' the Jidge are feckin murderers."

"It makes sense; the connection with the police; the way the Judge is protected, but we'll never prove it, Dougie."

"Ye're richt. Wunder whit the sentence is fur toppin' a heid o' polis' as weel as a Jidge?"

"Just remember I get first go."

Christine's arrival interrupts them. She looks worried,

but that increases when she notices MacLeod trying to slip the rifle into the gun cupboard.

"Well?" The pregnant pause emphasises the severity of her question, "and just *what* do you intend with the gun, George MacLeod?"

It's the first time he's heard his real name *and in full* in a fortnight. Delivered by Christine in *that* tone, has a marked effect. MacLeod speaks before his brain is in gear. No backtracking's possible then. Christine'll smell a rat if he changes his story, and she'll not let him out of her sight. He places his cards on the table, all face up. As he outlines his plans, Christine shows mounting concern.

"There's too much danger. It .. it's suicidal."

MacLeod explains that he'll only monitor the situation until Dougie and Sandy appear.

"What then? Do you think they're going to come out with their hands in the air?" Her sarcasm's all the more cutting because it makes sense. "You're prepared to shoot, aren't you?"

"You don't understand. A lot of water's gone under the bridge since we spoke last."

"I doubt I could live with you if you're prepared to kill, no matter how evil they are."

She'd made her statement, issued her ultimatum. She looked resolved, unwilling to listen. He cursed himself for stupidly divulging his intentions to secure the Judge and his thugs at any cost.

"Christine. This vermin continues to destroy lives, apparently, in our case, without much effort." She remains beyond reach. Ignoring her he turns to Dougie. "I'll see you tomorrow as soon as you can manage. Leave the car in the large lay-by and then head for the gorge. You'll be hidden most of the way. I'll be waiting at the top, opposite the lodge." Christine spun on her heels and left. "Dougie, maybe you'll get a chance to explain? I don't want this to be our last memory. Who knows what's going to happen? She'll take a lot of convincing about how ruthless these guys are. I doubt she'll ever understand. Tell her that my life's meaningless without her."

MacLeod was caught in a 'catch twenty two': succeed and risk losing Christine; fail and die and also jeopardise friends' lives. MacLeod hopes Dougie'll make Christine more aware of the choices forced on him.

MacLeod makes his final preparations. His day sack contains clothing to cover weather vagaries; balaclava, Dachstein mitts, waterproof jacket and trousers plus food and, finally, five boxes of Sako ammunition. The rifle and his day sack lifted, MacLeod bids Dougie farewell.

He's just placed the key in the ignition when Christine appears in front of the car waving a carrier bag. MacLeod steps out.

"For you." At arms' length, like a peace offering, the bag's held open for inspection. "There's some food and a couple of flasks and ... oh, I'm so mixed up. I don't want to lose you."

In his arms, she sobs. Glad they haven't parted with cross words he tries to reassure her.

"I'll be back, I promise and I'll not fire unless ... unless it's unavoidable. You're everything, but I *have* to go. *Please* understand."

Her sobbing doesn't ease the task of parting, but, to have any future other than that of a fugitive, he *needs* a result. Their parting kiss lingers until he grips Christine by the shoulders and steps back. Her moist, dark eyes haunt him. Abruptly he turns, closes the car door and doesn't look back.

Consumed by anger at the damage those bastards wreak, darkness fills his heart until he remembers his pledge. He mustn't allow emotions to dictate his actions. Before Tor'buie he crosses the bridge and turns left onto the single track, past the stone quarry towards the lodge. The track's full of deep ruts and potholes, insignificant jolts compared with the traumatic problems he anticipates.

Twice he cuts the engine and leans out the window to listen, but the only sound is the river surging down the gorge. He's reminded of the encounter with Luke. In a strange way Luke's discovery had removed the uncertainty of what to do: no longer the need to feign amnesia and dupe others;

that acting charade was past, but it had brought dividends and bought extra time. Now Colin was implicated in Alan's attack and also the avalanche, and both would lead to further enquiries. With the police confused by growing evidence that implicated a Judge in criminal activities, MacLeod had much to gain at this time. Colin had become a liability and would not be allowed to incriminate the Judge. Had that occurred to Colin, MacLeod wondered?

A passing place widened a corner where track and river bank met. He locked the car and hid the key in long grass at the foot of a fence post. Fine speckles of cold river spray refreshed his face and sent tingles down his spine. He was ready. There was no point in delaying as he moved along the river, his passage well hidden by trees and bushes. From a thicket a startled roebuck breaks cover and barks its warning. MacLeod takes the rifle off his shoulder: its contact is reassuring. He loads five rounds and waits. Five minutes pass with no apparent response to the roe's alarm call. MacLeod moves closer.

The lights of the lodge are visible. He sees people passing windows, but he's too distant to recognise individuals. In case guards are posted he decides to observe from a safe distance.

For two hours he watches. With no sense of urgency showing in the lodge, and its clientele appearing to settle for the night, MacLeod assumes the police have not informed the Judge about his disappearance. Expecting a long session he takes out the flask and washes down a salmon sandwich with hot tea. He assumes the salmon would have appeared on Hector's doorstep, its anonymous donation typical of the actions of that caring community.

The river sounds are soothing. MacLeod relaxes enough to doze despite his proximity to a viper's nest. His slumber is interrupted by urgent voices. On his belly he slides forwards for a better view. There's hectic activity. Colin, Donnie and Billy are rushing with boxes to the Judge's Range Rover. Before catnapping MacLeod hadn't noticed the Judge's vehicle. Its recent arrival suggests the Judge knows of MacLeod's escape and that he might head for the lodge.

Whatever the reason, everybody seems keen to leave.

In the growing light MacLeod sees further down the track. With no sign of Dougie or Sandy he *has* to delay the lodge's exodus. He gauges the distance to the Range Rover to be about four hundred metres; too far to guarantee hitting its tyres. Two hundred metres would offer a better chance, but that requires him to cross open heath with no cover until rocky outcrops are gained. If he can reach those rocks he's confident of immobilising the Range Rover and other vehicles. The frenzy of activity continues.

Leaving his position of security, MacLeod runs in a half crouched manner. His heart pounds more from anxiety than exertion. The toing and froing at the lodge continues but for how much longer? Another fifty metres in full view of the lodge and then he'll gain the outcrops. Only twenty metres from the nearest rock and the ground erupts before him. Peat and water mushroom to pepper his face and clothing. He hits the deck as another 'crack' raises a volcano of muddy water to his right. A third 'crack' as a bullet whistles over his head. The shots are too close. On his feet he's running in zig-zag fashion. Two shots pass so close that he feels their wind.

The high pitched 'whang' of a bullet striking rock is followed by a sharp pain in his forehead. His knees buckle. He's a squatting target as another bullet ricochets. Stone splinters fly wildly in all directions. MacLeod flattens into the heather then drags himself behind a small outcrop. His fingertips register warm sticky blood as it oozes fom a gash below his hairline; trickling it mats the sideburn at his right ear. At least his right eye is unimpaired, able to sight the scope.

Three more bullets whistle overhead. MacLeod steals a glance which draws another shot, the puff of smoke pinpointing the shooter's position as the lower right window. Releasing the safety catch, MacLeod slides the rifle around the rock. Raising the rifle until the scope's cross hairs are about two feet higher than the window he makes allowance for the bullet's descent over that distance. Squeezing the trigger the rifle butt jars into his shoulder just as another lump of rock disintegrates from his dwindling cover. The noise of breaking glass is immediately drowned by a nerve-jangling scream.

Colin and Donnie stop, immobilised by the blood-curdling cry. Donnie drops his box and runs for the lodge, closely pursued by Colin. MacLeod's shot has hit either the Judge or Billy. The sight of the portly figure scuttling to the Range Rover dashes MacLeod's greatest wish. Billy must have bought the bullet. The Judge has started the Range Rover. Colin and Donnie are rushing towards it.

The cross hairs of the Zeiss sight on the rear tyre. In the instant he fires, MacLeod knows he's jerked the trigger, the round hitting the vehicle's body. The Range Rover shoots forwards, self-preservation more important to the Judge than loyalty to hired hands. MacLeod cracks another round at the right rear tyre of the moving vehicle. Its rear side window stars. If the Judge had second thoughts about waiting for Donnie and Colin, that bullet decided matters. He accelerates down the track. With MacLeod's attention on the Range Rover, Donnie and Colin reach the lodge before MacLeod can fire again.

A period of inactivity is interrupted by the sound of a muffled shot. Without the whine of a bullet near him, MacLeod is puzzled: slowly realisation dawns. A feeling of nausea rises up his gullet. Billy's been executed. Wounded, unable to escape but able to incriminate others, Billy would be a liability. The dead don't talk.

A volley of shrieking 'zings' and 'whangs' shower MacLeod with stone splinters. He fears a ricochet. Five shots are released in rapid succession; *if* they all came from one rifle, its magazine should be empty. Cautiously, MacLeod raises his head. Colin is a hundred metres from the lodge and racing towards the suspension bridge that spans the gorge. The whistle of a passing bullet reminds MacLeod of his exposed head. He cowers down and considers the development.

The horrendous implications hit MacLeod like a thump in the midriff. Colin intends a pincer movement circling above and behind MacLeod. There he'll have a clear shot

211

over the very ground MacLeod is viewing; relatively flat terrain. MacLeod'll be the proverbial sitting duck, but, if he leaves his shelter, he becomes Donnie's target.

Sweat streams down MacLeod's body. An occasional tremor accompanies the tingling sensation along his spine. He imagines where Colin's first bullet might strike, and what his fate will be if he's incapacitated rather than killed outright. Colin will prolong his suffering, shooting each limb in turn. He'll maximise MacLeod's agonies with a stomach shot, then spectate and gloat before administering a final shot to the head.

Either MacLeod awaits a gruesome death or risks moving towards the lodge in the knowledge that the stalker will be a crack shot. MacLeod considers he's a better chance of survival as a jinking target for Donnie rather than a static target for Colin.

Breaking cover he makes a zany run towards a group of rocks that might offer shelter from both frontal and rear assaults. The 'zing' of metal whipping off rock gives added momentum. Racing in a half-crouched position, an unbalanced MacLeod tumbles and somersaults onto solid rock. It knocks the wind from him. Gasping, he lies on his back in an exposed position. Bullets pass overhead. Pained movements gain MacLeod a sheltered position between two large rocks.

With his back protected MacLeod risks a view of the lodge. He sees Donnie at an upper window. Donnie fires again but *down* the track! Rolling sideways MacLeod sees Donnie's target. Crouching behind Christine's car is Dougie. Another report and MacLeod sees the front window disintegrate. Dougie's pinned down, unable to move and with no means of defence.

MacLeod ignores the threat from Colin and adopts a kneeling position with his arms resting over a rock to steady the rifle. A puff of dust from the window's lintel shows MacLeod's overgenerous height allowance, but it causes Donnie to abandon his station.

A dull thud and ground vibrations alert MacLeod to a near miss. Spinning round, he looks for Colin. A bullet splays to erupt stone shards exactly where MacLeod had been a second earlier.

MacLeod registers the crouched figure as it prepares to fire again. Imperative to ruin Colin's aim, MacLeod fires from a hip position. His wild discharge is close enough to force Colin into cover: it buys MacLeod precious seconds to regain shelter. With time to aim, his next shot whangs Colin's sheltering boulder. Terms of engagement are balancing out.

"Dod!" Dougie's call of alarm turns MacLeod. He sees Donnie running in Dougie's direction. The scope cross hairs centre on Donnie's waist before MacLeod lowers them to the hip in case the bullet doesn't drop as much as expected. Keeping the cross hairs moving slightly ahead of target to allow for Donnie's travel, MacLeod squeezes the trigger. The rifle kicks. Donnie lies squirming on the track.

The searing pain and burning fire in his lower thigh consume Donnie. As he writhes painfully, his movements distance him from his discarded rifle. A smile graces MacLeod's lips. He's kept his word to Christine, and the result is even more satisfying. Had it been the Judge or Colin, the cross hairs would have centred between the shoulder blades.

Twisting around he sees Colin standing, stunned by what he's witnessed. The thump of MacLeod's bullet on the adjacent rock breaks Colin's trance. Colin ducks out of sight only to reappear screaming abuse while punching the air in defiance. He points to the mountain, to MacLeod and finally to himself but does not remain in view long enough for MacLeod to fire again. Several minutes pass without a further sighting. Colin appears to have left.

Cautiously, MacLeod retreats, constantly checking all around. Nearing the lodge he considers he's outwith Colin's range and abandons caution. Donnie's writhing has stopped, but both his hands grip a blood soaked knee, and his teeth are clenched in a painful grimace.

Dougie held Donnie's rifle, a Parker Hale .270: small wonder that MacLeod's rock cover had almost been blown away.

"Lower femur's shattered. Not nice." Dougie's concern angers MacLeod.

"Good. With a bit of luck, the bastard might bleed to death."

The horror on Dougie's face intensifies as MacLeod approaches Donnie.

"Okay, ass-hole, where's Colin holed up?"

A snarl passes Donnie's mouth followed by a scream as MacLeod's boot sinks into his shattered thigh. Dougie knocks MacLeod away.

"For Christ's sake, Dod. Whit's got intae ye?"

"In case it's escaped your attention, *mate*, I've been an Aunt Sally before you cruised onto the scene, and these fuckers weren't just trying to frighten me. No sir, .270 rifles doing their worst and you think I should be nice?"

"Okay! Ye've made yir point, bit he's still human, an' ye promised Christine." Dougie knew how to drive the point home. The mention of Christine and that promise to her had the desired effect. MacLeod's rage subsided.

"Sorry, Dougie. When you deal with shit some sticks, but I'll not guarantee this vermin's life if I don't get answers, and quick."

Donnie was still groaning, his seeping blood darkening the track. Dougie tried to comfort Donnie, but MacLeod brushed him aside, his unsheathed knife gleaming. The helpless, supine figure stares, his intense pain temporarily forgotten. Donnie's eyes reflect his growing terror.

"No, Dod, No!"

"Relax, Dougie. Perhaps later."

MacLeod hacks off Donnie's trouser leg to use as a tourniquet. The rough administration of first aid causes Donnie anguish with further pain promised if MacLeod doesn't get answers.

"Colin's rifle: the same as yours?" Donnie's eyes remain screwed shut, but his nod is confirmation. "Where's Colin hiding?"

Silence ensues. Cooperation is unlikely. MacLeod contemplates persuasion when the rifle crack and the cloud of dust arrive simultaneously. They hit the deck, MacLeod hissing at Dougie to pass the .270. With its superior range he might discourage Colin.

Preoccupied with Donnie, MacLeod and Dougie have failed to remain alert. Before MacLeod can return fire, Colin looses another round. Its dull thud confirms a hit. Dougie and MacLeod are unscathed, but Donnie is unconscious, blood oozing through his jacket. Mission accomplished, Colin is off up the mountain. His military training is evident; identify the target, hit and retreat before the enemy can recover. In that way your position is never compromised.

MacLeod would keep Colin waiting. He'd not be rushed into a situation where the odds were stacked against him, but he would pick up the gauntlet Colin had thrown. The immediate priority was to keep their potential informant alive and to avoid danger.

"Here, Dougie." MacLeod hands over the .270. "Use it, if you see *any* movement," but he's no confidence in either Dougie's willingness or ability to respond with effective fire. Conscious of their vulnerable position MacLeod works fast, ripping open Donnie's jacket and shirt. The bullet had missed the lungs but shattered the shoulder. MacLeod straps pads onto the wound to staunch further blood loss before fire-lifting Donnie onto his shoulder.

Inside the lodge MacLeod heaves Donnie off his shoulder in the first room they enter. Dougie searches for a first aid kit while MacLeod keeps watch. Bandages and slings along with plasters and ointments improve the hastily arranged field dressing.

Twenty minutes later and Donnie regains consciousness. In the intervening period Dougie has carried out a cursory inspection and made a grim discovery that confirmed MacLeod's earlier suspicions. Billy's body lay in an upstairs room. Not that anybody would recognise Billy without his face. The .270 round, fired through the back of the skull, had mushroomed to remove Billy's mask on its exit.

Dougie had thrown up. Forewarned, MacLeod was prepared for the spectacle but still found it difficult to retain his stomach contents. Also he noted a hole in Billy's chest and guessed that an autopsy would uncover a .223 slug from his Sako. The splayed .270 round should be traceable to Colin's rifle. *If* Donnie survived *and* testified, Colin and the Judge would rot behind bars. Donnie would be jailed but could look forward to a meaningful life after his sentence ended. With so much at stake Colin had no intention of leaving informants.

Dougie told Donnie that Colin's attempt to kill him had failed by five centimetres, the distance separating bullet and lung. Donnie became more cooperative offering evidence to incriminate Colin. When MacLeod demanded similar revelations about the Judge, Donnie had different ideas.

"You know that I'll do time": more a statement than a question.

"Without doubt."

"Well there's a high number of suicides in prison, ain't there?"

"Meaning?"

"Meanin' bloody nuthin'. It's easy to arrange 'suicides', when you've got a' that influence an' high connections. The Judge has friends inside. Naw, I'll testify against Colin after what that bastard done tae me and Billy, but there's nae way that I'd even think o' pointing a finger at the Judge."

"Not even if your safety was guaranteed?"

"Don't make me laugh. It hurts. There ain't no place safe from him. You'll find that oot even if you prove your case against the rest o' them. You did well. There are others who weren't so lucky."

"Okay, but you'll nail Colin?"

"Perhaps I should have said 'kill' Colin. You'll never take him alive. He's oot there just noo waitin' to kill you, or you him. You know, you've really got him worried. For the first time e'er I saw some type o' fear in his eyes when he was speakin' aboot coming in on you frae behind. He had a' the cards in his favour by rights, but you frighten him. He kept wanting me tae fire often tae make sure you kept your heid doon. Aye, you got him worried. Noo he'll be holed up waiting to bushwhack you, too scared to show himself first. Looks like you'll have tae smoke him oot."

MacLeod saw Donnie smile. Donnie disliked Colin *and*

MacLeod and was enjoying the prospect that one or both would die. MacLeod suspected Donnie knew where Colin would hide.

"Where would he lie up?"

There followed a long silence, Donnie eyeing MacLeod, enjoying every moment as he considered his options. If he told, there'd be a better chance of MacLeod killing Colin or the two shooting each other. If he didn't, Colin might kill MacLeod, but then he'd look for Donnie when he learned that his previous attempt had failed. Reading Donnie's thoughts, MacLeod told Donnie that he'd alert Colin to Donnie's survival and of Donnie's willingness to testify against him. Donnie's smile became a sneer.

"Feckin' bastard. You and Colin are the same."

"You'd better believe that. Now what's it to be; some of the earlier treatment or would you just like to shit teeth for the rest of the day?"

Fists clenched and standing menacingly over Donnie, MacLeod was on the verge of committing another barbaric act. Sensing MacLeod was not bluffing, Donnie offered enough information to avoid the dentistry work.

Armed with a vague description of some overhanging rock, MacLeod decides there's no point in further delaying the encounter with Colin. *If* Colin's captured, MacLeod remains unsure if Donnie will testify. Killing Colin will avenge Stuart's murder, but a dead Colin will be a scapegoat for *every* crime, and the Judge and Donnie will escape justice. The real issues will be lost where it mattered, in court, *unless*.... MacLeod knows he *has* to capture Colin to have any chance of securing a conviction. Putting a real judge in the clink for other inmates to 'look after' would have Stuart smiling.

Before leaving, MacLeod tells Dougie that, should he fail to return by nightfall then Dougie's to hide Donnie well away from the lodge and then alert the Tor'buie police.

"If only Sandy were here." Dougie's remark stops MacLeod in his tracks. He'd forgotten that Sandy and Dougie had arranged to meet.

"Just what *did* happen to Sandy?"

Dougie described Sandy's reactions on hearing Stuart's assumed fate, based on MacLeod's experience. The expected explosive reaction hadn't materialised. In shock, Sandy had remained seated and silent. Dougie had taken his leave, but not before he'd asked Mary to go into the room to comfort her son. Dougie had been unable to divulge any details to Mary.

"I hadn't expected a vacuum." Disbelievingly shaking his head, Dougie turned to find he was talking to himself. MacLeod, then ten metres distant, was striding purposefully towards the suspension bridge: alone; without help.

MacLeod moved quickly, occasionally sidestepping, occasionally darting faster than usual, varying both pace and direction, certain he was being observed by Colin. His legs raced. The blood pounded through his veins, and his lungs felt fit to burst. A feeling of bitter nausea rose from his stomach to the back of his throat, and the searing pain of a stitch in his side aggravated his distress. His feet clanged on the metal bridge, and then he was across and on the lower slopes amongst the sheltering hillocks where he rested.

Ten minutes elapse before he feels fit enough to continue. He's no plan but considers a mountaintop position will allow a scan of the lower slopes, but then reasons that he'll only see exposed ground, and Colin will *not* be out in the open. Also, on the higher ground he'll be outlined against sky and present a clear target for Colin. Better to traverse the mountain and gain height gradually: in that way he'll cover more ground and increase his chance of finding the flat-topped rock where Donnie believed Colin would shelter. MacLeod checks above, below and behind him every few steps and moves swiftly across any gap.

He imagines Colin skulking behind every rock. MacLeod's nerves are as taut as strained wire. Colin must be equally anxious. MacLeod makes longer stops to listen for a noise to betray another's presence and position.

A raven flies in his direction. Suddenly it tips a wing to drop sideways, 'cronking' its warning as it veers from the cause of its alarm. MacLeod recalls its flight path and the point where it stooped. He estimates fifty metres above and the same distance back; the *very* route he'd just taken. He shudders. Colin and he may have been within touching distance.

For half an hour MacLeod stays put. Confirmation of Colin's proximity arrives courtesy of a rock pipit piping its warning. A well aimed stone moves it on. Still chiding the missile thrower, it abandons its territory. MacLeod has spotted the projectile and retraces its trajectory to locate Colin's position.

Control lies with MacLeod, but he sees no safe approach. Colin occupies a recess surrounded and protected on all sides by rocks and stones: so much for Donnie's description of Colin's hiding place. Since Colin remains unaware of MacLeod's position, MacLeod decides to play the waiting game. The tables are then turned on himself.

'Chirp! Chirp!' MacLeod starts at the proximity of the warning call. The very notes so recently valued are cursed. Spinning round he 'shoos' the pipit away. 'Whang', the sound is accompanied by a stinging neck pain. Pole-axed, he slumps behind a rock as another bullet cleaves the air. The speed of Colin's reaction and the sudden reversal in fortunes amaze and frighten MacLeod.

Touching his neck he feels a small jagged object, either rock or metal. There is little bleeding, and so he makes no attempt to remove the shrapnel, but his position is dire. Colin has the advantage and will maximise it. MacLeod can't sit there all day; can he? It'll be several hours to darkness, but its cover will offer a safer retreat. MacLeod decides to wait but expects Colin will attempt to force him out before night falls.

"Give up. You've no chance." Colin's voice rings triumphantly.

"Join me for a cup of poison."

"Best to die quickly than painfully," the taunt of the uncertain bully.

"Luke thought the same. Remember what happened. Give yourself up. You'll get a fair trial."

A tirade of oaths follow, and MacLeod risks a glance. Still swearing, Colin's standing, looking not at MacLeod but at the lie of the ground to analyse his options. MacLeod's snap shot hits the rock in front of Colin's head. The cry of pain raises MacLeod's hopes, but they're short-lived as a four shot barrage is returned, the rounds screaming off rocks all about him. Those four plus the earlier shot; has Colin emptied his magazine in a frenzied fury?

"Nice try Colin, but I wasn't born yesterday."

"You're too smart for your own good, Horace. The magazine's full again. I *had* emptied it." Colin savours the chance to goad MacLeod.

Silence follows, each considering possible strategies. MacLeod steals fleeting glances to reassure himself that Colin remains in his eyrie fortress with its commanding view. Colin's rifle rests over a rock, immediately ready for an opportunist shot.

MacLeod brainstorms ideas on how to winkle Colin from his turret. He's gambling that Colin's impatience will increase as the light fades. Fanciful escape options are discarded as their risks prove greater than remaining where he is, but something niggles at the back of his mind. Donnie's involved, but MacLeod can not think how.

Colin's problems are how to devise a plan that exposes MacLeod while safeguarding himself. Then Colin smiles.

'Crash'; the startling sound is immediately above MacLeod. Instinctively he ducks. His ears are ringing, and his heart flutters. The missile is no bullet but rock. Another follows, and then another, until the fourth clears MacLeod's shelter and slices his left calf muscle. The sharp pain stabs repeatedly as nerve impulses echo from leg to brain. Blood soaks his trousers. Gradually the leg numbs and the pain subsides. Stones continue to rain down with several near misses. MacLeod's attention is divided between dodging missiles and checking that Colin stays in place. When the hail of missiles stops, MacLeod expects an assault, but Colin's fearful for his own life and remains in the same secure position. With no further salvo, MacLeod inspects the damage.

His tibia's undamaged, but there's a deep gash. The surrounding flesh has turned blue. MacLeod rips a piece off the torn trouser and ties it firmly over the wound, its direct pressure reducing further blood loss. The activity lull continues. MacLeod steals another look before whipping his head back as Colin aims the rifle sights. How long will this last before another onslaught? MacLeod feels fragile.

Again Donnie's remark niggles and irritates. Just what had it been? He was forgetting something important. Without warning the first rock of the next attack plummets and narrowly misses MacLeod's foot. *'Concentrate*, MacLeod. *Concentrate*, man.' A second rock lands uncomfortably close. The interval between successive missiles increases as each receives a more controlled launch. 'Zzzip'; the next rock parts ground, only centimetres from the damaged leg.

'Yes that was it.' Donnie saying "... you'll need to *smoke* him oot." MacLeod fumbles in his pockets for matches as yet another rock lands, again very close. The wind's blowing *towards* Colin: ideal. The matchbox spills from MacLeod's hand and rolls away. MacLeod endures an agonising wait for the next rock before he dares leave his shelter. 'Crash'; splinters of rock fly into the air as the projectile hits the top of MacLeod's main shelter before bouncing harmlessly over MacLeod's head and down the slope.

The box is snatched, and MacLeod dives back, his body pressed tight against the screening rock face. The box sounds hollow. MacLeod pauses and breathes deeply before opening ... three matches. What he'd do for petrol. Moving to the side he lights a match, his crouched body sheltering the flame as he attempts to ignite the heather. Briefly the bushy heather tops flame and then extinguish. MacLeod's heart sinks.

He rips off heather heads and compresses them to produce dense kindling. He *has* to maintain the flames for longer. So engrossed is he that the next rock is scarcely noticed despite it passing narrowly over his shoulder. The match is struck. Its head lights but careers off the stick, its blue flame extinguishing before it reaches the ground. Sweat moistens his back: *one match left*. Composure's needed. He imagines lighting the house fire where *every* struck match works. Striking along the emery side a flame hisses and holds. Sheltering the precious light in cupped hands he applies it below the ball of heather heads. His hands shake. Flames lick up and then, just as quickly, subside. His boot forces the dry heather stalks together. With more tinder in contact, the flames rise again. In a frenzied attack he grabs, tears and adds more heather, blowing on the flames to resuscitate and spread them. The fire's caught and is spreading as the wind fans the flames. As the flames soar so do MacLeod's spirits.

Colin sees smoke, hears crackling twigs and launches a furious attack. The entire reserve of his armoury arrives in quick succession; a wild deluge that lacks the accuracy of earlier attacks. MacLeod forces his body tight against his sheltering rock.

The flames are not only licking higher, but are penetrating the heather stalks as they seek fuel for their growing hunger. Colin's panicking. Soon the flames will reach and force him out.

The wall of orange is racing up the hillside. Blue smoke swirls ahead of its advance. Objects blur in the smoky haze and shimmering heat waves. An occasional updraught provides temporary gaps in the smoke screen before it closes its shroud to cover everything.

Holding the rifle, its safety catch 'off', MacLeod waits for the fox to bolt. Devoid of emotion, MacLeod anticipates the final act. He prefers to kill, but Colin's capture brings a glimmer of hope of convicting the Judge. Also, he's promised Christine. He'll try to incapacitate Colin.

Colin's coughing but sits tight. MacLeod grips the rifle stock firmly. The flames engulf Colin's lair. To the right a shadow appears to be moving downhill, the dense smoke screening the figure. A puff of wind raises the dense curtain, but the smouldering heather clouds Colin's lower body making a leg shot impossible.

MacLeod zeros the cross hairs on Colin's shoulder. The rifle crack is followed by a thump. Colin disappears as the striking bullet knocks him downhill.

As quickly as he can hobble, MacLeod covers the final few metres to where he last saw Colin. A wounded animal is at its most dangerous, and none would be more so than Colin. As he moves, MacLeod crouches to reduce his size, all the time scanning and searching. His caution consumes time but proves its worth. About to cross the lip of the slope a movement catches his eye. MacLeod steps smartly back as Colin prepares to fire. The shot flies harmlessly past. MacLeod sees Colin struggling with the breech while holding the rifle against his chest. Colin is fumbling with his left hand only, his right arm hanging limply by his side. MacLeod's shot must have shattered it.

"*Colin.*" Colin looks up to see MacLeod's rifle unwaveringly targeted on him. "It's no use, Colin. You haven't a chance. Drop the gun."

Colin discards his rifle, falls onto his back and slides downhill and out of sight. MacLeod pursues, his progress encumbered by his injury. At least he knows Colin's unarmed.

On reaching the middle of the convex slope MacLeod has a position that allows an uninterrupted view of the ground below. Colin's halfway across the flat expanse. MacLeod lies down to assume the steadiest shooting position possible. The cross hairs centre between Colin's shoulder blades. The temptation's great, but MacLeod moves the cross down to Colin's right thigh. He judges Colin to be one hundred and forty metres away. Another twenty metres and he'll reach rugged land that offers cover and an excellent chance of escape. With the light greying and darkness imminent, Colin has only a short distance to cross.

From his prone position MacLeod shouts a final command. Colin stops and turns slowly. He looks towards MacLeod and then the direction of escape. For a minute he deliberates before turning to run. MacLeod takes a slow breath, partly exhales then holds the remaining air to keep his thorax firm in preparation for the shot. His forefinger squeezes firmly, smoothly; the report of the shot. Colin's body lifts off the ground before crashing face down, motionless. MacLeod sees every detail but fails to understand. Another report follows. The corpse flinches.

Turning, MacLeod comprehends. Higher up stands

Sandy, his rifle raised skywards. MacLeod looks at Sandy, then at the motionless corpse, so near and yet so far from the gully that offered escape. Numb with disbelief, MacLeod has been a mere spectator, overtaken by events. A feeling of emptiness occupies his stomach where, so recently, emotional turmoil churned. At a stroke, all conflicts and doubts succinctly erased; terminated as clinically as Colin's life.

Sandy stoops to inspect his friend's injured leg, although MacLeod's oblivious to pain at that time.

"Seoras - for my family, for Dad, my thanks: Christine will be here soon."

Sandy's words fade, swallowed by a mist that cloaks and contains MacLeod. Drained of emotion and energy, MacLeod regresses into a world of purity and cleanliness.

"George?" His blank stare prompts alarm. "Oh Seoras, my dear, what's happened?" The warmth of Christine's body breaks the trance. His emotions flood out before self-control prevails. Fighting back tears of relief, he sinks his head onto Christine's warm, comforting bosom. Her tender caresses and soothing talk help him regain composure. Only then does Christine notice his wounded leg. As she examines the injury, they chat in a matter-of-fact way about friends: anything to distance him from immediate events although Christine appreciates his memories will need to be relived. In the sanctuary of the croft house she'll always be there to listen and help to heal those mental scars.

Sandy had raced ahead of Christine when they'd heard shots. Even if Christine had matched Sandy's pace, MacLeod doubted she could have prevented Sandy exacting his revenge. Sandy was unaware of the bigger picture and Colin's potentially explosive evidence against the Judge: MacLeod would never make Sandy aware of the implications of his actions.

Encouraged by Christine, MacLeod gets to his feet. Slowly they head back to the lodge. The noise of another shot halts their progress. Their eyes meet; they exchange looks of horror at the sound's possible implications. Another two shots dissipate MacLeod's fears: the traditional three shot salute of the Freeforester is Sandy's farewell to his much loved father.

Tiredness overcomes MacLeod: a hot bath in which to steep, a cool beer and a comfortable bed with clean sheets for an undisturbed sleep, are all he wants.

Near the lodge they're met by Dougie and three police officers. The most senior of the officers loses no time questioning MacLeod despite Christine's and Dougie's protests. He stops only when MacLeod utters, "I need a doctor," before collapsing.

MacLeod's half-carried, half-dragged to the waiting cars. The police drive at excessive speed down the track, each pothole jolting the car. It's a relief to MacLeod when they reach the police station where a doctor's waiting. The doctor forbids questioning and calls for the village ambulance to take MacLeod to Raigmore hospital.

For two days MacLeod occupied a single room enjoying excellent medical attention including psychiatric assessment in case he suffered emotional trauma. On the second evening friends were allowed to visit. Maggie, Jessie and Mary shed tears at seeing him alive. MacLeod evaded their questions, explaining that the police would be unhappy if others knew details before they did. Rumours abounded, but many villagers had interpreted events quite well. MacLeod was relieved to know that nobody blamed him for staying 'dead'. On day three he endured three police interviews, each lasting about an hour. His recollection of events and his answers were compared with others' statements as the police pieced together a 'truth' jigsaw.

MacLeod learned that Sandy's defence lawyer had stated that during his client's pursuit of Colin, Colin had tripped and lost contact with his rifle. Sandy had commanded him to remain prone, but Colin had lunged for the rifle leaving Sandy with no option other than to shoot. Sandy's action was accepted as self-defence despite two bullets having entered Colin's back. Later, Sandy told MacLeod that he'd pulled a sleeve over his hand before lifting Colin's rifle and placing it next to Colin's body.

MacLeod's testimony included reference to an exchange of fire, but he claimed he was unable to provide details of the final encounter since it took place out of his sight. Counsel for both the defence and the prosecution had heatedly debated a controversial decision, but moral justice had prevailed and neither Sandy nor MacLeod was convicted of any crime although both had their firearms certificates revoked and forfeiture of their rifles.

Donnie's evidence corroborated MacLeod's statement that Colin had executed Stuart and Billy. Donnie added that Luke had devised a plot to eliminate MacLeod, but, at the time, only Colin had known about it. After Luke's death, Colin had confided that information to Donnie. Donnie was careful to omit any details that might implicate himself or the Judge. Indeed the Judge did not receive a single mention in Donnie's entire account. Jurgen's evidence strengthened the case against Colin but did not implicate others.

The legal process was long, extended by a number of recesses that strengthened MacLeod's suspicion of external interference. The entire judicial proceedings left MacLeod bitter, a feeling aggravated by Dougie's research which showed the Judge and Assistant Chief of Police to be cousins.

Concluding court proceedings the presiding judge decided that there was no case against the 'Judge' and that any reference to his name, (mainly MacLeod's evidence), should be deleted from the records. Justice had been denied. The instigator and bankroller of crimes had his reputation intact and 'unblemished'. Everybody walked free. Colin, conveniently dead, was blamed for all crimes and misdemeanours that had sufficient evidence to substantiate them: a convenient and neat file to gather dust in some archive. The pimp, Cyril, whom MacLeod expected to spill the beans when deprived of his alcohol and drugs, appeared to be non-existent. 'Nobody' knew of such a person. MacLeod guessed that Cyril's corpse contaminated the moors.

Two months later the Judge 'sold' his Tor'buie estate, but locals believe he retained ownership, the 'purchaser' becoming a temporary custodian. Drug smuggling was too lucrative to relinquish. The Judge needed his west coast base.

MacLeod believed that the outdoor training was intended for drug collection and distribution. Night kayaking to moored ships would guarantee unobserved collections. Transport of high value, lightweight packages via old drove roads to the east would evade police road checks. The drugs could then be moved south via the greater east coast infrastructure.

On his release from custody, Jurgen had returned to Germany and his family for the rest of his vacation. MacLeod had been in touch and arranged to meet him in Edinburgh the last day of September before Jurgen resumed his studies. MacLeod intended to explain everything and hoped their friendship would continue.

As for the Judge, nothing was certain, but MacLeod sensed that their paths would cross again. MacLeod knew too much, and the Judge had to show the criminal world that no interference would be tolerated without a high personal cost being exacted on those who dared to challenge his power base.

Stuart's resting place was never found. The mystery continues to trouble his family and friends, although MacLeod senses that he is not alone when he wanders the moors and mountains in search of venison. The eagle and the raven have company.

MacLeod plans to spend quality time with Christine and her father. Their croft commands an idyllic view over Ardroan Bay and the Gannet Isles. There, on the horizon, the blood red halo of the setting sun sinks into the sea, its glowing fireball about to be extinguished. Such peaceful scenery belies the great treachery that skulks so near at hand.

Seated against the cottage wall, MacLeod surveys the beautiful scenery that stretches before him. The graceful shape of an expensive yacht glides elegantly through the strait as it heads towards the Gannet Isles. A cold shiver descends his spine, an eeriness unnerving him for no apparent reason. He goes inside to escape the night air although it had seemed warm a short time earlier. Perhaps he'd watched the yacht for longer than he'd appreciated?

Aboard the yacht, the telescope is set down. The portly figure raises a glass of champagne; the third finger of that clasping hand is adorned with a large, elaborately shaped gold ring. "Retire to your woman and your uncomplicated life. Sleep well, Mr MacLeod." The cold, hard eyes and the accompanying sneer contradict the words: a mock toast has sinister implications.

The warmth inside the cottage does not remove the chill feeling. "I'm not feeling great, Christine. Reckon I'll hit the hay."

Gently Christine's hands stroke his forehead checking for a temperature, removing his unease.

A large dram of the 'Famous Grouse' is shakily poured by Hector. "That'll help you sweat out any chill, and the best place is bed."

He sips the amber liquid, enjoying the inner warmth as it trickles down his gullet. In bed he's almost asleep when Christine joins him. The warmth of her body as she nestles against him should have made his sleep deep and restful: it was anything but …

On top of the sea stack the sleeping figure stirs as the delicate drops of rain awaken him to the real, less pleasant world. Slowly his eyes open. He's no watch, but the light is fading. Conditions deteriorate rapidly: soft rain hardens to large drops that strike and penetrate; the wind rises to gale force. Embers of his once wild and reckless behaviours are fanned; their glow increasing, a slumbering fire about to ignite.

His dark silhouette moves to the very edge of the rock platform. Below, waves boom against the defiant pillar. The screech of gulls is drowned by the shrieking wind which tears at his clothes, trying to push his charcoal outline back.

The movement has not gone unnoticed. Over the strip of sea, clad in camouflage fatigues, a figure lies prone on the clifftop. His patience has finally been rewarded. Beside him lies a rifle complete with telescopic sights.

Defiantly the climber teeters on the edge daring to lean against an invisible support: gambling his life he courts release, seeking inner peace.

The light gathering property of the Schmidt & Bender scope highlights the shadow; cross hairs align on the midriff, but the figure on the stack fades. Briefly, the sighting eyes shift their gaze to the side and then back without the slightest head movement; the marksman's focus is restored. The trained body position is well practised: prostrate and pointing in the rifle's direction, right knee bent to maximise stability; the rifle stock is held firmly, its barrel clear of any obstruction while the left arm is cushioned over a heather mound. Every detail suggests the true professional marksman.

Gently the finger squeezes, the pressure increasing until the recoil of the .243 is felt. The report of the shot is lost, spirited away in the high wind.

The hollow thud; burning heat and spinning torque are experienced at one and the same time. The sprawling figure twists and tumbles as it accelerates through space; the roar of breaking waves is ever louder, ever nearer.

His right hand reaches out: slim, graceful fingers touch and grip gently but firmly. He is not alone. Another shadow accompanies him on his dark journey. Her face is pale, its scars healing before his very eyes; her natural beauty is restored. His quest is now complete.

'Christine' he mouths. A smile of radiant beauty is returned.

The absence of any scream unnerves the marksman. The circumstances are so bizarre that even this assassin doubts his mission.

How many more must die before his debt is repaid? The threat of a long prison sentence for murder, like the sword of Damoclese, always hangs over him: he remains a prisoner by coercion.

Conclusive evidence of his guilt is held by the Assistant Chief of Police and would be unearthed if …. His thoughts return to the present. What, he wonders, had the silhouette done that demanded the ultimate price?

Preoccupied with those thoughts he rises to retrace his journey over moor and hill. The ejected brass cartridge lies forgotten in the heather.

Adjacent to the bottle of Glenmorangie and anchored by a rock, the corner of a clear polythene cover flutters: inside a personal message.

Already more than halfway to its destination, a letter sits inside a mail sack: one stamped envelope amongst many hundreds.

Awake, sitting bolt upright, MacLeod gasps for breath. Sweat streams down his face, and his body shakes.

Christine wakens. Equally alarmed she holds him close.

"George, you're okay, my love. You're home; safe with me."

He looks at her beautiful face, its image so recent. His breathing slows to a normal rate.

"What happened? Can you remember?"

"Just a bad dream. Can't remember. I'm fine now. Go back to sleep."

His squeeze of her hand is reassuring.

Christine kisses his cheek, lies down and turns. He slithers under the duvet, but sleep is out of the question. What does the nightmare mean? *He* was the figure on top of the rock pillar. What on earth was he doing on that sea stack, and what was the significance of Christine's spectre … and those scars?

He lies awake, haunted. The vivid images refuse to disappear.

CPSIA information can be obtained at www.ICGtesting.com
Printed in the USA
LVOW031556301211

261798LV00014B/88/P